At the royal summons, Shae mou.... and soars through the air to the high hold of Faeraven, where all is not as it seems. Visions warn her of danger, and a dark soul touches hers in the night. When she encounters an attractive but disturbing musician, her wayward heart awakens.

But then there is Kai, a guardian of Faeraven and of Shae. Secrets bind him to her, and her safety lies at the center of every decision he makes.

On a desperate journey fraught with peril and the unknown, they battle warlike garns, waevens, ferocious raptors, and the wraiths of their own regrets. Yet, they must endure the campaign long enough to release the DawnKing—and the salvation he offers— into a divided land. To prevail, each must learn that sometimes victory comes only through surrender.

The High Queen is dying.

DawnSinger

Janalyn Voigt

Ann,

Thanks for reading,
and I look forward
to your books!

Janalyn Voigt

DawnSinger

COPYRIGHT 2012 by Janalyn Voigt

The author is represented by and this book is published in association with the literary agency of WordServe Literary Group, Ltd., www.wordserveliterary.com.

Contact Information: titleadmin@pelicanbookgroup.com

Cover Art by Nicola Martinez

Harbourlight Books
a division of Pelican Ventures, LLC
www.harbourlightbooks.com
PO Box 1738 *Aztec, NM * 87410

Harbourlight Books sail and mast logo is a trademark of Pelican Ventures, LLC
Publishing History
First Harbourlight Edition, 2012
Print Edition ISBN 978-1-61116-200-4
Electronic Edition ISBN 978-1-61116-199-1
Published in the United States of America

Dedication

This book is lovingly dedicated to my mother, Marilyn J. Weise, who taught me to fly.

Praise for DawnSinger

Am I Imagining Things? In Janalyn Voigt's *DawnSinger*, I stumbled upon that old sort of storytelling magic. We find swords and dungeons, betrayal and love. We encounter enemies near and far. And, as Frodo and Gollum discovered, we realize that some of our most powerful enemies are those in our own minds. Janalyn puts her characters into one particular situation in which they fight shadow-wraiths. The more the characters fight the shadows, the stronger those shadows become. The darkness becomes darker when they give it that power. Are they imagining things? Or are these enemies real?

For nearly a decade I have made money as a novelist, but the full-time, quit-the-day-job moment didn't come until six years into my career. It's tough making a living this way. It's lonely. I spend a thousand hours alone in a room to research, write, and edit each novel. I still doubt myself on a regular basis. The dark shadows call my name: "Eric...Eric..." Just as I've heard my name in that UnderOath song, I hear personal doubts mock my abilities.

Who needs them?

I, like Janalyn, tune out the negative whispers and tune into the power of story. Imagination is a wondrous thing, and Janalyn, through *DawnSinger*, gives it a voice to sing.

Eric Wilson, *NY Times* bestselling author of *Valley of Bones* and *One Step Away*

Ravens with Names of Shraens and Raeleins

Whellein—Shraen Eberhardt and Raelein Aeleanor
Chaeradon—Shraen Ferran and Raelein Annora
Tallyrand—Shraen Garreth and (raelein not named)
Glindenn—Shraen Veraedel and (raelein not named)
Morgorad—Shraen Lenhardt and (raelein not named)
Braeth—Shraen Raemwold and Raelein Reyanna (last shraen and raelein of Braeth)
Daeramor—(shraen and raelein not named)
Merboth—Shraen Aelfred and Raelein Ilse
Graelinn—Shraen Enric and Raelein Katera
**Rivenn—Lof Ralein Maeven

    **High Hold

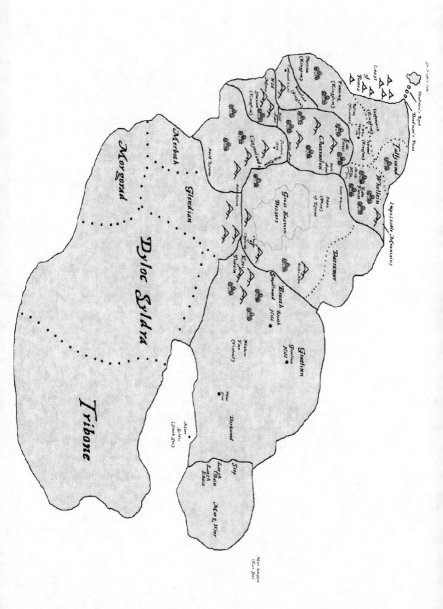

Part 1: Summons
1

The Whispan Tree

A crosswind caught Kai's *wingabeast* as lightning flared too near. Shrilling, the winged horse tilted in flight, and Kai's stomach lurched. A gust snatched the hood from his head and roared in his ears. He blinked to clear the stinging rain that drove into his eyes. Thunder boomed like a timpani, shaking the air. Flecht shuddered beneath him, and Kai placed a calming hand on his wingabeast's straining neck. He did not like this long flight through the wild night any better than did Flecht.

An image rose, unbidden—*Lof Raelein* Maeven, Faeraven's High Queen, upon her deathbed, her sea-green eyes surging with life. As a guardian of Faeraven and as a friend, he would die to appease the hope that had flared in those eyes.

Wind howled and lightning flashed close enough to blind. Kai wondered if his own death neared. He would not—could not—halt his journey, although it took him into the teeth of danger. Necessity drove him as he pushed onward, past endurance. If he survived the storm, he would deliver Maeven's last summons.

❦

Shae put up her hood and left the shelter of the stronghold to follow the graystone path. A chill wind rippled through the folds of her cloak, and she shivered. Overhead, clouds unfurled in a pearling sky. She passed into green scented shadow, where notes of damp moss and ripe humus met her.

She shouldn't have yielded to temptation and escaped into nature unescorted. In earlier days, she had roamed the grounds in freedom with no one caring. She couldn't get used to the strictures placed on her now that she'd grown older. When would she learn to be more like Katera? She couldn't remember her winsome twin ever causing their mother concern.

She would go back, but first she needed fresh air to ease the tightness in her chest.

Shae wandered beneath boughs laced with new growth and came at last to her favorite place at the garden's heart. Although the voice of a stream beckoned in the near distance, she paused beneath a stand of gnarlwoods, their ancient branches stretched wide. These trees had witnessed the construction of Whellein Hold, and they would remain when the stronghold's mortar crumbled and its stones fell away. She emerged from the copse into a meadow dotted with early flowers and bathed in morning light. The flutter of wings beat an accompaniment to the warbling of birds, and a wingen flitted through the lesser canopy to light in a nearby whispan tree. She stilled to avoid frightening the tiny bird, which dipped and bobbed its bright head to preen scarlet feathers. With its grooming complete, the wingen lisped into sweet-sad song.

Shae smiled. "Sing, small one."

But a shriek ended the wingen's song. Darkness extinguished its colors. Blood dripped from the foliage of the whispan tree, pure white only an instant ago. Terror gripped Shae by the throat, choking off her scream.

The giant raptor had descended from nowhere and now flailed ragged wings as it rose, screeching in victory, its black eyes trained on Shae.

Pulse thrumming in her ears, she crept backward. Back, back she moved, her gaze never leaving the leathery beast in the air.

This made no sense. How could a welke have ventured so far north?

Her heel caught the hem of her cloak, and she slammed into the ground.

Fear yanked her to her knees. Shock brought her to her feet.

The whispan tree stood pristine as new snow. No blood stained the smooth bark. No movement stirred the silken plumes. No sign lingered of wingen or welke.

And yet she had seen...*what?*

"*Lof Yuel!* Does this vision warn of danger?"

Wind stirred the leaves. Branches rubbed and creaked. A stone turned in the stream bed.

Another sound whispered at the edge of hearing.

Shae paused to listen. The sound resolved into a steady flapping, and her heart picked up its pace. She ran into the meadow and scanned the pale sky.

With a toss of its silver mane, a wingabeast spiraled toward her.

The rider sagged, and the spiral went amiss, but the wingabeast recovered with quick grace. With a ripple of muscles, its neck arched, and the feathered wings lifted. Shae rushed toward the rider before the creature's diamond-shod hooves found purchase on the ground.

She reached for his arm as he slid from the saddle, but he shrugged off her help and steadied himself against the shifting beast.

She searched his face. "Kai?" Strain etched her brother's features.

He turned and with one finger, traced forgotten moisture at the corner of her eye. "Shae?"

She shook her head to silence his question. "You've ridden through the night?"

He didn't answer but pushed her away with gentle hands.

"What troubles you?"

His long silver-gray eyes glazed with tears. "Lof Raelein Maeven lies on her deathbed."

She opened her mouth to speak, but no words came. What could she say to ease him when the news pierced her like a blade? Tears seeped down her cheeks, silent as the grave.

Kai touched her arm. "I'm sorry. I shouldn't have spoken so. You formed a heart-bond when she visited Whellein Hold."

"What other way is there to speak it?" The image of the wingen and welke returned to her. "Death is death."

His head bent in acknowledgment, the movement slow.

She touched his arm. "I'm sorry, Kai. I know she means much to you."

"Could but my hope and my prayers save her, she would live." He spread his hands in a helpless gesture.

"Such power is not mine."

"Only Lof Yuel has the wisdom to command life and death. We must leave such things to him."

He looked at her with a somber expression, but then tousled her tangled curls. "Truth from a babe!"

"One day, my brother, you may understand I am grown, or nearly so." She raised her brows at him, but then sobered. "Does Lof Raelein Maeven...suffer?"

"Little. She does not ail. Life ebbs from her, it seems, by choice."

Shae let out her breath. "I'm glad she feels no pain."

He nodded; his expression strange. "You love her, as she does you."

"How can such a thing come from one meeting?" She spoke again the puzzle that had long occupied her.

"Love has no logic. Come. I must tell Father this news."

"Then you must wake him." At his look, she added, "Last night's revelry kept him late."

"Revelry? Oh!" His eyes widened, and he gave a moan. "How could I forget the celebration of the founding of Whellein?"

She fell into step beside him as he led Flecht toward the stronghold. "Pay no mind. No one faulted you for not being here. You are given over to the Lof Raelein and must go or stay as she pleases." Struck by a sudden thought, she grasped his arm. "Her death will release you from your promise. Will you not then serve her son when he is made Lof Shraen of Faeraven?"

Kai turned to her. "I may serve Elcon...if I do not undertake our older brother's duties here at Whellein as Father wishes."

She considered his words. "Is it not possible to do both? For in serving one, have you not served the other?"

"Such a thing can only be in the realm of dreams."

"But not in wakefulness?"

He passed a hand across his eyes. "Such an ideal lies far from my reach. I can only hope Daeven will return from his adventures and relieve me from the choice."

Their older brother had been gone for what seemed an eternity, and she missed him with each passing day. Of her many siblings, only Kai held a closer place in her heart.

She smoothed a stray lock of Kai's hair. "You will know best when the time comes."

He sketched a smile. "Such blessed faith I cannot deserve!"

She gave him an arch look. "Faith has no logic."

His eyes widened, lightening from gray to silver. Laughter broke from him. "Such medicine I find in you!" He sobered. "Now tell me why I come upon you unkempt, unhappy, and alone outside Whellein Hold."

She gave no excuse. "I woke with the dawn and made my way to the garden to listen to the heartbeat of creation."

"In that you follow the habit of all Kindren. But you disregard wisdom to seek nature alone. I'll warrant our mother has no knowledge of your whereabouts. I thought you old enough to leave such mischief behind. You must stop this carelessness, Shae. Even within Whellein in these times of peace, the lands outside our stronghold are not safe."

She murmured an acknowledgment and broke contact with a gaze that had become too piercing. How could she explain the need that drew her from the constraints of life and into the freedom of nature, if only for a time?

"And the tears?"

She shrugged and looked past his ear. "I tripped on my cloak and fell."

"But you have no cloak."

Despite the morning chill, she'd been too preoccupied to notice its absence. She forced a smile that wavered. "I must have lost it when—when I heard you coming."

"Where did you lose it? I'll help you look."

"In the garden. Kai, I welcome your company but regret keeping you from your rest."

His hand cupped her chin and tilted her face. "What brings the tremor to your voice? Did something frighten you?"

"*No.*" She pulled away and ignored the puzzled glance he gave her. She still did not understand what she had seen. How could she explain the unexplainable?

"I'll lead while you ride Flecht." Kai guided her onto the wingabeast's back. "Now, where did you lose your cloak?"

She looked down at him, her hands tangled in Flecht's silken mane. She would have felt more secure if Kai had ridden with her, but he seemed happy to walk. Perhaps he meant to spare her contact with his sodden clothing. She guided him to the emerald cloak, puddled below the whispan tree. Kai gathered it, and she accepted the rough woolen garment with thanks.

Mottled light swept the garden, creating an illusion of movement. The air rippled, on the edge of hearing, with the bittersweet song of a wingen.

Shae sucked in a breath, and her gaze flew to the whispan tree, but its branches remained innocent and bare.

❧❧

Flecht quivered under Kai's hand. Shae must have communicated to the beast the tension he read in her face. Why did she stare at the naked branches of the small, white tree? He drew his brows together but didn't speak. Her eyes, so green they reminded him of deep shadows in an old forest, told him nothing. As she settled the cloak upon her shoulders, burnished tangles cascaded down her back. She looked beautiful and far too grown.

Something had upset Shae—that much seemed obvious. Equally obvious was her desire for privacy in the matter. Well, he didn't question such things. He already held enough secrets to quell any desire for more.

After his long ride, Kai relished the chance to walk. But he should not linger further. He swung into the saddle behind Shae and reached around her for the reins. Flecht adjusted to the additional burden with trained ease. Shae relaxed against him, and Kai smiled to himself at the small gesture of trust. Would that it could always be so between them.

Kai led Flecht to the path, and the wingabeast's hooves rang against stone in a steady cadence as the garden fell away behind them. The ancient fortress rose before them sullen and gray, while the fields and orchards beyond glowed with new light. The sharp scent of tilled soil and fresh herbs carried on the wind as they passed into the shadow of Whellein Hold.

They entered the ancient fortress through the gatehouse archway beneath the raised iron portcullis. Following the graystone path along the sward, they skirted the great hall, which rose to impressive heights.

As they neared the stables, voices, thuds, and the rustlings of crisp straw reached Kai. He dismounted and lifted his arms to Shae. Light as she was, he had to step backward when she leaned into him. He steadied them both, and then turned to instruct the groom. When Kai looked for her again, Shae was gone. A smile touched his mouth as he went through an archway in the inner curtain wall. He would keep his knowledge of Shae's morning activities to himself.

His mother's voice carried past her maid, Tahera, at her parlor door. "Let us start with soup of boar sausage and wild greenings dressed in sweetberry vinegar, then follow with smoked whitefish in savory sauce and—"

"I hope you have enough for one more." Kai entered the snug room.

A gold-edged mirror above the ornate mantle reflected his mother, Aleanor of Whellein's surprise and delight. She rose and pressed her slight frame into his swift embrace.

Kai held her at arm's length to gaze upon her. How long had it been since he'd seen her calm gray eyes and basked in her smile? He marked, with sadness, the progress of time across her face. Furrows marred a brow once smooth, and lines fanned from the corners of eyes that sparkled. His mother wore a simple woolen tunic of blue, girt with an embroidered sash. Her silver hair coiled in braids about her head.

She smiled. "We have stores aplenty for a Son of Whellein. But how come you by morn and not by eve?"

"I did not stop the night. I couldn't contain my excitement at nearing home." His gaze drifted past her to the muscular Cook garbed in a brown tunic, who smiled at their exchange.

Mother met Kai's look. "I think we shall continue later, Maeric," she said without seam. "I won't detain you from your duties longer. Tahera, please bring cider, cheese and bread."

The door to the raelein's parlor closed with a click behind Maeric and Tahera, and they were alone.

Kai went to the fire, grateful for its comfort as he steeled himself for what he would say.

"You must sit." His mother gestured in invitation as she resumed her seat on the bench. "Now tell me what has brought you on such a difficult journey."

"I've come for Shae."

Mother let out her breath in a long sigh. "And so I am to lose another child."

"Lof Raelein Maeven sends for her while on her deathbed."

Her hand flew to her throat. "The time has come, then."

"It nears, yes." He ignored a frisson of uneasiness. Of course, he spoke of more than Maeven's death. "It's long past time Shae learns her true identity as *Raena* Shaenalyn of Rivenn. On her dying bed, Lof Raelein Maeven yearns for her daughter."

His mother squared her shoulders as if recovering from a blow. "I thought I had prepared myself for this, and yet…" Her voice faded to a whisper.

"You've raised her well."

She looked down at the hands clasped in her lap. "I wish I'd done more to treat her as one of my own."

Kai knelt at her feet. "You did your best. Ever

since I brought her to you as a babe in arms, you've kept her hidden from those who would destroy her."

Aeleanor raised eyes shiny with tears. "She'll return to danger at Torindan."

"You have my promise to protect her." Each word fell from his lips by its own weight.

"When do you leave?"

He spoke with reluctance. "At first light."

She arose and took the place at the fire he had vacated, putting her arms about herself as if cold. "I will not say goodbye to her. It is better so."

Kai stood. For Shae's sake, he wished his mother would look beyond her own needs. But he cut short the reply that rose to his lips. How could he censure her when he did not know her pain? He hesitated, and then lowered his voice. "Have you word of Daevin?"

Mother lifted her head, and he read in her face what he should have already known. He need not have worried his question would quicken his mother's pain. She carried her missing son in her heart as surely as she had once carried him within her womb.

She shook her head and turned toward the fire. "None."

The word echoed through his mind. Kai shouldered its weight, but wished again for the freedom to search for his brother.

He crossed to one of the tall windows overlooking the inner ward with its herb garden. New growth burgeoned in all its beds, ready to erupt with life. His hands clenched into fists. He wanted to rejoice in such things. He wanted to comfort his mother. He closed his eyes, shut in by his own dark thoughts.

A touch on his arm, feather light, called him back. He turned and read the plea in his mother's face. "The

Lof Raelein's death will free you to return to Whellein, as your father wishes."

He met her gray gaze and told her what she already knew. "My duty at Torindan calls for my pledge of service to Elcon when his mother dies."

"Surely Elcon would not rob the House of Whellein so." She clasped her hands together so hard the knuckles showed white.

"Mother, let us leave this conversation." He put his hands over hers to still them. "You know I must decide my own course, for good or ill."

Tahera returned, bearing on a tray a tankard of steaming cider, a selection of cheeses, and a fragrant loaf. Kai cleansed his hands in the laver the servant provided and fell upon the repast.

His mother sat silent while he ate. She would not try again to win his promise, but he knew she ceded the battle only.

2

Whellein Hold

The heavy door groaned shut and Shae pressed against it while she caught her breath. The great hall stood empty, which was just as well. She should still be abed, waiting to be roused by her maid. Catching her breath, she watched dust motes float in bars of light slanting through the tall windows, which overlooked the inner bailey's herb garden.

Fresh rushes deadened her footfalls and sent up a warm scent overlaid with the pungent aromas of rosemary, mint, and lavender. Beneath a wide archway on one side of the chamber, Shae put her hand to the latch of a tall door carved with gryphons. She paused, caught by memory.

Beyond that same door, she'd once greeted Lof Raelein Maeven in her parents' absence. Maeven had at first seemed little older than Shae, but when the silver threading her copper hair gleamed in the candlelight, Shae saw that the transparency of her skin mimicked the tallow in the candlebranch beside her. Despite these ravages, Maeven's arching brows, fine nostrils and vivid eyes commanded awe.

As Maeven's image dissipated, Shae lifted the latch. The door gave with a creak, and she entered the Allerstaed, the place of prayer. A musty scent, the smell of dust and disuse, emanated from wood and stone. Faint light followed her from the open doorway and a few indifferent sunbeams penetrated the grime coating three high windows above the altar. Her steps whispered across the graystone floors, and she sank to her knees onto the stone step below the altar.

"I've come about Lof Raelein Maeven." Her voice rang loud in the stillness. She said no more, for words tangled in her mind. But Lof Yuel read her heart. If only she might read his in return, she could know the Lof Raelein's fate. Weak light ebbed and flowed over her as outside, clouds effaced the sun. Sorrow carried her in its current.

"Why do you weep?" A voice reverberated through the chamber.

Shae raised her head. She recognized this voice.

An Elder youth crouched before her. She studied him, taking in his burnished skin, rounded somber eyes, and black hair. How could she have thought she knew his voice? She'd never seen him before. Her breath hitched. "*Who* are you?"

Twin grooves in his cheeks deepened. "Don't be frightened. I am but a wayfarer."

She stared at him. "No. You are more."

He smiled. "Your heart speaks truth. I *am* a wayfarer...and I am more." He stroked the tears from her cheeks, feather-light, like the touch of a draft. "*Peace.*" The whispered word brought infinite comfort.

Shae closed her eyes and breathed deep.

"Remember, Shae, you must look to the light."

She opened her eyes, ready to ask how he knew her name.

She knelt alone in the Allerstaed.

What was this new vision? Perhaps prayer would

show her its cause. Time stretched away, uncounted.

"Shaenalyn!" A hard voice roused her.

She sat up and pushed hair from her eyes. "Katera?"

Her sister's delicate face framed by long, pale hair peeked around the door. "I thought I might find you here." Katera, resplendent in a tunic of yellow-dyed wool girded with links of gold, stepped into the chamber. "You should see yourself. You look like some spirit ready to fade if I blink."

"Hush!" Shae spoke with more vigor than she intended. She lowered her voice. "Don't say such things in this place!"

Katera made a face that failed to mar her loveliness. "You spend too much time in prayer. It has made you strange."

Dampness from the stone step chilled her, and Shae shivered. She stood on cramped feet and did her best to smooth her garments and hair. How she wished she better resembled her twin. Katera would never fall asleep on an altar step, see visions, or suffer the stirrings of a restless fate. She seemed made for marriage, motherhood, and the joys of a quiet life.

Shae tried to stifle her envious thoughts. "Why do you seek me?"

Katera stepped through the doorway. "Mother sent me to find you. You must ready yourself for the evening meal."

She noticed that hunger gnawed her stomach. "Is it so late then?"

Katera grinned. "You've been sleeping, have you? Such vigilance!"

Shae's face grew hot. "I rested little in the night. Exhaustion must have claimed me."

Janalyn Voigt

"Kai came early." The statement made a question.

"He did. Has he spoken to Father yet?"

"I think not." Her sister's eyes narrowed. "What news had he to say to Father?"

Shae shook her head and looked away. "Kai must give his own news."

❧

Kai's father, Shraen Eberhardt set his hands on the table in his meeting room and pushed to his feet. "You bring news of sorrow, but also, dare I say, of hope for Whellein." Father brushed past Kai as he paced a well-worn path between table, fire, and window.

Kai did not flinch, but such words grated against his grief for Maeven. He remained silent, for he did not wish to discuss his father's hopes now.

Father paused on his circuit to seat himself once more at the strongwood slab that dominated the chamber and dwarfed them both. He spoke, so low Kai leaned forward to hear. "I've had word of Daevin."

Kai held his breath as he waited for whatever news would come.

Father put his hands on the wooden surface before him. A groove beside his mouth deepened. "*His ship... The wreckers...*"

Kai sat forward. "What are you saying, Father?"

Father pushed off the table again and went to stand by the fire. "You have heard of *Muer Maeread?*"

Kai nodded. He knew the Coast of Bones as a place of dangerous currents and wild, subsisting Elder.

"The western shore to the north of Elderland has but poor land—sand dunes and salt marshes. The Elder there wrest a hard living from the sea, so hard it

16

is said they rejoice when a ship breaks against the rocks offshore, for salvage rights belong to them. Some even say they *guide* ships into the shoals with false lights. If any survivors wash ashore, they do not live long..."

Kai jumped to his feet. "But Daevin's ship should not have been anywhere near Muer Maeread!"

Father inclined his head. "The *Kestrel* journeyed west, but a storm blew it off course. Clouds obscured the stars and made it impossible to navigate. When lights appeared against the shoreline, the ship turned toward them. The captain must have thought they returned to harbor. By the time he knew his mistake, he had no time to turn back."

Kai joined his father before the fire, although it warmed him little. "How do you know these things?"

"*The Sea Wanderer* almost succumbed to the same fate. Its captain answered my inquiries. He witnessed the shipwreck."

"Could he not have given you falsehoods to gain a reward?"

"He asked nothing in exchange." Father spread his hands. "He brought proof."

"Proof?"

Father stood before the window's velvet hangings. "When the storm relented, Captain Ivan, at his own peril, returned to the site of the wreck to search for survivors. The Kestrel's fate would have belonged to his own ship had the other not foundered first and thus warned them of the shoals. The crew members he sent to comb the waters found none alive." He crossed the chamber to reach above the high marble mantle. "They fished this from the sea." Puffing a little with effort, he brought down a rough plank. "I've hidden it from your mother until I can bring myself to show it to her."

Kai received the plank, the rough wood biting into his hands. Ornate letters of scarlet spelled out *"Kestrel."* He shook his head. "This can mean nothing—or everything."

"I have confirmed its authenticity." In a sudden movement, Father slammed a fist into the palm of his other hand. The veins on his neck stood out. "Would that I had not allowed Daevin to go!"

"You did right, Father. Daevin longed for adventure and felt suffocated by duty. Had you not given your blessing, he might well have gone without it." Kai looked at his empty hands in puzzlement. His father must have taken the plank away, but he had not felt its weight lift. "When will you tell Mother?"

Father returned the plank to its hiding place above the mantle. "When the time is right. She has sorrow enough with Shae leaving. I tell you, Kai, so you will know your place as Whellein's only remaining son. I grow old and have need of an heir. Will you give your promise to attend such duties here at Whellein when the Lof Raelein's death releases you?"

Kai gazed into the fire, thus avoiding his father's searching gaze. A part of him wanted—*longed*—to make such a promise. He could rule and reign at Whellein rather than live the life of a second son in service. He ached to please his father, to help him shoulder his burdens. Besides, if none took up an heir's duties, Whellein could vanish as a separate entity at his father's death. His ancestral lands would pass to Kai's older sister, Ilse, and her husband, Aelfred, of neighboring Merboth.

But Kai could not bring himself to speak. Loyalty

to Lof Raelein Maeven and the House of Rivenn held him fast. He had dwelt within the embrace of Torindan since his early life. As personal guard to the Lof Raelein, he was expected to swear his oath of fealty to her son at Maeven's death. Kai could not, with ease, turn his back on such duties. Besides these things, something indefinable kept him silent—a sense of destiny— the simple understanding that a different fate awaited him.

"You will not?"

Kai shook his head and met his father's silver gaze. "I *can* not," he corrected, helpless in the knowledge his father would not understand, and that he could do nothing to ease his pain. He looked into the flames, watching them flicker and flare.

Footfalls sounded. The door whined and then thudded shut.

๑๛

Shae waited in the shadow beyond the torchlight. The door to her father's meeting room stood ajar, perhaps to release heat from the fearsome fire that blazed in the hearth. Light surged about the room in time to the leaping flames. It reached across polished floors, peeped into forgotten corners, and made ancient tapestries jump with life.

Kai was sprawled on the bench opposite the fire, and his fair head rested against embroidered cushions. Firelight played over his features, softening them. Shae itched to smooth the creases from his brow, but she curled her fingers into her palms instead. He would not welcome pity.

She knew a swift grief for the carefree youth who

had taught her the ballads of her people. More than once, he had kept her at his knee long after her bedtime as he spun tales of Torindan, High Hold of Faeraven. Shae sighed. She hardly recognized her brother in the weary sojourner before her.

She stepped into the light. "You summoned me?"

He nodded but did not turn his head.

"Are you not well?"

Kai gave a weak smile. "I require extra warmth to cure me of the cold, but I do not ail."

"You should perhaps have slept longer." She reproved him in gentle tones. "You give yourself little time to recover before journeying again."

"You are right, of course." He shrugged. "I leave at first light."

She gave him a searching look. "I don't understand. Why did you come with such urgency only to leave so soon? Surely any messenger could have brought news to Whellein of the Lof Raelein's illness."

Kai made no response. His eyes shut, and he went still so long she thought he slept. She crept away but his voice halted her at the door. "Do you remember how we used to sit together before the fire and search for the blue hearts in the flames, and afterwards imagine shapes in the coals?"

"I remember."

A smile stretched his lips. "Life seemed easy then." He opened eyes of deep gray touched with silver. "You are right. I didn't come to bring news of Lof Raelein Maeven. I came for you, Shae, to take you with me to Torindan."

She stared at him. "Why should you take me with you?"

"The Lof Raelein bids it."

"But I don't understand. Why me? Does Mother know of this? I'll miss Katera's wedding! What will Father say?"

"Mother knows, and Father agrees you must go. Even now, your maid packs a few things for the journey. Torindan will provide whatever else you need. You must travel with me on my wingabeast. I would not ask such a thing of you, but time presses." He hesitated. "You will come, won't you?"

The thought stole her breath, and she put a hand to her stomach to comfort its churning. She wanted to say no, to withdraw into the shadows and hide from the unknown threat that seemed to reach for her.

And yet…she'd never traveled far from Whellein. What would it be like to visit Torindan? Would she find more freedom there?

"Why do you ask when the Lof Raelein bids me? What choice do I have?"

He gave her a level look. "Shae, she would have you answer her summons of your own will."

She blinked away tears. "How can I deny her anything? I will come." As she spoke a strange awareness twisted through her, and she saw again, in her mind's eye, the welke drop upon the wingen.

3

Flight

The shadow of a hand suspending a comb above Shae's head stood in relief against the whitewashed wall of her chamber. She waited, but when the tug of the comb in her hair did not come, she glanced over her shoulder at her maid.

Lyse stood motionless, her pale gray eyes unfocused. "Danger waits for you."

Shae's mouth went dry. "What is it?"

Lyse gave a faint shake of her fair head. "It doesn't happen often, but sometimes I...sense things to come."

Shae stared at her. "Yes."

"Whispers from Lof Yuel."

"Tell me."

"An old evil seeks you." With a hand at Shae's shoulders, Lyse turned Shae to face her. "Must you go to Torindan?"

"How can I refuse my Lof Raelein's deathbed summons? That would be worse than ill-mannered, and I'd always regret disappointing Maeven."

"But if you go with Kai, you may not live long enough for regrets." Lyse stroked the brush through Shae's hair.

Shae's laugh sounded strained within the quiet room. "These are poor bedtime stories, Lyse." As the comb yanked at her tangles with sudden vigor, she winced. "Wake me early. I'm sorry, but I mustn't keep Kai waiting. If it makes you feel better, I'll tell him what you said. With a bit of caution, the journey should go well. And I'll watch myself at Torindan."

Lyse said nothing more but with deft fingers bound Shae's hair in a long braid, and then lighted the way into her bedchamber.

The feather ticking gave beneath Shae, and she lay on her back, content to let Lyse shut her in with the creatures embroidered on the heavy linen bed hangings. As Lyse rustled about banging and latching shutters, Shae gazed in the wavering lanthorn light at rampant gryphons, wingabeasts in flight and unibeasts with whorled horns entwined.

A golden gryphon batted its wings and pulled free of the bed hangings.

Shae backed against the carved headboard.

The gryphon swooped to perch at the foot of her bed and, stretching its sleek head, opened its beak in a roar much greater than its tiny size.

When the gryphon dove through a gap in the bed hangings, Shae waited for Lyse's scream, but none came. Before she could ponder what this might mean, a miniature unibeast leaped onto the counterpane and pointed its silver horn at her in challenge.

With a hammering heart, Shae held her cushions before her like a shield.

A fluttering shadow crossed over the unibeast.

Shae looked up in time to see a small white wingabeast circling at the top of the hangings before it, too, flew through the gap.

The unibeast followed in a graceful leap.

Shae strained her ears in a silence so profound it

seemed to pulse, and then, with a shaking hand, pulled back the hangings.

Her bed perched at the edge of a steep cliff that fell away into darkness.

She swung her legs over the side away from the precipice, and her feet met cold stone. Steadying herself with a hand to the damp rock wall that rose from the narrow landing between flights of stairs, she edged past her bed. Her foot slid forward as she searched in dimness for the first rising stair step. An air current stirred her hair, and she swallowed against the taste of bile at its fetid breath.

Somewhere near, something shrieked.

The edge of the stair crumbled beneath her foot, and its stones clattered away. Shae pitched forward, crying out as her knees struck the edge of a tread and her palms slapped moist stone.

She scuttled backwards from the edge and up several stair treads, but as the skin on the back of her neck crawled, turned her head to look behind her.

Darksome beings crouched above her on the stairs, ready to spring

A shudder laddered up her spine, and her legs went weak even as a whisper stirred the air.

"Find the light."

She moaned and thrashed, wrenching free of the nightmare to find herself on her bed's soft tick with the bedding tangled about her. The shutters rattled as wind whined into the chamber and lifted the bed hangings to billow against her. Lyse must have forgotten to latch one of the shutters.

Throwing back the counterpane, she pushed the hangings aside. Wind buffeted her face. But the shutters remained secured.

Shae trembled in her thin shift, an uncanny awareness lifting the hair at her nape. A dank odor assaulted her, and she sensed, rather than saw, the fell creature that slithered into the room.

Shae's knees went weak, and she slid to the floor as the unseen predator coiled itself around her mind — probing, squeezing, seeking entrance.

Her scream strangled in her throat.

ॐ∽

Kai snapped a sprig of rosemary and inhaled its robust fragrance. Sleep eluded him, despite his weariness. He tilted his head back and breathed in the green scent of life that permeated the garden. Stars burned into his eyes, so near it seemed he could pluck one from the velvet sky. As he watched, a tiny light arced overhead and extinguished. The lonely call of a nightbird pierced the darkness. He had tiredness enough to sleep. What he lacked was peace.

He would not let himself think of Daevin gone forever, lost in the cruel sea, or worse, cut down in cold blood after reaching shore. Dark fancies crowded his mind. He pushed them away. Better to remember kinder days, when he and his brother had tangled like puppies and bandied good-natured insults. *No.* He shook his head as if that gesture could clear his pain — better not to remember at all.

Kai pulled a handful of buds from spikes of lavender that rose beside the mossy path. They filled his mouth with sweetness. Perhaps the herb would ease his rest. He could not keep Shae safe if fatigue clouded his mind. He pictured her as she had appeared earlier — garbed in a garment of mossy green, plaited

25

hair hanging to her waist, a knotted band of doeskin circling her brow. Where had that engaging sprite gone? He glimpsed her at times in the spring of the maid's step and in the lift of her head, but the once-bright eyes now gathered shadows. He sighed and remembered a time, not so long before, when his young arms, aching from the unaccustomed task, carried her across the Plains of Rivenn. He'd sheltered her from wind and cold and the rain that mixed with bitter tears to stream down his face.

Kai turned away from the clutch of remembrances as the shutters at the raelein's parlor window grated open. His mother's face peered out, pale as a specter. What kept her awake in the night? Did she pray for Daevin's return? Perhaps she fretted over Shae. Or himself. He could not know. His mother had ever been an enigma. She'd wept at his father's decision to release him into service to Torindan, but had not bid him farewell. She'd flown to embrace him when he returned to visit, but held aloof when he offered her his comfort. Some thin cord of attachment still stretched between them, but he did not know its strength.

His mother withdrew, and the shutters banged shut. Had she failed to see him standing at the edge of shadow or simply decided to seek her rest? He should return to his own bed. Morning would come too early. Having determined his course, he cast one last glance at the night sky—and went still.

Wings unfurled against the moon's pale face as two wingabeasts bearing riders passed overhead.

A feeling of unease traveled Kai's spine. Had pursuers followed him?

As if in answer to his thought, a scream throbbed through the air, and he abandoned the garden to its mysteries.

He burst into Shae's chamber. Why was the door unlatched?

Lyse, holding a lanthorn in one hand and screaming, stood over Shae's prostrate body, which sprawled on the rug beside the bed. The maid lifted a frightened face toward Kai but, as recognition dawned, left off screaming and put a hand to her throat as if gathering herself to speak.

Kai crouched and placed his hand to the base of Shae's throat. He let out his breath on a sigh. "She's alive. What happened?"

Lyse bent closer, and the lanthorn she held cast fretful light over Shae. "I heard an odd cry, so I checked on my mistress and found her here on the floor." A sob shuddered through her. "I couldn't wake her."

He lifted Shae, laid her on the bed's feather tick, and then pressed his lips to her forehead. Her temperature felt normal. He stepped back, gazing at Shae in frustration. She seemed to have sustained some sort of wound he couldn't see.

As Lyse tucked the counterpane around her mistress, Kai stepped to one of the room's tall windows, drew the hangings and unlatched the shutters. He stared into the dark sky, where the feeble moon hid behind clouds. No sign remained of the wingabeasts and their riders.

He returned to the bedside, where Shae's maid knelt in prayer. He pulled her to her feet by her clasped hands. "Pray, but do it on the way to Praectal Aelgarod's chambers. She needs medical care." He pulled the knife from his boot and pressed it in her hands. "Go in darkness and watch yourself."

Her eyes widened, but then she nodded.

Kai latched the door behind Lyse, and then turned in time to see Shae's eyelids twitch. Her lips parted on a moan.

"Shae!"

Her eyes slitted open.

"Can you talk?"

"Something evil found me."

"What do you mean?" Kai struggled to keep his voice level.

"It strangled my mind and almost consumed my soul, but it released me when I called out to Lof Yuel."

"Lyse heard your cry. Her screaming alerted me."

Shae's gaze penetrated his. "I don't think I'll go to Torindan, after all. I don't think it's...safe."

He mastered his dismay. "I'm afraid it's too late to refuse. You're no longer safe anywhere."

❧⟨

"Will it be difficult to stay seated?" Shae eyed Flecht with new respect. It had been one thing to remain on the wingabeast's back while riding yesterday, but today they would lift into the air and fly like the birds. What had persuaded her to agree to such a thing?

Kai laughed. "You look as you did when you swung on that rope across the stream as it ran with water in the early spring."

She narrowed her eyes. "And do you recall what happened then?"

"You only got a little wet." The mirth left his face and he touched her cheek. "Pay no mind, Shae. This will come easier than using our rope swing. The saddle is built to carry two in safety, and I won't let you fall."

She hesitated, bit her lower lip, and then reached for the saddle. Kai steadied her as she placed her foot in the rear stirrup and pulled herself upward into the back seat of the double saddle. Now astride, she felt somehow better, although she couldn't unravel the hidden thread of logic in such a thing. Kai lifted into the saddle before her, and she put her arms around him. "Will we lodge the night somewhere?"

He spoke near her ear. "We will. I can't expect you to ride all night as I sometimes must. It would not please the Lof Raelein if I delivered you fainting to her bedside."

Shae smiled at such an image. Her spirits lifted, despite the danger, at the prospect of a journey. She had never traveled far from Whellein. The idea of going anywhere, let alone to Torindan, filled her with wonder. That she should go with Kai only increased her joy. But her happiness dimmed at the prospect of visiting the Lof Raelein upon her deathbed. And Shae could not shake the sense of foreboding that hounded her.

As they left the stables for the outer bailey and turned onto the path that would take them past the great hall and on to the west gate, Shae couldn't help a hollow feeling of loss.

"Wait!" A voice hailed them from the archway that led to the inner drawbridge. Mother ran toward them in the gathering light, the cloak of scarlet wool she carried trailing from her hands. Her silver hair flew unbound behind her, and she looked as if she had dressed in haste.

Kai turned Flecht, and his mother caught the wingabeast's bridle.

He reached down to take the hand she raised. "What troubles you, Mother?"

"I thought—" She gasped for breath. "I thought I had missed your going."

"It is well you did not." Kai chided her, but in a warm voice.

She turned to Shae. "Take this cloak to warm you in your journeys."

"Mother, I can't take your best cloak."

"*Please!*" she cried and put her face against the marmelot fur of the cloak's lining. "Pray, receive my gift."

Shae blinked away tears. "Thank you." When Kai helped her dismount, she exchanged her own cloak for the embrace of her mother's. "I shall return it unharmed."

Giving a wispy smile, Mother touched Shae's face. "Mind you do."

With a small sound, Shae went into her mother's arms.

When the embrace ended, Mother held her at arm's length as her gaze traveled over Shae.

Shae stirred. "I've had no time to say goodbye to anyone."

"I'll say your farewells, my daughter."

Kai helped Shae mount, and then joined her on Flecht's back.

Mother gazed up at Shae, her eyes bright with tears. "Submit to your brother's care. I would have you safe." With a last butterfly touch of Shae's hand, she stepped away.

At the west gate, Kai turned Flecht for a final goodbye.

Shae lifted her hand at her mother's wave and, as

they passed through the gatehouse, carried away the image of Aeleanor of Whellein wrapped in an emerald cloak with the early light threading her hair, watching her children depart from her.

∽∾

With beating wings Flecht leaped into the air. Shae's heart raced, and she held on to Kai with trembling hands until the wingabeast's flight leveled. Air washed over her in a rhythmic rush and flow. They must have cleared the trees by now, but she dared not look. She hid her face against the blue perse of Kai's cloak and clutched him with such fierceness his hand covered hers to soothe. Their flight leveled, and the flapping of wings silenced for so long she opened her eyes in alarm.

Vast landscapes unfolded on every side, just awakened by dawn. Pink-tinged mists undulated above hills washed in hues of green. The waters of *Weild Whistan* winked wavery light as they threaded in and out of the rich tapestry of the Maegran Syld, known by the Elder as the Hills of Mist. The weild passed into the Kaba forests and emerged to become the Elder's White Feather River where it entered Norwood. *Maeg Streihcan*, the "Broken Mountain," lifted its ragged head in the fore distance, where it floated and shimmered as if it might soon vanish. The other peaks of the *Maegrad Ceid*, the "Crystal Mountains," sliced the air to the south, beyond the mottled green of the Kaba canopy.

Whellein Hold dwindled behind them, its fields and lawns the only clearings of any size in the Kaba forest that ran to the foothills of the *Maegrad Paesad*, the

"Impenetrable Mountains." To the west and north, a nameless moorland stretched for lengths to reach salt marshes edged by sparkling sea.

She sighed, lost in wonder. Nothing could have prepared her for such exquisite beauty.

Flecht's wings stretched into a glide, feathers rippling in invisible currents. Their shadow chased them on the ground below, but the feeling of motion was gone. It seemed they hung, suspended, above the morning sun, which sat on the shoulders of the mountains and stained all in hues of red and pink and mauve.

As she relaxed against Kai, he released the hand he'd comforted. They flew lower, drawing level with the Kaba canopy where wingens and croboks darted and bushes rooted in the joints of the trees. Shae lost herself in the ever-changing vistas that unfolded below— plunging cascades, shallow rapids, and a wide place of many channels cutting between islets.

Flecht spiraled downward, and the rush of air in Shae's face roused her. They lighted on a small island where a flat shelf of rock jutted out to disrupt the current. Waves churned against their perch, only to curl around and lap the islet's shore. Beyond the wash, underbrush and thickets tangled in profusion and croboks nested beneath a sheer face of rock.

Shae stretched cramped legs and ate bread and cheese washed down with deep draughts of gamey water from elkskin bags. She wished they could linger in this pleasant spot.

"Come," Kai said all too soon. "We must press on while it is yet day." He called for Flecht.

As the wingabeast approached, Shae took the hand Kai extended and let him draw her to her feet, but then paused.

"What's wrong?"

"My foot's asleep."

Kai swung Shae into his arms. "Shall I lift you to Flecht's back? I promise not to dump you in the water."

"I've heard those words before!" She referred to the time when she'd managed to take him with her into the brook at Whellein Hold. Her lips curved at the memory, and Kai's eyes gleamed. But then her smile died.

Two hooded riders astride wingabeasts dropped toward them, dark against a blue sky. Steel glinted along swords held at the ready.

4

Along the White Feather

Shae landed in Flecht's saddle with a thump as Kai deposited her with more speed than grace. He bent and then straightened, and she caught the glint of metal.

Kai pressed something into her palm, and her fingers curled around a knife's hilt. "They'll need to dismount to attack with swords. I'll defend you, but if things go badly, take Flecht and follow the weild to the inn. You'll see it just back from the banks. You can trust the innkeeper."

Kai strode from her before she could point out that she had no idea how to fly a wingabeast. His sword rasped as he drew it from its sheath.

Just overhead, the riders split from one another. As they neared, Shae could see their eyes gleaming through cutouts in their hoods. Their wingabeasts' hooves touched ground, and they jumped from the saddle and onto the rock shelf with swords pointed at Kai.

The first rider advanced, a hair's breadth ahead of his companion, and as Kai met his lunge, swords clashed. Kai parried the second rider's thrust and spun to deflect the first rider's sword, which clanged against his armshield. Over and over, steel rang out.

Flecht snorted and laid his ears back, dancing beneath Shae. She patted the wingabeast's neck in an attempt to soothe him, but she felt less than calm herself. Although Kai fought well, how could he defend for long against two swordsmen? His knife weighted her hand, but she had no idea what to do with it. As a raena of Whellein, her training had included protocol and decorum, not fighting.

The riders closed in on Kai yet again, and the swordplay moved nearer. Flecht shrilled, and stones scattered beneath his churning hooves. One rider turned to point his sword toward Shae, but Kai's blade intercepted him. "Go *now!*" Kai called, and then whirled to stop another attack.

His words kicked her in the stomach, for they told her he didn't expect to survive. Her mind recoiled at the thought, and she sent a wordless plea to Lof Yuel. She turned Flecht's head westward but hesitated. Even if she knew how to send a wingabeast into flight, should she? Turning Flecht toward the battle, she gave up the notion of escape. She might have to watch him die, and then fall by the sword herself, but she could never leave Kai.

Anger flared through her with such radiance it pushed aside her confusion. She saw herself with Kai in her early days, throwing stones at a target on the far bank of the brook. The memory lifted her spirits, and she tightened her grip on the hilt of Kai's knife. Heart pounding, she drew back her arm but then lowered it. The fighting was too close. She might hit Kai.

A blade sliced through the air, just missing Kai's head, and she gasped. If she did nothing, he might die. She had to take the chance. The knife weighted her hand as, with breath held, she leaned forward, concentrating on the advance and retreat of combat.

Now!

The knife flashed through the air and thudded into flesh. Kai lurched and stepped backwards, and her stomach twisted. But when one of the riders collapsed instead, she released a shaking breath.

Kai flicked a glance her way, but then turned to meet a renewed attack from the fallen rider's companion. Steel ground against steel as they strained together. Neither gave way, and at last they sprang apart, panting as they eyed one another.

The rider feinted right but Kai thrust left, his blade cutting close to his opponent's side. The rider jumped back, and they circled one another with shields raised in a crude imitation of a courtly dance. When his opponent lunged, Kai deflected his sword, and they faced off once again. Shae sucked in a breath. Was it just her imagination, or did the rider's sword arm shake?

A hand grasped her ankle, and the pale eyes of the rider she'd felled glinted up at her through the holes in his mask. Blood seeped from his wounded shoulder to mar the front of his black surcoat. On his knees, he levered upward, the knife she'd used against him clutched in a bloody hand.

If she could find enough air she would scream. She kicked at him, but the rider dug his fingernails into her leg like claws and held tight. His arm drew back. The knife dripped blood.

Shae's hands convulsed on the reins, and a tremor traveled through Flecht. The wingabeast shrilled and reared, and the knife fell from the rider's hand.

A belated scream broke from Shae.

Kai's opponent lunged at him, but his sword

wavered. Kai's parry sent it spinning into a thicket of brambleberries. He turned toward Shae.

Flecht's wings unfurled above Shae as the wingabeast squatted on his haunches to spring into flight above the weild.

The rider dangled one-armed, his free arm flailing until he grasped the saddle. As his weight dragged her sideways, Shae gritted her teeth. She couldn't hold on much longer.

"Flecht, return!" Kai's call followed them.

As the wingabeast turned in answer, the hand slipped down her leg and fingernails dug into her ankle.

Screaming, Shae slipped further sideways, hanging on only by the saddle's pommel.

The crushing grip on her ankle released all at once and a splash sounded. The weild carried her attacker downstream.

She pulled herself fully into the saddle as Flecht descended. The wingabeast landed with a snort and a toss of his head, and Kai started toward them.

But behind Kai, the other rider lifted his companion's fallen sword.

"Watch out!" Shae cried.

Kai leaped into the saddle behind her. "Flecht, launch!"

Flecht rose into the air with a whinny.

Shifting restlessly, the two black wingabeasts neighed in response.

The remaining rider, running toward the wingabeasts, dwindled below them. Shae's neck ached as she alternately watched for him to follow and searched for the rider who had vanished in the water. As a bend of the weild took them out of sight, they veered and spiraled downward into a meadow set back from the banks of the weild. Flecht's hooves touched the ground, his wings folded, and they slipped into forest shadow at a meadow's edge.

"We'll travel the rest of the way to the inn through the forest, in case we're followed."

Kai's breath warmed her ear, although his words sent chills up her spine. What had she gotten herself into? "What is this all about anyway?"

Kai returned silence.

"You do plan to tell me, don't you? Why is my life at risk?"

"There are secrets at stake Shae, and I'm bound to them. Besides, one question leads to another, and we should keep quiet."

Shae sighed in defeat. She couldn't argue with his logic, or with his sense of honor.

An animal trail led them between towering trees and along a stream with banks curving over brown water riddled with mossy rocks.

At the softening of day, they emerged into a clearing and, where the track widened to a wagon trail near a ford, passed a fire-damaged structure. The homefarm must have burned recently, for smoke still spiraled from its charred wood. They passed the forlorn structure in silence. The path lifted clear of the forest long enough to show the sun, which hovered low in the sky. They skirted a narrow place where the weild cut deep, and then followed a bend.

A large house with smoke curling from a chimney of rounded stone stood on higher ground above a stable and a group of derelict outbuildings. Scattered cattle grazed in a pasture and waterfowl squawked in a small pond. Shae started. This must be the White

Feather Inn. Why did Kai's voice warm so when he spoke of this humble place?

When they reached the stable, Kai called out to the groom, who greeted him by name.

Shae studied the man. But for his rounded eyes and black hair, he might have been a Kindren.

The inn was smaller than she'd pictured but livelier than she could have imagined. A confused chorus of voices punctuated by laughter and an occasional shout carried to them as they entered. Light wended its uncertain way into the common room through deep, multi-paned windows. The smells of cooking and sweat permeated the smoky air.

As heads turned toward Shae, a hush fell. Her face went warm, and she longed to hide. She yielded to Kai as he guided her to one of the unoccupied tables. "I'll let them know we are here."

She lowered herself to the bench in gratitude, for in truth, her legs shook after the long day's ride. It would be unthinkable to spend more time in the saddle, as Kai sometimes must.

She looked up to find a man staring at her. A shock of hair the deep brown of gnarlwood bark covered his head, and hair concealed the lower half of his face as well. His eyes, a watery blue, shone as if with fever.

He reached for the tankard before him but missed. His companion threw back a head with hair the orange of rust and broke into hearty laughter. When the first man finally succeeded in hefting his tankard, he drank it down in a long gulp, and then sought for her again.

Shae returned his regard with grave attention. Did she look as odd to him as he did to her?

He jumped to unsteady feet, still gazing at her.

Shae's heart pounded. Did he mean to approach? But the man's companion clasped him, and they rocked in a jovial embrace. Shae sighed with relief when they sprawled at their table again.

She searched for Kai in the back of the room and found him deep in conversation with a muscular man near a door that must lead to the kitchens. The man flung an arm across Kai's shoulders in a casual embrace that spoke of friendship.

Shae stared at the muscular man, for he had hair of black. Belatedly remembering her manners, she pried her gaze away and closed her eyes for a respite from the jumbled sights and sounds around her.

Something thumped, and the aroma of food made her mouth water. "Now then, this will cheer you!"

Shae opened her eyes to find two wooden bowls of stew and a loaf of bread on the table before her.

The woman who had delivered them smiled, which brought apples to her cheeks. Her hair escaped its subduing brown kerchief, the locks red like licks of flame. She seemed friendly enough, and not much older than Shae herself. "I be Heddwyn, mistress of this inn. My husband, Quinn, delays your brother there, but give it no thought. I'll let Kai know his food's arrived and he'll likely be a' table afore the ale be poured."

Shae sat upright, ready to thank Heddwyn, but the inn mistress had already gone. Kai returned with the predicted promptness. "I'm sorry. I didn't mean to spend so much time talking with Quinn, but he had important news for us."

She gave him a weak, forgiving smile and offered him bread. "Will you not eat?"

He took the loaf, broke it, and returned a portion

to her. For a time neither spoke as they savored the warm stew. The coarse bread sat heavy in her stomach, but it would serve. After drinking today's stale elk-water, the hearty brown ale made a nice change. When they finished, Heddwyn withdrew the empty bowls.

"What news had your friend for us?" Shae returned to the earlier subject, raising her voice above the general ruckus, which had increased.

Kai looked past her. "I'll tell you later."

Her throat tightened. "Is something wrong?"

He gave a slight nod of his head, and she swallowed her questions.

Heddwyn returned bearing sweetberry crisp ladled over with cream. Putting the matter from her, Shae delighted in the treat. As Kai said, he would tell her later.

⊱⊰

Kai watched Shae's simple joy in the sweet dish and prayed all would go well this night. The news from Quinn was not good.

The inn keeper had shaken his head at sight of Kai and pulled him aside. "You should not have come here. Two nights ago a nearby homefarm burned. No one died, since none lived there, but folks be upset."

"I'm sorry to hear that." Kai pictured the burnt-out homefarm he and Shae had passed earlier.

Quinn stroked his chin. "There are those what saw two wingabeast riders in the air that night. Most say the Kindren be responsible. And now messengers from King Euryan of Westerland bring news that such things be happening there too." Quinn gestured with his head toward two men who drank together at one of the tables.

Kai had already observed the bearded messengers watching Shae far too closely for his comfort.

"I can feed you and bed you for the night," Quinn promised. "I'll not turn you away. But it be best you move on by morning."

Shae's sigh drew Kai from his dark thoughts. Another time and he might have smiled at the picture of contentment she made.

"Have you finished, then?" His voice held an edge. He stood and offered her his hand, which she took at once. Remorse went through him at her look of surprise and alarm. He had not meant to upset her, but furtive glances came their way often, and a nameless tension crackled in the air. They should leave.

Heddwyn's red-haired sister, Brynn, served the two messengers. She'd voiced objections to his presence at the inn before. He was, after all, a Kindren. Kai didn't know what Brynn said as she leaned down to the two men, but he didn't trust her, and the messengers had already imbibed enough to make them ready for trouble.

He and Shae must pass the messengers' table to leave the room. He took an unsteady breath and grasped Shae's elbow to guide her.

"We'll all be burned alive by those long-eyed *savages!*" Brynn's voice rose as they neared.

Kai's hackles lifted at the challenge in her voice, but he wanted no confrontation.

The men grumbled in agreement. "They be a blight on Elderland!" The tawny-haired one muttered into his tankard.

The dark-haired messenger staggered to his feet and blocked the way to the door.

Kai halted, ever watchful.

The messenger's hand went to the hilt of the dagger at his waist. "What business have you here?"

"That's none of your concern." Kai's voice, although quiet, sounded loud in the sudden hush. "Let us pass."

"I'll not." The man's chest expanded. "I be King Euryan's messenger. State your business."

"You ask amiss."

The man's gaze slid over Shae, slick as oil. "Who be *she*? Not your wife, I'll warrant. And yet she travels with you!"

"That has nothing to do with you."

The man's burly companion shoved to his feet, and others in the room made to rise.

Kai shifted into fighting stance. "We *will* pass."

5

The Stable Loft

The dark-haired messenger's hand snaked toward Shae's face.

Quick as thought, Kai struck the man's forearm.

The messenger snarled, and his dagger left its sheath.

Kai pushed Shae behind him, his sole thought to protect her, and then sidestepped to avoid the dagger's arc. His fist slammed into the man's jaw.

Brynn screamed and retreated in the direction of the kitchen.

The messenger careened backward, his dagger clanging as it hit the floor. His body caught the edge of the table, and it tilted over him. Crockery smashed. Ale spilled. He went down and lay groaning.

His companion's face turned red, and he surged forward, a dagger in his hand.

Shae screamed, but while springing out of reach of the blade, Kai couldn't look her way. Before his opponent could recover from his lunge, Kai shifted toward him and buried a fist in his stomach. The messenger grunted and bent forward, and Kai drove his knee into the man's face.

The second messenger slid down beside the first.

Kai glanced at Shae, relieved to find her

unharmed. She looked up from the slumped figures at her feet, her widened eyes dark with shock, and stared at him as if she'd never seen him before. Sorrow shot through him at what she had seen him do.

Quinn hurried in from the kitchen, followed closely by Brynn, and the swinging door banged to and fro behind them.

Kai wheeled toward movement in his side vision. Most of those who had made to rise at the start of the trouble now sat back down, but a burly man dressed like a farmer in ragged wool strode forward, his hands fisted and ready.

Quinn shook off Brynn and inserted himself between Kai and the farmer. "Calib, what quarrel have you here?"

Calib's face twisted. "This *Kindren* attacked King Euryan's messengers!"

The inn keeper pinned Kai with a glare. "Is that so? I'll not have such doings. Be gone with you!"

Surprise at Quinn's betrayal robbed Kai of speech.

Quinn turned back to Calib. "Let that lie between them. It has naught to do with you. I don't want trouble in my inn."

Calib chewed his lip while he glared at Kai. Finally, his posture eased. "For you, Quinn, but get him out of here."

Quinn sent Kai a wordless look, full of meaning.

Kai recovered himself. "As you wish." Grasping Shae's hand, he led her outside onto the porch but paused there to draw deep draughts of fresh air as his eyes adjusted to darkness.

꙰

Shae blinked but could not see beyond the pool of light spilling onto the porch from the oiled parchment window. The need to flee pulled at her, but her trembling legs wouldn't carry her far. An intense longing for the comfort and safety of her bed at Whellein brought her near tears. As she fought for control, a small sound caught in her throat, and Kai turned her into his embrace. She let him comfort her, putting from her mind thoughts of the violence the arms that held her had just wrought. She had never seen Kai in action before, and had not known he could fight with such deadly grace and precision. In truth, she had never seen *anyone* fight before, except in play.

A burst of bawdy laughter drifted from the inn. If she didn't know differently, she would think nothing untoward had happened. The disturbance had been but a wrinkle in the fabric of the evening to most of those within. Even the two messengers would shelter this night in the inn.

But where would she and Kai rest?

"Pssst…" The sound came out of the darkness below the steps.

Shae started, and Kai went still. "Who goes there?"

"Come, then!"

The voice belonged to a woman. By straining her eyes, Shae just made out below the porch a figure carrying something dark and bulky. She resisted the gentle pressure of Kai's hand at her elbow, but then she sensed that his tension had eased. Whoever called to them in the night, he must know her. Trying to quiet her jumpy nerves, she let Kai guide her down from the porch and toward the figure in the moonlight. Even as they neared, the woman's features remained hidden beneath the shadow of her cloak's hood.

Kai released Shae's elbow. "Why do you ask us to come when your husband tells us to go?"

"Be my husband what sent me, to settle you for the night. Come. We'll walk in darkness for I dare not bring a light, although I know the way well enough. Follow Heddwyn."

Heddwyn? Quinn had only just banished them from the inn. Why did his lady help them?

Heddwyn guided them to a hunched-over building, which they entered through a low door. The smell of leather, fresh hay, and manure assailed Shae. Unseen beasts thudded their hooves. Moonlight fell through the open doorway and around a slatted window above the loft, but the rest of the building reposed in darkness. Understanding dawned, and Shae gasped. *"Here?* We must sleep *here?"*

"Aye." Heddwyn spoke beside her. "You'd not be safe in the inn this night. The stables will serve, but take yourselves away early. Those two from King Euryan likely won't wake until midday, and with thick heads and bruises, but others could bring you sorrow."

Heddwyn stepped into the moonlight. She struggled to drag her dark burden up a ladder toward the loft. Reaching its top, she stepped from the ladder and paused to catch her breath, then beckoned to them as bars of moonlight from the loft window slatted across her. "Come."

Shae hesitated. Must a raena of Whellein sleep in a stable loft? What would Mother say about this night's events? But then, Mother had urged her to submit to Kai's care. When Kai touched her elbow, she sighed, kilted her skirts and climbed the ladder. She heard Kai following.

The hay dust in the loft made Shae sneeze.

Heddwyn lay down her burden, panting as she spread the thick furs on the hay where it spilled into drifts. Shae gave the makeshift beds a speculative look. She and Kai would stay warm enough beneath those furs, but something rustled among the bales of hay in the loft's dark recesses—rodents?

Finished with her task, Heddwyn bid them good night and disappeared down the ladder.

"I know it's not the comfort I promised you…" Kai's voice came out of the dimness that followed the lantern's withdrawal.

She banished the thought of furry bedmates as best she could, for his sake. "We must accept such comfort as we are given." She braced herself and removed her cloak, and then surrendered it to Kai, who hung it on a peg protruding from the wall. Shivering and shuddering, she slid beneath one of the piles of furs and pulled it to her chin.

But Kai knelt in prayer.

As Shae edged closer to him, the hay crunched beneath her, sending up a grassy scent. "What prayer did you give? Or should I not ask?"

"You may ask. I prayed for our safety. Tomorrow we cross the Maegrad Ceid."

"The Ice Mountains? I will join my prayers to yours, but do we have cause to fear?"

"The icy peaks offer peril enough for sojourners, but ancient lore tells of Erdrich Ceid, the Ice Witch who dwells in the passes. Truth to tell," Kai's voice warmed, "I have not met her in all my journeys to and from Whellein, but we should nonetheless keep watch."

Shae smiled at the child's tale, which she'd heard many times. A yawn took her by surprise, and her eyelids drooped. "What *else* have we to fear?"

"Only the cold and weariness that comes at such altitudes—and wind shears. But I know the passes well."

He didn't mention the possibility of encountering wingabeast riders bent on killing them, but she knew it existed. Even now, the dark riders might track them. She closed her eyes to pray with zeal but soon fell into the languor of warmth and drowsiness. "My thanks," she said, her tongue thick with sleep.

"Thanks?"

"You protected me this night."

"Sleep, Shae." She heard the smile in his voice. "Tomorrow's journey will try our strength."

꙰

Her steady breathing stirred the silence, a touching sound that comforted. Kai lay beside Shae, enveloped by the scent of hay, and reviewed the night's events. If the messengers had not imbibed too much, he might this day have suffered more than bruised knuckles. Something worse could have happened, too, had not Quinn stepped in.

He frowned. He didn't like to think how close to danger he'd brought Shae. He must watch over her with more care. Although he couldn't have known about the situation at the inn, he might have guessed that, sooner or later, the hostilities arising within Westerland would reach Norwood.

Here now in Norwood, as in Westerland, accusations of mischief by wingabeast riders flew. How could such a thing happen? In all Elderland, only the guardians of Rivenn, high guard of Torindan, commanded the wingabeasts. True, the creatures existed in the wild beyond Whellein, inhabiting the reaches behind the impassable peaks of Maegrad Paesad. Could others have tamed them? Or—distressing thought—could traitors exist within the guardians? Creating strife between the Elder and Kindren of Elderland at this time could threaten and weaken Torindan just at the transition of power from Lof Raelein Maeven to Elcon, her son.

Kai willed himself to let go of such unquiet thoughts, and a thread of song wove through his mind. *"For when the DayStar shines while discord darkens Elderland, hearken to the signs and rest within Lof Yuel's hand."* He had never understood its meaning. At a time of discord, how could one rest? And yet, in sleep at last, he did.

❧

Unspeakable evil groped toward Shae. Her heart drumming, she lifted her head in slatted moonlight. Where was she? A strange lump crouched, ready to spring, at the edge of shadow. Fear twisted her stomach.

His even breathing reminded her that Kai slept near, and she sighed her relief. It had been only a dream.

But even as her body relaxed toward slumber, her mind snapped a warning. A horrible creature from the world of shadows still sought her. She felt it.

Shae sat up in alarm, straining to see in the darkness.

The loft's wall faded away to reveal two wingabeasts flying toward the inn out of a moon-

50

washed sky. Dark riders clung to their backs.

The image melted into the walls, which solidified.

"Kai!"

He stirred. "What's wrong?"

"Our pursuers draw near. I saw them."

He sat up and ran a hand through his hair. "You must have had a nightmare."

"It was no dream."

"How do you know that?"

"I just know!" She struggled to stand, hampered by her tunics.

He pushed to his feet and steadied her. "All right, then. Tell me what happened."

"Some *thing* searches for me, Kai. I can't explain it—"

"That's all right. I believe you."

"I saw, as if in a waking dream, two wingabeasts fly toward the inn. I couldn't tell for certain, but it looked as though their riders wore hoods."

He pushed her away with gentle hands. "Wait here."

The creak of the ladder told her where he'd gone. She shivered. Where had Kai hung her cloak? There! Two darker shapes stood out in the dimness. With trembling legs she crept toward them, and at last her hand closed on wool. She gave a tug and her cloak came free. The hair at the back of her neck lifted, and she wanted to run back into the moonlight beneath the window. But Kai would need his cloak too, and there was little time to waste. Ignoring her sense of foreboding, she pulled the second cloak from its peg.

Darkness slithered around Shae's soul.

Her knees gave way, and she fell, twisting her hand beneath her. But she bit back her cry, fearful the wrong ears would hear. A chill crawled over her in woeful contrast to the flare of pain in her wrist. Fingers of fear probed her mind, as if to capture her thoughts, and her throat went dry.

A rush of air reached her, and she realized Kai must have opened the door to the stableyard and gone out. She drank in the cleansing flow, but then the stench of death returned. She could barely breathe and didn't dare call out, but would the strange presence suffocate her within hailing distance of Kai?

Lof Yuel! The name, more a prayer, sounded in her mind. As her ears rang, she knew she would faint....

દેન્ઐ

"Shae, wake up!"

She moaned and shook off the creeping blackness.

Hands gripped her arms. "What's wrong with you?"

"It's—gone."

"Tell me what happened."

"I—don't know. A fell spirit somehow touched mine." Her voice strangled in her throat.

Kai gathered her against him. "You're safe now. We must keep you so. You were right, by the way. Two hooded figures slipped into the inn, and I could just make out dark wingabeasts in the clearing between the stableyard and the porch. I hope Quinn and his guests bolted their bedchambers this night. I wish I could warn them somehow, but more lives are at stake than those contained within the inn."

There it was again—that hint of a greater purpose. But even if she had time to ask questions, did she want to know the answers? A shudder walked up her spine.

"Will they search for us?"

"We have to assume so. We don't want to give away that we slept here. Are you well enough to hide our bedding? There's not much time, and I have to saddle Flecht with little light."

Whatever had attacked her was now gone, but the last thing she wanted was to be left alone again. She bit back her protest. "I'll manage."

Kai caught her wrist and pulled her to her feet. "Be careful on the ladder when you come down."

"Wait!" She snatched up his cloak and pressed it into his hands. "Take this."

Kai touched her face. "Thank you." Bars of moonlight slanted across him as he strode toward the ladder.

Forgetting all about rodents, she burrowed into the hay until she'd made a hollow large enough to hide the furs. She covered them over, the task taking far too long. Hay dust tickled her throat, and she sneezed as softly as possible, then paused to listen with her heart beating in her ears.

The rustling of hay alerted her. Kai, with Fletch beside him, waited at the bottom of the ladder. The angle of Kai's head conveyed his tension, and as she descended, he caught and lifted her onto the wingabeast's back. Flecht clopped toward the stable door.

Shae sucked in a breath. "Must we go that way?"

"The back door is barred from the outside. We'll have to sneak out through the stableyard."

"But anyone can see us in this moonlight."

"Only if they happen to look. There's even more danger of being overheard. Remember, voices carry far in the night."

They approached the stable door, and as alarm tingled through her, she said no more. The door, already ajar, swung inward with a moan. Shae winced at the sound. Beyond Kai in the widening gap, the stableyard shone blue in the moonlight. As Kai led Flecht through the opening, a brisk wind slapped Shae's face. Despite its chill, she resisted pulling up her hood. She might need to rely upon her hearing.

Kai slipped back into the stable, and Shae waited alone in the stableyard. The skin on her arms prickled, and she eyed the silent inn, but found no sign of the intruders within. She could almost doubt they existed save for the dark shapes of their wingabeasts grazing beside the porch. One of the creatures lifted its head and knickered. Although his ears pricked, Flecht did not respond.

The stable door shut behind Kai and, as dark shapes crawled up its rough surface, Shae's breathing hitched. But when Kai led Flecht forward, the shadows copied their motions, and relief washed over her. The cloak of darkness waited for them beyond the stable's corner, just steps away.

A rasp drew her attention, and she held her breath as the inn door swung inward.

Running now, Kai pulled Flecht around the corner and to a halt in blessed shadow. Blinded by sudden darkness, Shae understood his caution. And yet, with every nerve strung tight, she had to restrain herself from urging Flecht into a run. Only when Kai touched her arm did she hear the ragged sound of her own breathing. She kicked away the panic baying at her heels as Kai lifted into the saddle before her and took up the reins.

They had gone only a few steps when the stable

door creaked. As Shae hiccupped on a gasp of hysteria, Kai's hand clapped over her mouth. When she nodded, he released her. She mentally scolded herself. She would do neither of them any good if she didn't get her nerves under control.

Flecht reached the rear of the stable, and then carried them into a small meadow. Although moonlight picked them out, the stable's few windows all faced the inn. If they could only reach the stand of Kabas between the meadow and the weild, they could hide.

As the stable door thudded, Kai urged Flecht into a run.

The hooded riders rounded the stable's corner, but Flecht moved into the darkness beneath the trees and paused. Shae pressed her face against Kai's back, and his hand slid over hers where they rested at his waist. Warmth went through her at his touch, and she sat straighter.

A murmur of voices rose and fell in the shifting wind as the hooded riders ventured farther into the clearing. They seemed to peer straight at her, and she held her breath. But the riders, muttering together in angry tones, reined in short of the trees. Their wingabeasts leaped upward into flight and soon dwindled into black dots against the pewter sky.

"Are you all right?"

She nodded, but her body shook.

"They're pointed southward, which makes sense if they *borrowed* those wingabeasts from the stables at Torindan. Even if they ride without stopping, they'll be hard-pressed to return before the wingabeast keeper stirs. Let's give them a head start to make sure, and then we'll follow."

Follow? She should have listened to Lyse's warning, after all.

6

Torindan

"Torindan!" Shae breathed.

The stronghold of Rivenn perched below them on an arm of rock that thrust into the swirling waters of Weild Aenar. Its bulk rose from the mist like some noble bird of prey. Sand-pink wings fanned backward to water's edge, and white plumage fluttered from atop its many towers. Walled fields stretched from the gatehouse to the granite cliffs that towered overhead. Beyond the fields and near the river, a collection of roofs huddled behind a town wall.

A humbler Torindan lay in eternal summer surrounded by rolling hills and flowering meadows, at least in her imaginings. This monolith crowded every vista and tinged the very air with its pale colors. She blinked away tears and swallowed against the tightness in her throat. Torindan. High Hold of Faeraven. Seat of the fabled guardians of Rivenn. Center of music and learning. Archive of history. Allerstaed of Worship.

Flecht lurched in a sudden gust, and Shae tightened her arms around Kai, grateful for his warmth. He would be the only person she'd truly know at Torindan. She'd understood that from the start, but now the reality faced her. When a downdraft caught them, the thrill in her stomach wasn't entirely due to the unexpected drop.

Kai's back muscles flexed as he tightened the reins, and Flecht's great wings batted to bring them up level.

Despite her misgivings, Shae welcomed their journey's end. This rugged land of snow-bound crags, cirques, and valleys seemed to stretch on forever.

She could still see in her mind's eye the jagged shafts of ice-encrusted stone pushing against the sky that were the Maegrad Ceid, the Ice Mountains. Nature's pulse beat with a wild rhythm there. Mysterious under-shrouding mists, the passes had revealed themselves in glimpses of a forbidding landscape where rocks thrust upward through the snow.

Flecht banked, and Shae swallowed against a new bout of nausea, grateful she would soon find rest.

Their approach from the river took them past the postern water gate. Its hewn steps, walled and flanked by defensible platforms, ran from an upper gate to water's edge. They rounded the side of the castle to come upon the barbican, an impressive gatehouse with wide towers and twin turrets. Dampness and the smell of fetid water greeted them as, with a final batting of wings, they landed before the drawbridge that jumped the moat to the barbican.

A voice called from the turrets. "Kai returns!" Metal rasped, and the wood and iron doors swung inward. Kai guided Flecht across the drawbridge. They entered the barbican, and the wingabeast's hooves clattered across a plank floor riddled with trap doors. As the massive doors thudded shut behind them, Shae glanced back. The two guardians dropping the iron bar into its rest wore the same surcoat of green and gold as

Kai did—the uniform of the guardians of Rivenn.

They passed beneath the iron teeth of a raised portcullis to enter a corridor where light fell in strips through arrow slits and around closed "murder holes" in the ceiling. At the end of the corridor and beyond a second raised portcullis, a sunlit patch of cobbled road took them onto a drawbridge spanning a smaller channel of the moat.

They entered the inner gatehouse through an archway and beneath a third raised portcullis. A short corridor with a row of doors on either side led through the center of the gatehouse, but before they reached the archway at its end a flame-haired figure emerged from one the guardrooms.

"Kai! You return. The Lof Raelein already asks for you." The youth gazed with undisguised curiosity at Shae.

"Aerlic!" Kai greeted him. "I present my sister, Shae."

"Welcome, Fair One!"

She smiled at his intensity but dutifully inclined her head in response to his courtly bow.

"How fares the Lof Raelein?" Kai asked.

Aerlic's roguish face sobered. "Her body weakens."

Kai frowned. "And her spirit?"

"It remains strong."

"That, at least, comforts." Kai turned to Shae. "Aerlic is First Archer of the guardians of Rivenn but in my absence, set aside his bow to take my place at Lof Raelein Maeven's side." His words held an edge.

Aerlic frowned. "I kept my duty. I only came to the gatehouse for a quick word with Craelien while Freaer visits Lof Raelein Maeven. When she rambles, a strangeness overtakes her that only his music can soothe."

Kai slid from Flecht's back. "Craelin is First Guardian of Rivenn, and Freaer is First Musician of Torindan." He raised his arms to Shae, and she let him take her weight and swing her to the ground.

"What do you think of Torindan?" Kai asked near her ear.

"It's all I'd thought and more. And yet it seems— *different*."

He pulled away to look at her. "Different?"

"Not as—kind."

"Ah!" His face lit. "Children often picture what should be."

Shae pushed back her hood and shook out the burnished tangles that had long ago escaped their plait. "But I am no longer a child."

"True enough."

She lowered her hands from her hair, caught by something in his voice. But he already turned away.

"Let me tend to your wingabeast," Aerlic offered. "The Lof Raelein looks for you."

Kai surrendered Flecht's reins to Aerlic with a weary smile. "Thank you."

Kai escorted Shae through the archway into the outer ward. Aerlic followed behind them, leading Flecht, but turned onto the side path that cut to the stables while Kai and Shae continued along the main path toward the gateway to the inner ward.

Shae gasped at the tiered fountain beyond the gateway's arch, which rose from a square pool of dressed stone amidst budding roses.

Kai smiled. "A wellspring supplies the fountain and feeds water through pipes to the kitchens. The stables have a separate well. The source for both lies deep underground, and so may never be poisoned in a siege."

As she neared the pool, Shae saw the bronze figures topping the fountain—a rearing wingabeast with a youthful rider.

Kai paused beside her. "Talan's wild ride."

She had known that particular tale since her early days. With the sun behind him, she squinted at Kai. "The statue puts your description to shame."

"I did my best to show it to you with words."

Shae gazed with longing at paths wandering among early flowers, strongwoods and roses, but Kai pressed her onward. She yielded, but she would return to explore this exquisite garden.

A square structure with four corner towers dominated the inner ward. This keep dwarfed the one at Whellein Hold thrice over. The gated archways behind it must be the postern and upper water gates. Every hold had a postern gate—a way of escape from the rear. Kai told her that Torindan's watergate could receive delivery of goods by boat from Weild Aenor, which would make a siege more difficult.

A smaller building of the same pinkish sandstone connected by means of a vaulted corridor to the side of the keep—the Allerstaed. Stained glass windows looked out from arches over the doorway and ranked down the building's sides. Beside, and bending away behind it, lay a garden of vegetables and herbs in square plots.

They ascended a circular stairway within a corner tower of the keep, and then followed a paneled corridor. Their footsteps echoed above a faint thread of music—an intricate weaving of voice and instrument, which grew in volume.

Kai knocked on a carved and gilded door at the end of a short corridor. A round-faced maid bowed her head and admitted them. Shae followed Kai into what must be the Lof Raelein's chambers. Exhaustion lent her a curious detachment, as if she walked in her sleep. The elaborate chambers themselves added to the illusion, for their exquisite beauty did not seem quite real.

In the Lof Raelein's outer chamber, a seating area waited before an enormous marble fireplace where a fire glowed. Upon the mantle twined carven images of unibeasts and gryphons. Above it perched a variety of stuffed fowl—pheasants, wingens, and graylets among them. The birds appeared so life-like, Shae imagined they might spread their wings and take flight at any moment. On the wall over the mantel hung a tapestry that showed the first of the Kindren entering Elderland from Anden Raven at Gilead Riann— the Gate of Life.

The maid opened another carved and gilded door and led them into the inner chamber. Details imprinted themselves in brief flashes on Shae's tired mind...white furnishings....mats in deep colors...vibrant tapestries...a prism turning in a stray draft at the window embrasure and refracting rainbows through the chamber.

The music ceased as they entered, but flaemlings flitted from perch to perch in a hanging golden cage and trilled their own melodies. A fire of fragrant draetenn boughs in the marble hearth snapped and crackled its percussion.

A movement drew Shae's eye to one of the window embrasures, where the changing light of late afternoon obscured the figure of a musician bent over his lute.

"Kai." A voice rasped from the carved bed that dominated the room. "You have brought her?"

Shae started. In a combination of weariness and awe of Torindan, she had all but forgotten the purpose of her visit.

The musician came away from the window, and light slanted across him to reveal a lithe figure and features of surpassing beauty. Vibrant hair of gold sprang above a well-formed brow. Fathomless eyes held her. Shae caught her breath, and her hand went out in a blind motion.

Kai's arm braced her. "I have brought Shae—by too long a journey."

"She will rest then, after greeting me."

Shae tore her gaze from the musician as the Lof Raelein made her pronouncement. Shae approached the bed to give her bow and hid her shock at sight of the shrunken figure lying there.

"Lof Raelein." She took the dry hand proffered and, on an impulse of pity, touched her lips to the pale skin. "I greet you."

Maeven's face softened. "Such a gentle child. Perhaps my mind will settle now you are here. It's taken with wandering of late…" Her face wrinkled in lines of perplexity.

"Kai said you wished for me. I have no idea why I should deserve such an honor, but if my presence brings you comfort, I am glad."

"I have not forgotten our other meeting."

Shae smiled. "Nor have I."

"I only wish there had been *more*—more time…" Her features twisted as tears washed the seawater eyes, but then the Lof Raelein's face smoothed. "You will sing my death song."

"Oh no!"

"Promise me!"

Shae hesitated, but then inclined her head in defeat. Who was she to deny the Lof Raelein's request? "As you wish."

"Thank you." Maeven's voice weakened. "Go now. I tire, and you must rest as well. We can speak again, should Lof Yuel allow it. Freaer, stay and comfort me with music."

Shae looked toward the golden musician who waited in the embrasure, his head bowed as his fingers ran silently over his lute's strings.

Maeven beckoned the servant. "I give Chaeldra over to you."

Shae murmured her thanks, eager to end the meeting. Shame filled her at the self-serving desire, but in truth, the trying journey had left her no reserves with which to face the reality of life's passing. She longed only for food and rest and must, of necessity, turn from death to tend the needs of life.

She stood, but hesitated as her gaze collided with Freaer's.

Kai bowed to Maeven and inclined his head to the musician. "Freaer."

The musician returned Kai's gesture with a touch of melancholy. Soft strains followed them from the chamber.

❧⸱❦

At the first sight of her outer chamber, Shae exclaimed with delight. Kai watched her move about the room, admiring its tapestries of unibeasts and maidens, running a hand over carved strongwood benches, and sighing over window hangings adorned with the gilded rose of Rivenn. But as her gaze met his, the joy in her face extinguished.

She did not touch any of the food Chaeldra brought them. When she spoke, he leaned forward to catch her whisper. "Have I somehow erred?"

The quaver in her voice stilled the harsh remark poised on his lips. He set down his goblet, for his appetite fled at the trembling of her chin. Chaeldra stepped forward to refill his goblet.

"Leave us." He winced at the harshness in his own voice.

Chaeldra obeyed but cast a sullen look his way before going through a side door that led to her own quarters.

Kai chided himself. Would he now rail at servants? He took a long breath. Exhaustion, tension and the weight of secrets had combined to unnerve him. He brought his thoughts back to Shae's question. "She should not have asked you…."

"…to sing her death song?"

He spread his hands. "Such an honor by custom belongs to Torindan's First Musician."

"*Freaer?* She asked me in front of him! No wonder he looked—well, he seemed…"

"Unhappy?" Kai passed a hand across his eyes. "Death often forgets courtesy."

"Which carries more weight—custom or Maeven's wishes?"

"A Lof Raelein has the power to change custom. Her wisdom in doing so might draw scrutiny."

Shae gave him a fretful look. "What should I do?"

He lifted a joint of pheasant and taking a bite,

chewed and swallowed before answering. "I don't know."

"How can that be? You always know what to do!"

"I'm sorry, Shae, that you find me so—diminished." She did not look at him, and he thought she fought to quell tears. He berated himself yet again. The day's journey had provided Shae trial enough without the added shock of seeing Maeven so ill. Just as well, then, that Maeven had kept other revelations to herself, although he could hope she would not wait too long to give them.

She made a small sound in her throat. "I'm sorry, too." She looked at him, her eyes shadowed. "I've created difficulties, haven't I?"

He shook his head. "Forgive me. I'm out of sorts, it seems. I don't blame you for Maeven's error. I should have kept the matter to myself. Now, forget such concerns and take food, Shae. You must hunger. We've had little to eat the entire day."

Shae raised her goblet from the small table before her and sipped the ginger beer. With murmured thanks, she took a portion of pheasant Kai cut for her, and they completed their meal in awkward silence.

He left her then, carrying away an image of her framed in a tall window, hair escaping her plait. Sunset fell across her shoulder and lent its mysteries to the quiet garden with the fountain at its center behind her. Fire limned the high peaks beyond. Kai shut the door between them, caught by a feeling she'd already slipped away from him.

∂∽∾

"Trouble with the Elder has arisen in Norwood."

Elcon, warming himself before the fire, looked up at Kai's words. Sometimes when he glanced at Elcon, Kai found himself lost in memories of Lof Shraen Timraen. Elcon had his mother's sea green eyes and pale burnished hair, but his father's features.

"*What* do you say?" Elcon seemed too young for such burdens but, like Timraen, must carry them. "*More* trouble?" He jerked his head toward Craelin, who moved toward the door.

Kai gave a belated bow. "True, Lof Frael. Two hooded riders on wingabeasts attacked me between Whellein Hold and the Whitefeather Inn. Also, witnesses report that two wingabeast riders burned an abandoned homefarm in Norwood. And then I had a— ah—an encounter with messengers from King Euryan of Westerland, come to warn Norwood against Kindren attack."

"More trouble." Weariness laced Elcon's voice.

Craelin turned from bolting the door. "Yesterday, a messenger brought word of disturbances from Westerland."

Kai shook his head. "This makes no sense."

Elcon pressed the pads of his fingers against his temples. "The Kindren have lived in peace beside the Elder since coming from Anden Raven so long ago. Will we now have discord?" He spoke with restraint, but his words penetrated.

"Could there be some mistake? Perhaps the raiders only *appeared* to be Kindren."

Elcon shrugged. "Kindren blood sometimes runs diluted in Elder veins. That could perhaps account for appearances, but what of the wingabeasts?"

Craelin left his position at the door and joined Kai on a green and blue woven mat near the benches before the fire. They stood much the same height and met at eye level. "Did you learn anything about the riders?" Craelin asked. "Did the witnesses describe them?"

Kai shook his head, wishing he'd had the presence of mind to query Quinn in detail. "I didn't speak to the witnesses."

Elcon paced before the fire. "As far as we know, only the Kindren have tamed the wingabeasts of Maegrad Paesad. And, among the Kindren, only the guardians have access to the creatures. Could things have changed?"

Kai spread his hands. "That question has plagued me since Norwood. Anything is possible, but wingabeasts have declined in the wild since Talan's time and now dwell only in the farthest reaches of Maegrad Paesad. Any who sought them would risk life itself crossing ice fields and glacial moraines, and then must lead unwilling beasts out by the same route."

"Such a thing is close to impossible!" Craelin's expression darkened, his jaw tightened, and his clear blue eyes misted. "More likely, the traitors dwell within the ranks of the guardians. We must find them at all costs."

Elcon paused in his pacing. "What do you suggest?"

Craelin squared his shoulders. "We should allow the traitors to trap themselves."

"*How?*"

A small silence grew out of Elcon's question, but Craelin roused at last. "We can question the guardians, one by one. Someone may have noticed something unusual on the nights the raids took place, or perhaps the guilty will betray themselves if questioned."

Elcon inclined his head. "It's worth a try."

Kai rubbed his chin. "Should we not watch from the bastions and double the stable guard?

"We would only alert the traitors if we made such changes. And yet..." Craelen's face lit. "We could place spies in the stable loft each night."

"We could." Elcon agreed. "But who can we trust with such a mission?"

Craelin grew thoughtful. "I can name no guardian I do not trust, and yet all are suspect."

Elcon sighed. "Then take your spies from outside the guardians."

Craelin nodded and glanced sideways at Kai. "But who?"

This question overtaxed Kai's tired mind. The fire had burned to coals. Elcon called a halt and enjoined them to return to his chambers tomorrow night.

Torindan lay in slumber as Kai returned to the comfort of his small bedchamber. Strains of music drifted to him, for his room connected to Maeven's outer chamber. He went to the window, pushed aside the hangings, and opened the shutters.

Striding through the archway and into the outer bailey, Craelin leaned into the wind blowing from the snowfields as he headed for the gatehouse where his sleeping chambers lay. As Kai watched, roiling blackness blotted the stars from the sky, one by one.

The storm broke with a howl, and he closed the shutters and let the hangings fall into place. He settled into his cold bed and thought not of traitors, but of Shae. He had noted her silent exchange with Freaer earlier. She would find suitors at Torindan, he supposed, but the idea filled him with dismay. He had enough to think about without keeping her out of that kind of trouble. He could even wish for her return to Whellein, but such a decision lay beyond his reach. With a sigh, he accepted the truth. There could be no turning back for Shae—or for him.

❧

A foul wind breathed over Shae, and the hair on the back of her neck raised in warning. A hissing from the broken stairway sent prickles walking over her skin. Eyes gleamed in the shadows, and long shudders traveled her spine.

Somewhere, something shrieked.

Shae stumbled on the stone stair suspended between a dark void and a wall of living stone. She called for Kai, but her voice made no sound. Where was he?

"Find the light and be saved..." The whispered words stirred the air.

She strained to see in the dimness. Who had spoken?

And then the broken stairway with its stench and the eyes of death dissolved away. Chest heaving, she lay trapped between waking and sleeping.

Light flared around the shutters. The pattering rain echoed the thrum of her pulse. Wind rattled the window and whined into the chamber through cracks. Drafts scuttled across the floor and sent the bed hangings swaying.

Darkness seeped into the room and wrapped around her very soul. She longed to escape, to flee, but her leaden legs would not carry her. Cold tendrils wrapped about her mind, probing, seeking entrance...

"Lof Yuel, protect me!"

An inner light flickered, and the weight of darkness shifted.

She felt it then—a second, quieter soul. Without hesitating, she welcomed its soothing touch. In the daylight, she would likely question everything, including her own sanity. But here in the dead of night, questions would not find answers.

7

Sword and Scepter

Craelin's expression reflected Kai's own frustration as Dithmar, another guardian who had seen nothing and knew nothing, left the gatehouse guardroom with a spring in his step, whistling.

Like Dithmar, each guardian had seemed innocent under questioning.

Kai sighed. While relieved to find no hint of duplicity among the guardians, he couldn't help his disappointment at failing to discover the traitor's identity.

A rap at the scarred strongwood door announced the arrival of the last guardian to be questioned, Guaron, keeper of the wingabeasts. Like the other guardians, Guaron did not ask why they summoned him but waited before them with quiet dignity.

Craelin rose from the bench that flanked the rough table centered in the sparse chamber. "Greetings, Guaron. We have questions for you."

Emotion, at once repressed, crossed Guaron's rugged face. Surprise? Or something more?

Craelin's face remained neutral. "Have you noticed anything unusual from the other guardians?"

Guaron shook his head and his fine hair, straw-colored and cropped at chin level, followed the movement. "I've noticed nothing untoward. Should I have?"

"And the wingabeasts? Have you noticed anything strange about their behavior?"

Guaron drew breath as if to respond, but checked. His gaze swept from Craelin, who circled him, to Kai, waiting in silence at the battered table. "I think—well, yes I have."

Craelin halted. "Pray tell us."

Guaron rubbed his chin, and one index finger found its cleft. "Now you mention it, I *have* noticed a certain restlessness in the stables of late."

Craelin's eyes, nested in squint lines, glinted blue. "How long have you noticed this?"

"Not long, but it started before the Lof Raelein fell ill."

Craelin tilted his head. "Restlessness, you say?"

Guaron's glance flitted to Kai. "It reminded me of times in Glindenn Hold, before I came to Torindan, when the horses I tended sensed the approach of garns. Lately it's seemed…"

Kai sat forward on the bench.

"Sometimes I could almost swear…" Guaron's index finger again sought its rest. "Certain wingabeasts can seem out of sorts for no reason, almost as if… as if something keeps them from sleep."

Craelin clasped his hands behind his back. "Have you heard or seen anything to shed light upon such observations? Anything out of place? Any sounds you might have disregarded at the time?"

Guaron's forehead furrowed, but he shook his head. "I can think of nothing."

"What about yesterday morning? Were all the wingabeasts accounted for?"

"Yes, but I thought two of the blacks might be sick. They improved with food and rest, though."

"Thank you, Guaron. Seek either Kai or me should you think of anything else. Say nothing of this to anyone."

After Guaron murmured assent, Craelin dismissed him. His step in the corridor didn't spring as Dithmar's had, but Kai couldn't fault him for that. He didn't feel particularly lighthearted either, given what they had just learned. He rose from the bench he'd occupied throughout the interviews and flexed his tense shoulder muscles.

Craelin stood also. "What think you?"

Kai shrugged. "Guaron appears truthful, and he confirms the wingabeasts have been upset of late."

"Our plan to post spies may well yield results. Have you given thought to who might assist in this?"

"What if we take our spies from among those who hunt and track for Torindan?"

Craelin put a hand on the back of his neck and bowed his head. "Your idea has merit. Trackers know best the art of watching." He dropped his arm. "Let Dorann be among them."

"And his brother, Eathnor."

"All right, but let's keep the number of spies low. The fewer who know they exist, the safer they'll be. Two can take turns watching over the wingabeasts from the stable loft at night." Craelin gave a nod of dismissal. "Tonight we will tell Elcon our strategy."

Kai sought food and drink at the great hall and filled his trencher full of savory bruin stew. Abandoning his normal habit, he sat alone. The morning had soured him on conversation. Not that any of the guardians who sat nearby were talkative. Honor-bound to silence, they would not speak of their questioning, even to one another. And so they spoke of nothing. Kai did not linger over his stew.

On his way to Maeven's chambers, he stopped to tap at Shae's outer door. Silence followed for so long that he turned away. But the door swung inward and Chaeldra peered out. The apple-cheeked maid, unkempt and breathless, appeared not much older than Shae. She looked at him with bright eyes as a flush crept up her neck and hair the color of honey escaped from her cap. Before he could speak, she put a finger to her lips. "Shae sleeps."

"Yet?"

She averted her gaze. "The Lof Raelein said she might sleep as long as she likes."

With a bob of her head, she made to shut the door, but he stopped it against his foot. "Send her, when she wakes, to the Lof Raelein's chambers."

"Just as the Lof Raelein wishes."

He released the door and it swung shut with a final click of the latch. He examined the rampant gryphons carved into its surface. Did Chaeldra's words hold a touch of resentment? He'd not treated her well the night before. He turned toward the corner tower, putting the servant from his mind. A smile touched his lips at thought of Shae still abed. Well, she'd earned it. She'd endured with fortitude the privations of their journey and suffered with grace his ill humor.

Eufemia, the willowy serving maid, admitted Kai to the Lof Raelein's chamber. Maeven seemed stronger and more focused today. Elcon knelt at his mother's bedside and smoothed the hair from her brow, speaking to her in quiet tones.

Eufemia poured water into a goblet from a cut-glass ewer, but Maeven waved both glass and servant away. "Go at once upon my *other* errand."

Eufemia bowed and left the room.

"Good day, Kai. You look somewhat improved. Take your ease here beside me, if you will."

Kai sank into the red velvet cushions of the bedside chair and, as mother and son returned to their conversation about some bygone hunt, gave them his silence. He had learned long ago to remain at hand but detached and vigilant. He seemed, by nature, suited to keeping his own company.

When a rap sounded at Maeven's outer chamber door, Kai answered it in Eufemia's absence. Benisch, Steward of Rivenn, clad in blue and girdled with links of gold, swept past him into the room. Adorning Benisch's feet were fine blue slippers sewn with tiny gold bells that jingled when he walked.

"Good Steward, you honor me with your visit." Maeven gave a fleeting smile.

Clinking and jingling, Benisch bent over her hand with pretty manners.

Kai resumed his seat at Maeven's bedside while he repressed a chuckle at the chagrin on Elcon's face. Benisch, Kai guessed, came not to visit Maeven but to remind Elcon of his duties.

Benisch straightened and favored Maeven with a smile. "I am grateful for the opportunity to wait upon you."

He would have spoken again, but Maeven forestalled him. "How fortunate you should come just now when I have need of you."

"If I can serve you in some way—"

"You may stand witness." Maeven hesitated. "I've put this off, but I can do so no longer. The time has come. I shall bestow the Sword of Rivenn and the Scepter of Faeraven upon the next Lof Shraen of Faeraven. By now, Eufemia will have given Craelin a missive stamped with my seal asking him to retrieve them from the strongroom. They should arrive anon."

Kai had no doubt that Benisch misliked having his afternoon spent for him, and indeed the steward scowled, but protocol demanded he accept such a duty with grace. To his credit, he took a seat in a window embrasure and folded his arms to wait.

Benisch intrigued Kai, who could read most people with ease, but not Benisch. The steward, a poor and distant relative of Timraen's, had advanced to his present position at the former steward's death. Benisch stood in less favor than Riechardt had, for his more literal interpretation of the law. Not that any steward culled popularity. Even kindly Riechardt had known criticism.

A tap came at the inner chamber door, and it opened to admit Eufemia, followed by Craelin bearing the Sword and Scepter. Two of the guardians, Dithmar and Weilton, entered behind him, swords at their sides.

Out of respect for the ancient emblems of the Kindren, Kai stood, as did Elcon and Benisch. Craelin crossed to Kai and placed the Scepter of Faeraven in his hands. Kai's fingers curved around smooth metal as the gleam of rubies, diamonds, and emeralds met his eye.

Maeven waved a hand. "We shall begin!" All drew near, and Elcon knelt at her bedside. "I remember a time when Timraen carried Sword Rivenn into battle. With this Sword, forged by Kunatel in the Viadrel, the Flames of Virtue, he freed me from the garns at Pilaer." Maeven's face glowed as if with youth, and her voice throbbed with vibrancy. "Neither can I forget the sad night when Timraen passed Sword Rivenn into my hands. Locked away during an era of peace, it has waited for stronger arms than mine.

"Listen well, my son, for the time to once again wield Sword Rivenn approaches. This twin-edged Sword divides joint and marrow, spirit and soul, bringing judgment and destruction in its wake. And yet, it can break magics and act as a beacon to guide the lost to safety." She held out her hands, and Craelin laid in them the bejeweled hilt of Sword Rivenn. But she strained to lift it, and Craelin lent the strength of his hands to hers.

Maeven laid the flat of the blade on Elcon's head. "In this sword find birth, death, and life."

Elcon stood, received Sword Rivenn from his mother's hand, and sighted down its gleaming length. His sea-green eyes shone. "I will strive for worthiness to carry such a blade."

Maeven smiled. "My son, as Timraen's son, you already possess the worth you seek."

She beckoned to Kai, and he gave the Scepter into her hands, but steadied them with his own.

"Elcon, son of Timraen, open heart and hands to Faeraven, the ancient alliance of *ravens,* lands joined of necessity and choice."

"I receive and will keep the alliance of Faeraven." Elcon accepted the Scepter as he recited the ceremonial words and added, "with all my heart."

"Well said." Maeven's voice quavered, and she fell back against her scarlet cushions.

"I am honored and humbled to hold a thing of such beauty and history in my hands." Elcon raised the golden Scepter, its many jewels catching the light. The staff terminated in a gryphon with wings aloft. In its claws it clutched an orb of sapphire with a white star blazing at its heart.

Maeven's eyes gleamed in a white face. "My son, you shall make your own history."

8

Freaer

As a trick of light contrived to make Maeven look young again, Kai smiled at her sleeping form. He spared a brief thought of pity for Elcon, drawn away at the conclusion of the ceremony by Benisch on some trivial matter or other. The others had dispersed also, leaving Kai to keep silent vigil at the Lof Raelein's bedside.

Maeven stirred, and her eyelids opened. "Have I slept long?"

"Not long, but well." He smiled and took in the restoration sleep had wrought. The tremor that had taken her earlier had ceased, and she looked strong. Incredible as it seemed, she might yet rally. Hope died even as it sprang forth within him, however, for her heightened color spoke of fever.

She returned his regard. "You should go and rest, Kai. Eufemia can stay with me until Elcon returns."

"I could find a use for food and drink."

"Go, then. Shae will come soon, as well. I long to see her, but she must rest as much as she needs. Coming all that way on the back of one of those wingabeasts can only have worn on her."

"Shae is not as fragile as she seems."

"I don't doubt that."

He leaned forward in his chair and lowered his voice. "She can bear the truth."

She flinched, and her face went white.

He cursed himself for unsettling her, although his words had wanted saying.

"I will see if I can bear to give it."

When she put out a hand in a childlike gesture, Kai cradled it in his own. He gazed into eyes of drenched seawater green and remembered the lilt of her frequent laughter and how she'd looked in his early days while Timraen still lived. He searched in vain for some hint of the winsome creature she'd been before schooling herself to sanction duty above all else.

He released her hand and stood. "I will send Eufemia to you."

∂∾∽

A tall serving maid opened the heavy door at Shae's knock. She glanced at Chaeldra and inclined her head to Shae. "Greetings. I'm Eufemia of Morgorad. Praectal Daelic, the healer, visits the Lof Raelein, but I will let him know you wait." Eufemia stepped aside to allow them entrance to Maeven's outer chamber. She gestured toward the seating area before the fireplace. "Pray, take your ease."

"Thank you." Shae gave a polite smile.

The inner chamber door shut behind the serving maid with a gentle click.

"Eufemia will look after you should you need anything." Chaeldra said in a breathy voice as she slipped from the room before Shae could recover the wit to call her back.

She really should speak to Kai about Chaeldra.

The servant continued to overstep and often went missing. She wandered about the outer chamber, struck by the beauty of its rich tones, which gleamed in light slanting through tall windows. The marble fireplace with its twined unibeasts and gryphons drew her. She warmed herself before the modest fire and studied the tapestry that hung above the mantel, which showed the first Kindren entering Elderland from Anden Raven. The group of Kindren in outdated garb pictured in Caerric Baest, the Cavern of Wonder, included her own ancestor, Whellein. He stood with Chaeradon, Tallyrand, Glindenn, Morgorad, Braeth, Daeramor, Merboth, and Graelinn—all those who had followed Rivenn from Anden Raven into Elderland, so long ago.

Rivenn, father of Kunrat, father of Talan, father of Shaelcon, father of Timraen, stood apart from the others with his bride, Gladreinn, on a natural bridge that spanned a chasm in which flames leapt. The bridge reached to a mysterious opening in a sheer face of rock. Light so strong as to veil the opening poured through it and bathed each face. In her early days, Shae had learned how the Kindren came through Gilead Riann, the Gate of Life, only to find the way closed behind them and their homeland lost forever.

She sighed. Only since leaving her own homeland did she begin to understand what it would mean to be cut off and never return. A chill touched her despite the warmth of the fire, and she averted her gaze from the tapestry, no longer pleased to view it.

When Eufemia still did not come, she looked out the window over the bailey at the hustle and bustle of activity. She had not considered that she might have to wait to see Maeven. At home, needlework and conversation would have kept her hands and mind busy. Perhaps she should ask for something to occupy her. Renewed irritation flashed through her. Chaeldra should not have abandoned her. Had she remained, Shae could have sent her to fetch something to occupy her instead of having to summon Eufemia. She raised a hand to knock, but hesitated, not certain she cared to reveal she could not handle her maid.

The door flew open. She had time to recognize the musician, Freaer, before a solid, heaving wall slammed into her face and a boot ground into her slipper-clad foot. Arms came hard about her and took her weight but robbed her of air. She struggled against them until reason triumphed over instinct.

The arms about her loosened as the quality of the embrace shifted.

She fought to breathe, managing to gulp in air just as blackness closed in. She rested against Freaer while her vision cleared, her face warming at so familiar a contact, but she couldn't stand alone. She held her injured foot just off the floor, for the initial pain had not yet lessened.

"Are you all right?" His voice vibrated under her ear, adding melody to the percussion of his heart.

She lifted her head, ready to speak words of assurance, but as his gaze ensnared hers, the words fled. No, she was not all right. A small sound started in her throat, and she pulled away, wincing when she put weight on her injured foot. "I've suffered little harm." She spoke the untruth in a rush, her voice pitched high.

"I'm sorry. I should have taken more care. Here, let me see your foot."

"No!"

He gave her a puzzled look.

She swallowed. "Thank you. No. It's not bad. I'm certain it's just a bruise."

Ignoring her protest, he took her by the arms and guided her backward to a bench. As she sat, he bent to remove her slipper.

Eufemia emerged from the inner chamber to hover beside the connecting door. "Is all well?"

Shae gritted her teeth. She would not make a fuss in front of the servant, but Freaer's long fingers running over her injured foot seemed an intrusion.

"Nothing broken, I think, but you're right about the bruising." As he bared strong teeth in a smile, Shae lost both thought and breath.

He murmured something to Eufemia, and the servant returned to the inner chamber.

As Shae examined the reddish bruise blooming on her skin, a footstool thudded before her and Freaer lifted her foot to its embroidered cushion. "Rest. Praectal Daelic will soon tend you."

"That's not necessary. It will heal well enough without care."

"There's no harm in having him take a look."

Suddenly too weary to fight so strong a will, she gave in with defeated ease, leaning against the cushion behind her. Her eyelids drifted shut.

"You look like Meriwen of Old, whose beauty upon awakening drove Iewald to forsake an army." His voice washed over her in a smooth tide.

"I wasn't sleeping." She protested, although she found it difficult to rouse. She could by no means picture herself as he painted her. Katera might merit such praise. She never could.

"Do you know the tale?"

"I know it—and its sorrowful end. Iewald

betrayed the Kindren for love of Meriwen, who wove a web of magic to ensnare him. But I prefer to think of honor and love as allies, not opponents. And would true love need any other magic?"

His eyes glinted. "What do you know of such matters?"

"As much as any, but less than some." Uncertain of her answer, she fell back on the common saying.

He gave a soft laugh. "Well spoken."

She hesitated, not certain if he mocked her. "Speaking of honor, I must tell you.... The Lof Raelein's death song—"

"Leave the subject!" His expression grew remote. "She has made her choice."

"But —"

"Leave it."

Shae's protest died.

Freaer stirred the fire, which sent up showers of sparks and released the cloying fragrance of Draetenn wood. He added a log and rocked back on his heels, outlined in profile against the flames.

The inner door opened to admit a large fellow with a kind face. A satchel of elk hide hung by a strap slung across the front of his brown overtunic.

"Praectal Daelic!" Freaer said by way of introduction. "Shae, sister to Kai."

Daelic's face lit with a smile. "So you are Kai's sister. I hear you've run afoul of Freaer." He eased himself into a kneeling position beside the footstool and made a sympathetic sound in his throat. As he prodded her foot, Shae held her breath. "Hurts, at a guess."

She nodded. "It does—especially when you touch it."

His smile settled into well-worn grooves in his face. "Let me stop then. I'll give you a drought to help the pain, so you can sleep. At least nothing's broken." He rummaged in his satchel and brought out a small bundle wrapped in dried Draetenn leaves. "Take it as an infusion last thing at night."

She took the packet with a polite murmur.

"I'll rub arnica salve into the injury and wrap it to stop the bruise from spreading." Daelic bent to the task. "Keep your foot raised, walk little, and it will heal faster. A soak in vinegar mixed with water will fade the bruise faster."

Shae gave her thanks, grateful when he stopped pressing her injury.

Daelic stood to his feet, huffing. "What kind of brother does Kai make?"

She tilted her head to look up at him. "You ask that as if puzzled."

He smiled. "I've known Kai since his early days and have seen him in many roles, but not as brother."

Shae considered his words. "I find no fault in Kai as a brother except for his long absences from Whellein."

"At least he is loved enough to be missed." Daelic's smile widened, but then his expression sobered. "Kai seems too alone and little given to tender mercies—except, of course, when duty calls for tenderness."

"You describe him as cold!"

Daelic shook his head. "Not cold—just practical. Kai entered into service as a guardian of Rivenn in his early life, remember. Weapons and endurance tests don't well replace a mother's arms. He excelled and trained under Craelin, which gave him little time for anything save duty. Small wonder his heart remains intact, although some have vied for it." He cleared his throat again. "But I forget I speak to his sister…"

Shae laughed. "I'm fascinated. You make me wonder if I know my brother at all."

"I wonder if I know him any better. He keeps much to himself. It has made him a little…strange."

The memory of Katera calling her "strange" for spending so much time in the Allerstaed made Shae smile.

Daelic looked inquiring. "I amuse you?"

"It's nothing but some wraith of memory come to haunt me."

"Tease you, more like, judging by your smile."

Shae laughed at such fancies, but sobered when she caught a glimpse of Freaer. Incredible that she had forgotten him, for he claimed her thoughts when near. She did not altogether understand her preoccupation with him, nor did she trust it. She looked past Freaer to Eufemia, waiting beside the inner chamber door. "I'm well enough to see Lof Raelein Maeven, if she will receive me."

"She will see you now if Praectal Daelic—"

"Yes, I've finished." Daelic helped Shae to her feet and steadied her.

She limped forward, leaving behind her slipper, which would not fit over Daelic's bandage. "How does she fare?"

"She seems much recovered." Daelic frowned. "But since I have not been able to find the cause of her illness, I can't know for certain it has mended. Time will show us more."

Shae hobbled into the inner chamber, surprised to find Maeven sitting upright, her hair newly brushed and falling in waves about her. Maeven wore a simple overtunic of lavender embroidered with black and gold at the cuffs and collar. She seemed no less regal, propped in bed, than if seated on the ancient seat of carved strongwood in the Presence chamber.

Maeven rested her hands on the counterpane. "Have you recovered from your journey?"

Her face warmed. "I slept far too long, but I do feel better."

"That is well." Maeven gave a vague wave

Shae took the gesture as invitation to sit and perched on one of the bedside chairs. "And you, Lof Raelein?"

Maeven smiled. "Daelic tells me I improve, and I do feel better."

"I'm thankful."

"Freaer, play something on your lute, if you will. Then I wish to spend time alone with Shae."

Shae started. She hadn't seen Freaer follow her into the chamber and occupy his place in the window embrasure. At Maeven's request, he took up his lute and strummed it as weak light sifted through the tall window. A bright melody wandered above dark notes. He sang, and the tale of "Iewald's Betrayal" unfolded.

"Heed a tale of woe and dread,
And learn of sore defeat.
There now lies a warrior dead,
With dishonor on his head,
Brought low by low deceit.

"Iewald, Talan's trusted friend —
First Guardian of Pilaer —
In fear's name he'd never bend

Although garn fighters would descend,
Riding welkes from the air.

"Iewald fought and won the day
By wit, by speed, by might,
But death came, perfumed and gay,
In beauty leading him astray,
And Pilaer lost the night.

"What then of mortal might?
What then of faithful art?
Meriwen whispered of delight
And Iewald fell without a fight,
Overcome by his own heart."

A musical interlude of melancholy beauty followed, ending on a sustained note, unresolved and fading.

Freaer made his bow and left the chamber in silence.

Maeven stirred. "Such a tale of sorrow brings memories. Sit there in the window, Shae. I delight in looking at you, especially when the light touches your hair with gold."

Shae obeyed with a smile. "It's pleasant here in the sun."

"You are a sweet child. I'm glad I sent for you. Now tell me of your life at Whellein. Have you found happiness there?"

She considered. "Happiness is but one thread woven into the tapestry of life at Whellein."

"Tell me of this tapestry, Shae. What other colors twine there?"

"Let me consider….the gold of happiness gleams

alongside white threads of honor that touch the red of sacrifice made in the name of that honor."

"Our tapestries are similar." Maeven's voice was dry. "Tell me more."

Shae warmed to the game they played. "Purple threads mark the pageantry enjoyed and endured by a daughter of Whellein. But black also wends its way through the tapestry, to mar it with grief."

"Ah, yes…threads of black… I have seen too many of those. But surely your tapestry holds lighter colors. What of hope?"

Shae smiled. "Hope comes in yellow and lies across days of green, whiled away in the solace of nature."

Maeven smiled. "I once spent many such days."

"I hope you will tell me of them."

Maeven waved a hand. "Go on. Now I would hear of you."

Shae mused. "Orange bespeaks a young girl's wish to find worthiness by her own merits, but blue tells of failure." Swift understanding settled on Maeven's face, and Shae finished in a rush. "Silver threads glint within the cloth and show unmerited pardon. I think my tapestry must hold more of blue and silver than all the other colors combined."

Maeven's brow furrowed. "Tell me of your early days, Shae, and of your family."

"I hope you will still think well of me after I give the tale. I would like to say I proved a good and biddable child, like my twin sister, Katera, but I cannot. All of my five sisters have impeccable manners, and of course, Kai could not disappoint in that regard. My older brother Daeven and I suited one another better. I don't know from whence such waywardness comes. It led Daeven astray. I can only pray it will not do so in my case."

Maeven gave a tender smile. "You remind me of—of someone I knew in my youth." Her voice throbbed with emotion. "*So long ago…*"

Shae's throat caught at the sadness that haunted Maeven's face. Words clamored, unspoken, just out of hearing. "Tell me."

Maeven grew silent. Shadows of memory flitted across her face. "Such feasts! What pageantry!" Her words fell in soft cadences. "It seemed each raven must outdo the next in welcoming Shaelcon, our new Lof Shraen. Allandra, his Lof Raelein, matched him in nobility and in grace and charm. Faeraven prospered and forgot the earlier days of struggle. Kunrat's defeat and the rout of the Kindren from Caerric Baest lived only in legend. The Cavern of Wonder became known ever after as *Caerric Daeft*, the Cavern of Death and none, save fell creatures, inhabited its reaches. Even Iewald's betrayal of Talan at Pilaer shrank to a small tear in the fabric of history.

"The Kindren were glad to hunt and fish and till the soil, glad to marry and bring forth children. Few thought of the garns of Triboan at all, except as a brief shadow across the face of a glorious day. The garns, engaged in war elsewhere, left the Kindren in peace—but not forever. The day came when garns, no longer sated with the flesh of the southern Elder, turned their grotesque faces northward. They came first to the High Hold of Pilaer. Lof Raelein Allandra lost her life in the attack, and Lof Shraen Shaelcon fell captive. The Kindren grew faint of heart then, for an untried youth now wielded Sword Rivenn."

Maeven paused, her eyes aglow. "He was a son of

kings. Authority sat with ease on him, despite his youth."

Shae stretched in the warmth of the window. "You speak of Timraen."

Maeven smiled. "Untested and untrained save in the war games of his early days, yet Timraen stood in battle. He rallied the shraens of Faeraven and took the garns by surprise at *Krei Doreinn*, the place where three canyons meet, and there won a victory. They could not know that the main thrust of the garns that day would take Braeth, the fortress from which they had ridden forth. All the best fighters had gone to Krei Doreinn. When the garns came to Braeth, they killed and ruined all.

"My mother, Raelein Reyanna, had no chance. My father, Shraen Raemwold, never knew of the devastation that day, for he fell in battle alongside my brother, Seighardt, at Krei Doreinn. In but a day, I became both orphan and heir to a vanished kingdom."

"I am sorry." Shae's voice softened and she blinked away moisture. It was one thing to learn this history from her tutor, and quite another to hear it from Maeven's lips.

Silence fell, thick with memories Shae knew nothing of, but that formed a cast across Maeven's features.

At last Maeven stirred. "In truth, my own life would have been forfeit had I not tricked the garns who planned to slay me, saying I knew the location of great treasure. They took me in chains to the garn king at Pilaer. He had little time to question me about treasure, however, for Timraen engaged him at once in battle and soon freed me. After that, I became Timraen's bride."

Maeven sent Shae a look that glinted. "The tale grows sad."

"Oh surely not sad all the way through!" Shae protested, caught up past discretion. "You must have had joy in motherhood even after—"

"Timraen's death?" Maeven supplied the words Shae hesitated to speak. She shook her head, the light picking out strands of silver in the cloud of brushed copper that framed her face. "Sometimes motherhood pricks more than it blesses."

"Such a thought!" Shae had heard only good of her son, Lof Frael Elcon. "How do you have cause to utter it?"

A distant expression settled on Maeven's face. "I have cause."

9

Inner Garden

Shae ran her fingers through the row of strange garments, here and there picking out a fabric of interesting texture or pattern, touching cool silks, smooth linens, and fine wools. With a sigh, she let her hand fall to her side and turned away from the wardrobe. Her own familiar belongings waited for her at Whellein.

Kai leaned against the doorframe, although she hadn't heard him approach. "What are you doing here?"

He straightened with a laugh. "Such a greeting! I could say brotherly concern brought me, but that's not my whole motive. I came to tell you Lof Raelein Maeven sleeps and will not require your presence until later this day."

She frowned. Daelic had spoken of Kai as lacking in tender mercies. *Except when duty calls for tenderness.* If he had no message to give her, would Kai have sought her out?

She pushed the question aside but tested him. "You could have sent any servant to tell me that."

He smiled, once again the brother she knew. "True enough. Now let me see your foot, Shae. Daelic tells me you injured it."

"No." She smiled back. "It's nothing, and you should not be here in my inner chamber, brother or not. Where is my servant?"

"She must have slipped out on some errand. Your outer door stood open."

Uneasiness ran over her. "I'm not sure about Chaeldra, Kai. She does not take her duties to heart."

Kai smiled. "I've heard the same spoken of you, dear one."

"Heed me!"

Kai's smile died. "I'm sorry, Shae. If you mention your concern to Maeven I'm sure she'll provide you with another maid."

She hesitated. "I'll wait and see. I hate to bring dishonor to one who may only need guidance. Perhaps something important occupies her just now. I'm certain she'll return soon. When she does, however, she should not find us closeted here. Will you please leave?"

Kai sighed. "Shae, we slept alone in a hay loft, and you never once worried about seemliness."

"That was different."

"You defy convention at every opportunity."

His words stung. "I don't mean to do so."

"Let me see your foot."

Something in his tone answered her earlier question, and she gave him a soft smile. "All right, but let's at least go into my outer chamber."

He lifted an eyebrow as she passed him in the doorway, but followed in silence. When she sank onto one of the fireside benches, he fetched a footstool and, kneeling, unwrapped Daelic's bandage with gentle fingers. She winced at sight of her bruise, which bloomed in shades of purple.

Kai whistled. "Does it pain you?"

"Not much at all, though Daelic thinks it may when I try to sleep tonight."

"Daelic can give you an infusion to aide you."

"He's already done so."

He wrapped the bandage again, bending to the task.

"Kai?" She spoke to the top of his head. "Tell me of your life here at Torindan."

He looked up, and his silvered gaze meshed with hers. "What do you wish to know?"

She hesitated, choosing her words with care. "Your life—has it been hard?"

A change came over his face, making him look...guarded. "Why do you to ask such a thing?"

She shrugged, not sure how to answer.

Bending once more over her foot, he rewrapped her bandage. "Hard by whose standards? The definition of 'hard' varies."

"Don't be difficult."

"What do you want me to say? My life has been—as it has been."

"Have you missed Whellein?"

His fingers paused. He nodded, and a shaft of fading sunlight from the window tangled in his silver-gilt hair. "At first I did, but I accustomed myself to Torindan."

"Did you find that difficult?"

"Difficult enough." His fingers finished their task, and he rocked back on his heels. "Tomorrow you'll not need a bandage."

She waved a dismissive hand. "More has been made of my injury than it perhaps deserved."

He watched her out of eyes more gray than silver.

"What's brought about these questions anyway? Are *you* homesick?"

Tears pricked. "A little…"

"You will adjust." He gave her a lopsided smile, and then pushed to his feet. "As it is, your visit may not be over long."

"Kai!" Her voice halted him in the doorway. "You've always taken care of my troubles. I-I've never given much thought to yours."

He turned back to her. "That's as it should be, Shae. You were but young. Remember when you made that pathetic raft and spent the night stuck in the reeds in the middle of the slough? Good thing I was home at the time or who would have guessed where you were?"

She blinked away foolish tears. "I remember." Kai always knew where to find her when she was lost.

"If you weep for me, save your sorrow. I'm happy enough." Cupping her chin, he dried her cheeks with gentle fingers, and then dropped a kiss on her forehead. "I'll see you in a while."

She waited for the sound of his footsteps to fade down the corridor before fetching her cloak. The bandage he'd wrapped with such care unwound easily. Without this encumbrance, she could just stretch her soft slipper onto her swollen foot. Standing, she tested her foot, pleased that it didn't pain her unduly. Kai wouldn't approve of her going about unescorted, but she wouldn't go anywhere unsafe.

∞

The wind breathed through the inner garden, molding Aeleanor's scarlet cloak against Shae. Leaves hissed and strongwoods creaked as twisted branches thrashed against a fading sky. She raised her face against the wild current, letting its force revive her, and then, as elder petals drifted across the fieldstone paths at her feet, wandered with time forgotten. The splash and fall of water eventually drew her to the garden's heart.

"Who's this?" The challenge came from a youth who sat at the pool's edge with his burnished head tilted, his sea-green eyes fixed on Shae. He wore a cloak of emerald wool edged and lined with mustela fur, its hood thrown back. Twin golden roses adorned this garment on either side, joined by a bejeweled strap. Fine scarlet wool showed at the cloak's opening.

Something about this youth seemed familiar. "Who are you?"

"I'll have my answer first!" He chided with a smile that nudged her memory. "Sit." He indicated a place beside him.

She gaped at the bronzed statue of Talan astride his wingabeast in the fountain's center as she perched on the pool's wide rim of stone a little distance from the youth.

"I await your reply." His voice made her jump. "Who are you? I'll vow we've not met before. Are you some creature of magic? You sprang from the garden like a wraith, and I'll swear you carry mysteries."

She laughed, the sound loud in the gloaming. "I hope it will not disappoint you to learn I am merely Shae of Whellein, sister of Kai."

"Kai's sister?" The youth smiled. "Are you rested from your journey, then?"

"You're Elcon!" She placed him at last. "I-I mean, High Prince—Lof Frael Elcon." She bowed her head.

Elcon inclined his own head. "How do you know me when we've never met?" His voice carried an edge.

"By your smile."

"Oh yes?"

"It belongs also to your mother."

A shadow passed over his face. "True, I'm told. And what do you know of my mother?"

"Enough to love her."

"Well said." He smiled at her. "How have we not met before this?"

"I've not ventured far beyond Whellein."

"And Whellein lies across the Maegrad Ceid—so distant I've not ventured much that direction."

"Your mother came but seldom."

"I've traveled a corner of Whellein. I remember great mountains and flats crowded with gnarlwoods and kabas and cut by a rushing weild." He frowned. "It seemed a good, simple land."

"And Rivenn is not?"

He tilted his head. "Rivenn is complicated and difficult—but also wonderful."

She gave no response, not wanting to call him back from whatever vistas of memory he wandered. Birdsong filled the silence between them until Elcon at last stirred. "Kai must show you more of Rivenn than Torindan Hold. How long do you stay?"

She shook her head and bent to trail a hand in silken water. With a glimpse of silver, a fish darted to the surface, then dove again as ripples sparkled across the pool's surface. "I don't know when I'll return to Whellein. Your mother summoned me to comfort her last days."

He looked away. "In that case, may your stay be lengthy."

She watched a flurry of white elder petals from a limb arching overhead cascade into the pool. "I join my wish with yours."

"'If wishes be true, what claim have we to glory?' After quoting the ancient saying Elcon gave a wry smile. "This day, the Lof Raelein passed to me the Sword of Rivenn and the Scepter of Faeraven. Rulership now rests on me."

"Then I spoke amiss. I should have called you Lof Shraen Elcon."

"You name my position, but not my title until my coronation." His silence sketched what he failed to say—that his coronation would take place after his mother's funeral.

A finger of wind ran along Shae's collarbone and made her shiver. "Lof Raelein Maeven seems much improved."

He inclined his head. "She does, but I should return to her. I slipped away for a time only."

"I'll accompany you, if I may."

"Yes, come with me. You should not seek the garden alone. It may seem safe within the walls of Torindan, but welkes can venture this far west and may even slip past the archers who keep watch. There's no danger now, since they seek their roosts by twilight, but welke attacks are not our only reason for caution." The obscure remark and his shadowed expression reminded her just how far from home she'd come.

"You warn me, yet risk yourself freely." The words came without thought, and she wished she could take them back.

Elcon's expression warned her she went too far, but then he laughed. "Well spoken, Shae of Whellein. I should heed my own words and use more caution. In truth, I sought nature's solace to escape duties I should embrace." He turned. "*Look* at the sky."

She watched with him the fiery death of day.

Night blackened the sky, lighting moon and stars and turning shadows purple. They walked beneath blackened strongwoods where starflowers glowed with pale light and released a heady fragrance. From somewhere near a night bird gave its lament, long and low.

10

Storm and Fury

A burst of sound and a flurry of movement mingled with the tang of smoke and spices to invade Shae's senses as she entered the great hall. Flames leapt in the hall's three fireplaces. Torches flared and flickered against the stone walls. Velvet hangings covered tall, arched windows against the night. Servants scurried to serve those who made merry at over-laden strongwood tables. The dissonance of instruments being tuned in the minstrel's gallery rose above the din.

Kai cut a swath through the crowd to a table where several guardians lounged. Shae, trailing behind, jumped at a touch on her arm. She glanced down. Freaer's eyes, shaded into darkened pools, snared hers. She shifted to step away, but he caught her arm. Her heart kicked up a beat, and a tingle of discomfort ran down her spine. She tried to pull free, but his fingers tightened.

He spoke, but the noise swallowed his words. She bent forward, and his breath caressed her ear. "Your foot—does it pain you?"

She summoned a smile. "It feels better, thank you." She tried again to pull away, but his fingers on her arm tightened again, biting into her muscle.

Unwilling to create a scene, she went still. "I really should join my brother."

"You look beautiful by torchlight."

She said nothing, but at the beauty of his slow smile could not slow the rapid rise and fall of her chest. His gaze traveled over her and then onward to Kai, who laughed with Craelin, oblivious of her plight.

The pressure on her arm eased. "Go to your brother if you must, but mark you, our conversation has just begun."

She fled from him, her face warm. Kai hailed her, drew her to his side, and presented her to the five guardians at the table. Breathless and grateful that speech was not necessary, she smiled and inclined her head to each in turn.

Kai seated Shae beside him, but ignored her as he entered into a discussion of marksmanship. Servants brought platters of venison with roasted onion, winterberry sauce, creamed yellowroot, an unfamiliar green vegetable and dainty blue crobok eggs. Kai tackled his food with appetite, but Shae picked at hers. After the encounter with Freaer, her stomach churned.

The cup of cider warmed her hand as she sipped from it, and she let the babble lull her, content to watch Kai consume the last of the honey cakes.

The torches flared with sudden zeal to brighten all but the upper reaches of the cavernous hall. They wavered and dimmed to bring an uncertain half-light. A storm built outside, it seemed. Kai's discussion progressed from hunting to the taming and handling of wingabeasts.

Shae hid a smile and gazed at the animated faces about her, careful to keep her gaze averted from Freaer. She couldn't shut out the sound of his voice, though, and it threaded through many voices to find her. His laugh rang out, and without thought, she turned her head toward him. She recognized her mistake too late, for his gaze waited to capture hers.

She pressed a hand to her brow, surprised she had no fever. What madness assailed her? The harder she tried to ignore Freaer, the more she noticed him. When he reached for his cup, she caught the movement. When he laughed, she heard it. The gleam of torchlight gilding his hair did not escape her. Worse, he seemed to sense—even revel in—her attention.

"What's wrong?" Kai asked at her sigh. "You seem flushed."

She avoided his light, probing gaze. How could she explain what she did not understand? "It's nothing."

He touched her forehead. "Are you fevered?"

She shook her head.

He looked her full in the face. "What then?"

"Please, it's nothing." But she couldn't keep from glancing past him to Freaer

"I *see*." With a nod to Freaer, who raised his cup in mock salute, Kai turned back to her. "Does he trouble you?"

She looked at her hands, which clasped one another in her lap. "What do you mean?"

"Only that you're—unsettled. Is your discomfort about Lof Raelein Maeven's death song or something more?"

"The death song?" In truth, she'd all but forgotten it. "Freaer *wants* me to sing it."

His brows lifted. "You've spoken to him? What did he say?"

"Little." She remembered the way Freaer had

studied the flames in the fireplace while she questioned him. He looked anything but pensive now. Laughing as he jumped to his feet and took up his lute, he bounded to the minstrel's gallery and joined in a rousing chorus of "Lof Shraen Timraen's Glory."

> *"Risen son of Rivenn's sons,*
> *Lof Shraen while still a youth,*
> *Timraen spent his time in prayer—*
> *Seeking wisdom, guidance, and truth.*

> *"He shared his bread, gave his gold,*
> *Listened to the downtrodden,*
> *Comforted the overcome,*
> *Called every Elder friend.*

> *"None could find a mark so true,*
> *Nor wield a sword as well,*
> *Yet the strength he found in mercy,*
> *No other shraen can tell."*

> *"When garns besieged Pilaer,*
> *The fortress could not stand,*
> *And Lof Shraen Shaelcon fell*
> *At the garn chief's hand.*

> *"His father lost, Timraen fled*
> *To cheat the garn's demand.*
> *He came at last to Braeth*
> *And sheltered in that land.*

> *"Timraen, son of Shaelcon,*
> *Led Faeraven's shraens to fight*
> *The Battle of Krei Doreinn,*

There to break the garn's might.

"Braeth now lay in ruin.
For as battle raged without
The fortress fell within,
Bringing forth a rout.

"His Krei Doreinn victory
Now tasted like defeat.
Yet Timraen persevered
To regain the ancient seat.

"Timraen, son of Shaelcon,
Led Faeraven's shraens to fight
The Last Battle of Pilaer
There to break the garn's might.

"Tales of shraens and glory
Begotten in Pilaer
Ever tell the story
Of victory most fair.

"Timraen won fair Maeven
From the garn chief of Triboan.
He stood in war but fell to love.
Maeven's heart became his own."

"Timraen, son of Shaelcon,
Found his father, not yet dead,
In the dungeons of Pilaer
And brought him life instead.

"Risen son of Rivenn's sons,
Brought low while still a youth—

A false arrow cut him down,
But could not steal his truth."

The music ebbed. The crowd, caught by its mood, did not stir as the last strains faded to silence.

"Did he seem angry?" Kai asked.

Shae stared at Kai and forced her mind back to the conversation about the death song. "I'm not sure."

Freaer leaped from the minstrel's gallery to land beside Shae. With his head tilted at a rakish angle and enticement in every line of his bearing, he smiled and offered her his hand. Guffaws and good-natured suggestions rang out.

She stared back at him while her cheeks flamed. She could neither take the hand nor refuse it.

A murmur of discontent arose from the crowd at her hesitation, but with it a counterpoint of approval.

Shae swallowed against a dry throat. "I cannot."

With a veiled expression, Freaer stepped back. His arm dropped to his side. He turned away, bearing her rejection with apparent ease, and drew another maiden, golden-haired and plump, from the crowd. Laughter followed. A burst of music from the gallery filled the hush that fell. Other dancers jumped up to join in.

The touch of a hand recalled her. She knew without looking that it belonged to Kai. "Come. It grows late." He pressed her against his side, and she leaned into his warmth, a haven from her turmoil. He escorted her from the hall and accompanied her down corridors and up staircases. His silence weighed upon her but, absorbed in her own thoughts, she could think of nothing to say.

What wordless thing had happened between

herself and Freaer? She'd felt the first, wonderful-awful stirrings of infatuation before, when Pawel, a son of Daeramor raven, visited Whellein. Nothing had come of it, of course, but vague dreams. Those feelings had been like a sweet-sad nocturne. She put a hand to her throat as if the action could quiet her racing heartbeat. The feelings that gripped her now weren't sad, nor were they sweet. A wild strain infused this music with dark fascination.

❧

"What do you want?" Shae did not mean to sound curt, but Kai's request for a word with her came as unwelcome. She sought the hearth, as if the fire might lend her its strength, and then remembered her servant. "Chaeldra, you may go—for now."

Chaeldra hesitated, but strode into her own chamber—leaving the door ajar.

Kai leaned against the mantel with nonchalance, a tilt to his head she knew well. "What do I want?" His tone denied his casual posture. "We can only wonder what our mother would say about your behavior tonight."

"*My* behavior?" she cried. "So you fault *me*?"

"How can you stand there looking the picture of innocence and outrage—as if you didn't invite Freaer's attention?"

"I didn't—" She paused, mid-protest. *Had* she invited Freaer's attention?

He pushed away from the door and paced toward her. "You didn't *what*? I saw you watching him. Do you not know what a maid's eyes can do?" He caught her shoulders and turned her toward the gilt-edged mirrorglass above the mantel. "Look at yourself! You've grown to a woman."

Somehow Shae found no joy in his acknowledgment, although she'd sought it in recent days. They stood together, framed in the mirror, something they'd done before, but never like this. How often she'd measured herself against him, a slender reed next to an ironwood, stretching to make herself taller. She came to his shoulder now, still slender, but with a rounded figure beneath the tunic she wore. Her face had lost its baby fat. Her expression held innocence, but also the beginning of knowledge.

She searched Kai's face in the mirrorglass. Where was her familiar, unruffled protector? Here was a stranger with more than a hint of danger about him. She caught her breath, shaken by the change in him.

He released her and stepped backward. She continued to watch him in the mirror, caught by the play of emotions that chased across his features. "Let this attachment die," he urged. "Nothing good can come of it."

"Why not?" She felt the need to challenge him, although in truth she agreed with his assessment.

He shook his head. "Just let it die." Unspoken words churned near the surface. She could hear their whisper.

"Tell me!"

"Must you plague me?" He ran a hand through his hair, abandoning all pretense of calmness. "You make me regret bringing you to Torindan!"

She flinched, both at what he said and at the raggedness in his voice. She couldn't bring herself to ask for answers again, but went to the window, keeping her back to him. She fingered the hangings, not really seeing them. Wind buffeted the pane and drafts leaked in, making her shiver.

A scrape and thud carried to her, and she rushed across the chamber to bolt the door behind Kai.

Drawn to the window again, she opened the shutters and measured the storm's progress. Blackened clouds boiled over peaks above moonlit snowfields as they flowed toward Torindan. Strongwoods in the garden tossed their heads like skittish ponies. Their branches glistened in the first pattering onslaught of rain.

This wild prelude must mark the inception of a fierce storm. She placed her hands on the pane as rain struck. Such a thin barrier to separate her from the storm's fury. She bowed her head and touched her forehead to the cold glass. Perhaps she should remove all barriers and join herself to the storm. Its strength might serve to overcome her own inner turbulence. It was an odd thought, not quite sane, but not quite crazed. So many mysteries lurked in Torindan— unspoken words, distant echoes, restless dreams, souls touching in the night—and now she did not even understand the fabric of her relationship with Kai. She preferred the honest energy of nature to these nameless, shifting realities.

She donned her cloak and pulled its hood over her hair, then slipped out of the room. The clunk of her outer door shutting behind her echoed through the deserted corridor. She found her way with ease, as if guided by some other hand. The strongwood door leading outside resisted, groaning in protest. *'There are other reasons, too, for caution.'* Elcon's voice spoke in memory, but his warning went unheeded. Nothing mattered now but her need to escape.

The door gave at last, a gust tearing it from her hand, and it banged open. She hurried to secure it.

The wind snatched her hood away and combed through her hair. Rain washed her face. She lowered her head and fought the wind, grateful to find the path, although it was slick and flanked by drowned starflowers. Her feet slipped on an incline, and she put out a hand to save herself. Thorns pierced her palm and pain twisted through her injured foot.

"Steady, there!" A masculine voice came out of the darkness. Arms slid around her and rough fabric ground against her face. "I knew you would come!"

Shae jerked her head back, but blinded by rain, still couldn't see who spoke. The wind tore her breath away, and then cold lips slid over hers.

She sank her fingernails into the soft skin at the back of her attacker's neck.

He flinched and jerked her hand down.

She fought to free her other hand, crushed between them. Her pulse drummed. Pressure built in her chest. Air—she needed air. She plucked at her assailant's cloak as blackness swirled about her and the storm's thrashing faded to silence...

"Shae!"

A voice roused her and she saw, in a flare of lightning, Freaer bending over her. His grip shifted, and her feet left the ground. With an effort, she dragged her arms upward and put them around his neck. A world of noise and fury, illumined by flashes of light, swung around her. The storm lashed at her back and every step Freaer took jarred. She hid her face against his neck with a sob, glad to be rescued.

The wind, rain, and noise abated, and Shae raised her head in sudden and profound silence. The glow of an oil lamp wedged in a niche revealed a ceiling that hung low. Its raw stone surface glistened with moisture that dripped into circular pools. A smooth floor stretched to lamplight's edge, where stone steps led down into darkness. Opposite the stair, and beyond a gaping black maw, the storm still raged, sending wild currents to lift her hair.

Freaer set her on her feet, and she rested in his arms. He hooked a finger beneath her chin and turned her face to the light with a smile. "Will you faint if I kiss you again?"

Freaer? *He* had been her assailant? She had never been kissed in such a way before. It seemed a strange business, and she couldn't say she liked it. She watched him, captured by the emotions that played across his face as his thumbs traced a path from the hollow at the base of her throat to her lips. His next kiss, when it came, did not match his hands in gentleness.

He lifted his head, his breathing unsteady. "Don't hold back, Shae. You can't stop this."

Tendrils of sensation curled about her soul, a soft seduction. How easy to surrender…

"No!" She voiced her alarm. "I should not be here with you."

He rested his forehead against hers and his hands stroked her temples. "Shae, I called you to me tonight and you came, even in the storm." A whiplash of reigned-in power brushed the edge of her mind as he let her feel the strength of his will.

She tried to pull away, but he held her fast. "Who *are* you?"

"The end of your journey." His kiss was violent this time, tearing at the roots of her being. She whimpered but just managed to curl into a hiding place in her inner being.

Freaer groaned and put her from him. "I should have given you more time."

She shook her head. "This is very wrong. I want to go back to my chambers."

"Through the downpour?"

She took a shaky breath. "Better the rain than this."

His lips smiled, but his face looked bleak. "How you flatter me."

She could say nothing as she stepped out of the puddle formed of droplets from their clothing.

Freaer sighed. "All right, Shae, I'll give you time." He reached for the lamp, and it swung in his hand. She saw then what lay hidden in the shadows, a bed of furs. Freaer steadied the lamp and tilted his head. "But know this—I won't wait long."

She jerked her gaze from his and caught sight of droplets of moisture streaming down the smooth stone wall behind him. Teardrops on a tender cheek?

As the chill penetrated her cloak, she shivered and pushed away the strange fancy. "What place is this?"

He lifted the lamp, and the movement raised grotesque shadows. "We stand in a sallyport, a hidden gateway in the curtain wall that leads through the motte. It was built to provide escape from the hold, or access to it, in time of war, but few remember this place of secrets."

Secrets. The word hissed in Shae's mind.

"Why bring me here?"

His mouth quirked. A feather-light touch brushed her soul and withdrew. She pictured the bed of furs. He'd meant to lie with her tonight. Mother had told her of such goings on between a man and woman, but within marriage. Not like this. "You will meet me here, Shae, when the time is right. Our souls have touched."

"*You?* That was you? But I felt *two* souls."

He shook his head, his hair gleaming in the lantern light. "I am only one soul, but with many sides."

She stared at him, remembering. "You terrified me."

"I'm sorry. I can't always control it."

"I don't understand."

He looked at her, his eyes shadowed. "You will come to trust our bond."

"Our bond?"

"You cannot deny we are joined."

"No!" she cried, and then, "Yes! What binds us?"

He touched her face, and her knees went weak. "Can't you guess?"

She stepped away. "A fool trusts another who answers with a question."

Freaer threw back his head and laughed. "Another ancient saying? Your words prick like thorns that guard a tender rose." He caught her hand and carried it to his lips. "Never mind, sweet flower. A few scratches won't turn me aside. But I've promised to wait, and I shall. Come."

She hesitated, but took the hand he extended. His fingers curled around hers, lending warmth. Light from the lamp rushed ahead to show the way out of shelter and into the storm. As they crossed the bailey, wind snatched her breath away and rain slapped her face.

Freaer flung open the keep's side door and pulled her into the corridor.

Shae pushed back her hood and shook her hair

free, blinking rain from her lashes. The corridor lay mantled in the stillness of deep night. The torches flared, then guttered and hissed, on the verge of extinguishing. Her stomach knotted. How long had she been gone? "I must return to my room! I never meant to leave for so long. What if someone looks for me?"

He gave her a light shake. "Peace, be still. Think of the worst that could happen in that event."

Her mind reeled at the suggestion.

His smile steadied her. "You'd have to wed me, of course. Would that be so terrible?"

She stared at him, unable to answer, taken by the memory of Kai in her mirror. *'Just let it die.'*

Freaer accompanied her up a flight of darkened stairs and down a silent corridor. She sighed when they reached her chamber door, relieved they'd met no one and that the night's adventures were over. A pang went through her. What had she gotten herself into this time? Why had she promised Maeven she would learn to behave, only to break her word at once? She meant to prove herself to Maeven and if she could bear the truth, Kai—but she seemed incapable of following her best intentions.

Freaer caught Shae's wrist when she would turn away. "You look weary. Make an excuse to lie abed tomorrow."

She shook her head and spoke to the image of Kai, which would not leave her. "I deserve to suffer for my recklessness."

Freaer's lips curved. He put a hand to her cheek, and his gaze probed her face.

Heaviness settled over her. She must pull away, get away. There was more here than she knew.

The door to her chamber opened and there, as if

her thoughts had summoned him, stood Kai. "Shae! Are you well?" His voice carried an edge. Firelight spilled over him, revealing an alertness she'd seen in him once before—when he faced the messengers at the White Feather Inn.

Freaer must have noticed it, too, for he stepped away from her. She registered this almost as an aside, her whole attention given to Kai. A heedless impulse to run to Kai and shelter in his embrace shook her, but such a move would find no welcome. Something had shifted between Kai and herself, and she feared they could never go back to what had once been.

"I am well," she answered as she brushed past him, not altogether certain she spoke truth. Something had also shifted between Freaer and herself.

࿐

Kai's gaze locked with Freaer's. He stepped into the corridor and shut Shae's outer door. "Leave…Shae….alone."

Freaer strode toward him, drawing a quick response from Kai's nerves. "How come you to tell me this? You wrong me. I found your sister wandering in the storm and brought her again to safety."

Kai hesitated. Shae did have a tendency to stray into trouble, but something rang false in Freaer's assertions. "Thank you, but I expect you will not approach Shae further."

Freaer stood his ground. He seemed, by some trick of torchlight or imagination, to grow in stature, and the hair on the back of Kai's neck stood on end. Time seemed to expand and contract.

"I will follow Shae's wishes in the matter." Freaer

turned away with a curt nod.

"I'll thank you to keep Shae's honor. Speak of this night's events to no one."

Freaer turned back with a faint smile. "Would that Shae had your concern for her honor."

Although his hands balled into fists, Kai kept hold of his temper. "I will see she does."

Kai returned to Shae's outer chamber and bolted the door. Leaning against its solid wood, he breathed in quick gasps. What had just happened? Something uncanny had wended its way into that corridor to wound his spirit. Even now, shut behind a locked door and embraced by the comfort of fire and hearth, he did not feel quite safe.

11

Place of Prayer

Shae threw open the shutters. Moonlight flooded the room, washing into a pool at her feet. Drafts lifted her hair, their chill a marked contrast to the feverish thoughts that kept her from sleep. The world below lay in savage beauty. She recalled the pastoral setting she'd once imagined surrounded Torindan and smiled.

The rain had ceased, taking with it the clouds. Jagged peaks stood in relief, and the full moon, glaring white against a pewter sky, made spider's webs of weaving shadows. Silver edged the eastern horizon like a whispered promise.

When she could tolerate the cold no longer, she reached for the shutters but paused and scanned the horizon. Had she seen...? Yes, there—darker shapes against the sky resolved into two wingabeasts with riders. They approached from the west and landed within the outer bailey, passing from view.

A wave of energy hit Shae with such force it brought her to her knees. Anger, excitement, and triumph rushed headlong through her. Another soul clung to hers like a parasite. As she fought to breathe, Freaer's words came in memory. *I'm sorry. I can't always control it.* Swept before a force she neither knew nor understood, she floundered, eroded by the strange tide engulfing her.

❧

Leaning forward in his chair, Craelin steepled his hands and rested his forehead on them. "Traitors flew wingabeasts on some foul mission last night."

"You're sure?" But Kai asked without hope.

Guaron, across from Craelin on the bench in the main guardroom, nodded, his straw-colored hair swaying. With one finger he tapped the cleft in his chin. "I know the wingabeasts well. Two of the blacks, Saethril and Morgraen, journeyed far in the night, I'll swear. They showed signs of fatigue, and their coats bore flecks of sweat this morning. Whoever rode them either grows careless or lacked time to cool them down."

Craelin narrowed his eyes. "Did you see or hear anything?"

Guaron considered the question, and then nodded. "I can't say I did."

"You're sure? Think back."

Guaron obeyed, with the same result.

"Thank you." Craelin said in a defeated voice. "Pray advise us should you find anything more."

"I will." The door shut behind Guaron.

"By Timraen's grave!" Craelin slapped his hand on the rough wood of the table. "We will get to the bottom of this!"

Kai narrowed his eyes. "Our decision not to increase security for the stables seems a poor one now. But time may bear us out."

Craelin shook his head. "I fear time will only teach us more of last night's evil."

৵৵

Light descended like a benediction from stained glass windows that reached toward a vaulted ceiling. Shae paused in its rear archway and took in the splendor of Torindan's Allerstaed. How unlike Whellein it seemed. No dust intruded, and no grime marred the glowing panes repeating beneath arches down either side of the building. Even the silence seemed inhabited—more a pause than a period.

Shae stepped into the sanctuary, her slippered feet making little noise on the floor of polished strongwood. "Oh, Lof Yuel, I've been such a fool." She whispered the words, and then fell silent. What more could she add? That she had broken her word to Maeven and alienated her brother? That she'd disregarded both honor and integrity? That she suspected Kai and Freaer might yet come to violence on her account?

She reached the golden railing at the foot of the altar, knelt, and bowed her head. "I should never have left my chamber during the storm, except to come here. Oh *why* couldn't I have come here?" Her tears flowed, silent and solemn. She wished with all her heart she had not added to Kai's burdens by her rash behavior. She regretted, not for the first time, that she didn't better resemble her more obedient twin. Katera would never find herself in such a position. Tears fell to bathe her clasped hands.

"And so I find you."

Kai stood silhouetted in the rear archway

Shae came to her feet. "Why are you here? Chaeldra said you would be in a meeting all the morn."

He sighed. "So much remains obvious. Why does it surprise me when you ignore my wishes? I asked you to remain in your chambers until I came for you."

"You can't have meant to deny me the Place of Prayer."

"I would rather find you here than...elsewhere. I meant only to keep you safe until we could speak."

"Safe?"

He stepped toward her. "You met no one on your way here? Spoke with none?"

She found her voice with difficulty. "What makes you ask?"

He paced from light to shadow and then back into light as he crossed beneath one of the high windows. "Freaer and I came to...an agreement. He will not speak of what happened. But others helped search for you in the night—Craelin and a few of the guardians. They heard a tale I devised. I wanted you to know of it before you speak with anyone." He stopped before her, his voice crisp. "Now tell me, Shae—did you or did you not encounter anyone?"

She hesitated, and then spoke with truth. "I met no one on the way here."

"That's well then."

She crossed her arms over herself. "Am I forgiven?"

"Always, Shae, but I'd rather, for both our sakes, you had no cause to ask." With a hand beneath her chin, he lifted her face to the light. "Do you weep?"

His gentle tone unsettled her. She had expected harshness. She should tell him how wretched she felt about the mess she'd created. She opened her mouth to speak, but the words stuck in her throat. "Mine are selfish tears," she said instead. "You shouldn't regard them. What tale have you given Craelin and the others?"

He stepped away. "I've explained that your foot pained you in the night and, loath to wake your servant, you left your chamber to find me, only to become lost."

Shae shuddered at such lies spoken in the Allerstaed. Did all secrets start with lies? Did lies feed them until they grew into dragons ready to devour their creators? "What if we told the truth?"

He shrugged. "Your reputation would suffer, and you might have to wed Freaer to still gossip." The words fell, each a weight, to lie like stones between them.

Heat rose in her cheeks as she recalled what Freaer had said. *Think of the worst that could happen. You'd have to wed me.* The prospect hadn't daunted him, but it troubled her. She couldn't deny the depth of her fascination with Freaer. Neither could she overlook the confusion she felt in his presence. Would a union with Freaer bring joy or would it, indeed, be the worst that could happen?

Kai's eyes narrowed. "Put the thought from your mind!"

She bristled at his tone, although she tended to agree with him. "Why should I? At least I would then keep Whellein's honor."

He shook his head. "You are not for Freaer."

She eyed him. "You speak as one who knows my future?" The words, meant as a challenge, came out a question.

"I do, at least a little."

"And do you not think such knowledge would

interest me?"

"I'm sure it would." He turned away.

"Wait!" She caught his arm but he didn't turn back to her. "*Look* at me! You speak in riddles and tell me nothing. Am I only a duty to you? Can't you see I need more? I need to know, to understand—"

"Peace, be still." He shook free of her grasp. "Love is not duty, but you know not what you ask."

Hypnotized by the play of emotions across his face, Shae stared at Kai. Stepping backward against the prayer rail, she put out a hand and found the comfort of its smooth wood.

"All right, I'll tell you. By all that's holy, I've wanted to often enough. Only answer this and I will speak: Are you certain you want to know?"

Her intake of breath rasped in the silence. She'd never imagined Kai would give in to her demands. Now that he had, she hesitated, less certain she should abandon the shield of ignorance, however flimsy it might be. She pressed her hand against a bud of fear blossoming in her stomach. The gleam in Kai's eyes told her he read her heart, and she bent her head with the knowledge of defeat.

"I didn't think so." His words, although tender, jarred. "Nor should I have offered. Such a right belongs to another."

"Go, then." She could have stood before his censure, but his gentleness unraveled her. "Leave me alone to pray."

"I'll wait to escort you to the Lof Raelein's chambers when you finish."

"I can find my own way."

"Shae, you must take better thought for yourself. Elcon told me about your meeting with him in the inner garden. Promise me you'll stop going about alone. There's no need since the Lof Raelein has given you a maid. The freedom allowed you at Whellein has hindered your grasp of decorum or even prudence. But you are no longer in Whellein. You speak of leaving childhood behind, yet conduct yourself with the carelessness of a child. You must stop getting into adventures."

Such a lecture from one who had rescued her from many adventures without complaint made Shae blink back tears. Her fingers cramped around the prayer rail. She let go and stretched them, and then lifted her head with dignity. "As you wish."

A scuffling came from the darkness behind carved marble pillars in a darkened side passageway, and Shae's heart pounded.

Kai took on the watchfulness she now recognized. "Come out!"

"Very well." Elcon, wearing a surcoat of blue and gold over a rumpled tunic, stepped from behind a pillar.

"You!" Shae forgot her manners in surprise. "What are you doing here?"

The smudges beneath his eyes made their light green color stand out. "Trying to avoid embarrassing you."

"I—I—you startled us." Heat crept up her neck, and she bowed her head. "Lof Frael." She flashed a glance at him. He wore weariness like a mantle. Had he spent the whole night watching over his mother?

A fleeting smile touched his mouth. "I came to offer prayers but seem to have entered at an...awkward time. You and Kai were...preoccupied and failed to hear the side door."

Her face warmed further, and she cast back over her conversation with Kai. "How long did you hide there?"

"Not long. I learned little I did not already know, except that Kai can lose his patience."

She attempted a smile. "I suppose we all can. I've tested his fortitude often enough."

He gave a bark of laughter. "You do Kai a service. I've often thought him too perfect. Mother held him up to me as an example in my early days."

She smiled with true warmth. "Mine did the same."

Kai rubbed his chin. "I regret displaying my ill temper, although it does disprove your false images of me."

Elcon stared at him. "You are fortunate to have a sister. Treat her well."

Drawn by the wistfulness in his voice, Shae imagined Elcon in his early days—an only child growing up fatherless and in the isolation that accompanies privilege. She should say something on Kai's behalf. "I am fortunate to have a brother who guards my welfare with diligence."

Elcon directed his light-eyed gaze to Shae. "Well spoken, fair maiden. I hope you will heed his advice. I remember you risked yourself without chaperone the night we met, also. I brought you to safety and spoke of the matter to none but Kai. Not everyone would do the same."

She bowed her head in acknowledgement and, having no defense, made none.

"How fares the Lof Raelein?" She looked up in gratitude at Kai's change of subject.

"She spent a peaceful night and has improved."

Elcon's face clouded. "I cannot say the same. I spent the night on a chair at her side. I did sleep, but only little. Images passed behind my eyes."

"Images?" Kai asked.

Elcon's forehead puckered. "Only shadows— things hissing in the dark—insects crawling over my flesh." He shook his head. "And behind it all a foul thing waits."

He seemed to describe Shae's own dreams.

Elcon ran a hand through his hair, leaving it rumpled. "I'm out of sorts, but I came anyway to pray for my mother's recovery. Will you join your prayers to mine?" He turned to the rail, and Shae knelt beside him. Kai went to his knees on her other side.

It felt somehow right to kneel between Kai and Elcon, although she did not pause to ask herself why.

☙◦❧

Wooden shutters and embroidered hangings shut out the fading light, giving the room over to the soft glow of candle branches and oil lanthorns. Eufemia moved from the window with quiet grace and covered the flaemling cage with a sheet of fine linen before turning to the Lof Raelein in inquiry.

Maeven waved a hand. "Thank you. You may go."

Kai drew closer to the bed where Maeven sat propped against pillows. "You look much improved."

She smiled. "I almost dare hope for life. There are those for whom I would linger."

"Not for yourself?"

"I think sometimes to join Timraen and leave this struggle."

"Forgive me. I should not have asked."

Maeven's voice strengthened. "My wishes don't enter the matter. Lof Yuel decides such things, and I would not hasten or stay His hand."

"And what of Shae? Have you enjoyed your visit with her?"

"She comforts me."

"I'm glad. You spoke with her, then?"

Maeven's eyebrow arched. "I did, but not on the subject you mean."

"No?" He couldn't keep the disappointment from his voice.

"She returns anon, as does Elcon."

He met her look. "I see."

"You may see less than you think."

He returned silence, uncertain how to respond to her pettish remark.

She sighed. "Words elude me just when I would speak them."

He opened his mouth to comfort her, but a tap came at the outer chamber door.

"Please remain."

"You honor me."

"Honor doesn't enter into it. I need to lean on your strength."

He smiled. "I think you will find your own strength. You are, after all, Lof Raelein of Faeraven and a daughter of kings."

"Which is why I find myself at such a pass."

Kai could find no reply for the truth of her words. If he could shoulder her burden he would. In some ways he had borne it with her since his early life. Perhaps he would always carry the weight of her secrets, for they had molded his life.

At the outer chamber door, he admitted Elcon

with a bow. Shae brushed past him, looking much as she had in her early days when chided for some mischief. Despite his irritation, his heart softened. He understood well enough the part of her that could not settle to routine. Truth to tell, he found its echo within himself. How could he fault her when she'd experienced the freedoms of neglect since her early days? He wished, not for the first time, that Mother could have brought herself to give Shae the benefit of the same affection she lavished on Katera.

Shae warmed herself at the aromatic draetenn fire. On the wall above her, flames pirouetted in wall-mounted lamps, courted by stray drafts. In the changing light, the colors of the tapestry above the mantel, which told of the ancient pilgrimage from Anden Raven, deepened and its figures took on life.

Kai remembered his manners. "Lof Frael, I understand you have already met Shae, my sister."

Elcon removed his cloak. "We met yesterday in the garden when we both stepped out to seek an interlude of peace and beauty." He took Shae's hand in a courtly gesture. "I'm sure I saw more of beauty than did she."

She extricated her hand. "The Lof Frael was—"

"Charming?" Elcon's eyes glittered. "Chivalrous? Intriguing?"

"Kind."

"There you have it." Elcon spoke in heavy tones, but he smiled. "I was kind."

Kai returned a fleeting smile, and then indicated the door to the inner chamber, which stood ajar. "The Lof Raelein looks for you both."

Maeven waited within, upright against her cushions, hands clasped before her. She smiled in greeting.

Elcon bent and embraced his mother. When he straightened he kept her hand. "I am glad to find you so well."

Maeven extended her other hand to Shae, and Kai smiled at the picture they made. Maeven had shed the heaviness of illness and now appeared well and whole, if weak. He pushed away the thought that, earlier, in the harshness of daylight spilling through the window, her bloom of recovered health had seemed less true.

At Maeven's invitation, Shae perched on one of the bedside chairs. "Did you rest well last night?"

Maeven's eyes glowed. "I did indeed. I have not rested so well in a long time."

Shae dimpled. "I worried I overtaxed you yesterday with my eagerness to hear your tales."

"I counted it joy. And you? How have you occupied yourself while I rested?"

A blush colored Shae's cheek. "I kept to my rooms but then stole away to the gardens, where I met Lof Frael Elcon."

Kai gave her a stern look tempered by mercy, for at least she had not hidden the truth in lies. Elcon laughed outright.

Maeven sent Elcon a reproving look and shook her head at Shae. "I can see that those committed to protect you cannot find the job easy. Sweet child, you must take more care for my sake."

Shae had the grace to look abashed. "I'm sorry." Her gaze included Kai in her apology. "I didn't understand the dangers until the Lof Frael warned me of them. Nevertheless, I should have used more caution."

Kai spread his hands. "I'm afraid Shae has had too much of her own way at Whellein."

Maeven's eyes crinkled at the corners. "We can hope that time and wisdom will remedy such a lack."

Shae murmured something in response, looking far more demure than Kai had thought possible. Perhaps the time spent at Torindan would prove the tonic she needed.

Maeven's smile reached her lips. "I'm glad, anyway, that you and Elcon had the chance to meet."

"As am I." Elcon took a seat beside Shae. "Had I known Shae resided there, I would have found more time to visit Whellein."

"Yes." Maeven spoke in a distracted voice as she glanced at Kai and then back to Shae.

Kai gave her a sharp look, hoping her mind did not stray again into paths of its own, but her voice, when she spoke, was lucid. "Tell me of the garden at shadowfall. I long to wander such paths of beauty again."

Shae's face lit with quiet intensity. "I pray you shall."

Kai withdrew to the window embrasure and stopped listening to their words. Shae's voice rose and fell to mingle with Elcon's deeper tones and Maeven's murmurs. When silence fell it roused him.

'Will you play and sing?" Maeven asked him.

He took up the lute in the embrasure, one probably left by Freaer. By the fading light from the window behind him, he bent to pluck the instrument into tune.

Maeven answered his look of inquiry. "I would have *DawnSinger's Lament.*"

His head came up at her choice, but he bent to strum the lute, and then sang the ancient words.

"Long ago and once before,
In another homeland,
A Contender waged war,
In a bloody demand.

Misbegotten of Meriwen,
Son of Rivenn but not heir,
Birthed in forgotten dreams,
Lord of Darkness, Lord of Air,

The Contender fell,
But not by might—
Kunrat's loss
Would end the fight—

Within Virtue's Fire
By Lof Yuel's Breath
At the Well of Light,
In the Cave of Death.

The Contender fell
'Til the wane of Rivenn,
For when released,
He will bring division.

He will gather armies
And bring forth war
Devouring Elderland
Forevermore.

Unless Son of Rivenn
Wed Maid of Braeth
To birth a daughter
Of overcoming faith.

Daughter of Rivenn,
Daughter most fair
Bring forth the DawnKing
Through Kunrat's air

In the Cave of Death
At the Well of Light
By Lof Yuel's Breath
Within Virtue's Flame.

For when the DayStar shines
While discord darkens Elderland,
Hearken to the signs
And rest within Lof Yuel's hand."

The plaintive strains thinned and passed out of hearing. Kai set aside the lute.

Maeven held herself in stillness, hands clasped together against the red-gold counterpane.

Elcon spoke. "Hearing that ballad makes me sad, for it speaks of prophecy unfulfilled."

"No, my son. It speaks of promise."

He stirred. "Forgive me, Mother, but Braeth Hold has fallen to ruin. Only the smallfolk known as the *Feiann* dwell in the smallwood of *Syllid Mueric* that surrounds the hold. It's no longer possible to fulfill Prophecy. Even if I would, I could not wed a maid of Braeth and bring forth a daughter."

"True enough." Maeven held out a hand to Shae. "But hope lives in your sister."

12

Betrayal

Shae stared at Maeven. *What* had she said?

Elcon drew in a breath on a hiss. "But I have no sister."

Sorrow shadowed Maeven's face, and she looked to Kai, although, from the expression on his face, he already knew her tale. "I gave birth to your sister long ago, Elcon. She died in birthing, or so Timraen and I said. We had to preserve our daughter's safety—and Elderland's. We knew she would one day fulfill Prophecy—*if she lived*.

"We could not ignore the signs—the Contender of Prophecy had escaped from *Lohen Keil*, the Well of Light, to hide at Torindan. Having cheated death by fell arts, he would do anything, it seemed, to also cheat Prophecy. He made several attempts on my life during my pregnancy, always without revealing himself. We knew he lived among us. Timraen searched, but could not discover the traitor in our midst, so I kept to my chambers under constant guard until my daughter's birth."

As she looked at Shae, moisture glistened in Maeven's eyes. "We sent you away the day you were born." Her tears spilled. "How my arms ached to hold my baby."

Maeven's face set in stern lines, and her voice grew brisk. "You almost didn't survive our efforts to protect you. The guards who accompanied you on your journey met an ambush. None survived the skirmish save Kai, who was little more than a child himself. Your wet nurse died shielding you with her body. After the attack, Kai took you on to Whellein, where he placed you in his mother's arms.

"Raelein Aeleanor had just given birth to Katera, and so she passed you off as her true daughter's twin. Those who attended Katera's birth kept your secret well. No one in Elderland suspected that a daughter of the House of Rivenn lived. For a time, even Timraen and I did not know, for we thought you perished in the ambush..."

She grew silent for so long Shae thought Maeven's mind must have wandered. But then she stirred. "Kai returned with the news you lived. We gave it about that he saw you torn apart by wolves in the aftermath of the ambush."

Maeven sighed. "I wish I could have known you better. I longed for you, as every mother longs for her child. But I had to release you to another's care. I could not even visit you as I wished, for I dared not draw undue attention to Whellein, for your sake. I should not have brought you here even now, but I couldn't bring myself to leave this world without seeing you again."

Shae's thoughts turned inward. Kai's protectiveness toward her, her quick bond with Maeven, and the reserve Aeleanor had shown Shae alone of her children all had new meaning. Even the sense of calling that haunted her made sense in light of her true identity.

She clung to the cool, dry hand of her mother, and a tear fell from her cheek to bathe their clasped hands. "This is too cruel, learning of this now. You might have told me sooner! Did you think I couldn't keep my own secret?"

Maeven frowned. "What kind of life would you have lived, always looking over your shoulder? I wanted you to grow up without fear."

"Shae—" Elcon touched her shoulder, but she pulled away.

Tilting her chin, she met Kai's gaze. "And you! How could you pass yourself off as my brother when all the time you knew—" She broke off, unable to speak the horrible truth. They didn't belong to one another at all. Her entire life had been a lie. The room swung, and she put out a hand as Kai stepped forward.

He caught her, his arms steadying her. "Stop it, Shae."

"These burdens fall to those who serve a throne and a people, my child." Maeven's voice throbbed with sudden passion. "How I have longed to call you my child."

Shae turned in Kai's arms.

Tears rolled down Maeven's sorrow-creased face. "Will you forgive me for sending you away, my daughter? I never meant to hurt you."

Elcon folded his arms. "Why do you ask Shae's forgiveness? You didn't abandon her but acted as a true mother."

Maeven's eyes widened. "How can you speak with such grace? I kept your sister from you."

"You did what you had to do."

Shae looked away from Elcon's unflinching gaze. She couldn't mistake his message. She ground her teeth. His life had changed little. If he had been the one whose life was devastated, would he be so quick to excuse Maeven?

And yet, Maeven had finally told the truth. Could Shae live with herself if she allowed her to go to the grave with words of anger between them?

Shae stepped out of Kai's arms. She had no right to lean on him ever again. "I don't fault you." Even as she spoke the words, she knew them as false, spoken from pity rather than mercy. But she wouldn't take them back, not with Maeven's face alight with joy.

"I ask but one thing more—" Maeven's voice thinned.

"You tire yourself." Elcon spoke with swift concern.

"I have already promised to sing your death song. Is there something more?" Shae couldn't keep a hint of reproach from her voice.

Elcon sent her a disapproving look, and then bent over Maeven. "Rest now, and perhaps a death song won't soon be needed."

"It's not of the mael lido that I speak. But rather I ask your promise, Shaenalyn, Raena of Rivenn, that you will travel to Lohen Keil, the Well of Light, and by your song release the DawnKing into Elderland."

"Who is this DawnKing?" Shae asked.

"The identity of *Shraen Brael*, King of the Dawn, remains unknown." Kai spoke from beside her, although she hadn't heard him move closer. "Some say Kunrat waits to rise from Lohen Keil where he fell with the Contender long ago, but no one knows for certain. We only know from Prophecy that if a daughter of Rivenn and Braeth sings Kunrat's song at Lohen Keil before the DayStar completes its arc of the sky, the

DawnKing will enter Elderland to save it. But if she fails in this, Elderland will fall to the Contender."

Shae felt like a small leaf blown about in a maelstrom. "It seems I have no real choice in the matter. But even if I go to Lohen Keil, I've never even heard Kunrat's song." Her words fell like drops of rain into darkened pools.

"I wish I could guide you." Kai's voice soothed her. "But Kunrat's song has been lost in time."

The room seemed airless. "How can I sing a song not known?"

Kai's gray gaze held hers. "Trust Lof Yuel to provide the song."

∂∕◠

"Kai, come near."

When he glimpsed Maeven's white face, concern touched Kai, but he knew she would find no peace until whatever new matter pressed her mind had settled.

"You pledged yourself to Timraen's service in your early life, and to mine at his death." Maeven's lips barely moved as she spoke. "You have served well as both a friend and servant. I have already released the Scepter and Sword to Elcon. I now release you from your service to me. *Hear me!*" She stilled his protest. "I release you. If I could command the allegiance of a guardian of Rivenn, I would do so, but I cannot. I can only ask you to pledge fealty to Elcon."

The time of decision had come sooner than Kai anticipated. An image of his father rose in his mind's eye, and his thoughts clamored so loudly he could barely think. He lifted Maeven's hand for his kiss, but he would not speak to appease her. "I will consider your wishes."

"I have no doubt you will make your choice with wisdom."

Her face sank into lines of weariness, and he gave her a quiet smile. "Will you rest now?"

"I will rest. Shae, will you stay and watch over me while I sleep?"

"I will stay."

Maeven's eyes lit with tenderness. "Thank you."

Elcon pressed forward beside Shae. "I can return later and escort my sister to her chambers, after I take care of certain other duties."

Kai remembered that Elcon's duties included a meeting with Craelin and himself. He bowed and excused himself, stepping into the outer chamber.

Freaer waited before the hearth.

"How long have you been here?" Kai heard the edge in his voice. The inner door had been shut, but could Freaer have overheard somehow?

Freaer's eyes glinted in the firelight. "I've only now arrived. Since no one came at my knock, I admitted myself. Maeven requested my music this night, but when I heard voices, I decided to wait before entering.

"You did well to wait. Maeven will want no music tonight."

"Are you certain?"

"Yes. She's about to sleep."

"Then I'll return to the great hall."

"I'll come with you." Kai stepped into the corridor with Freaer, but paused. "I'll take my leave of you, after all. I've remembered an errand."

Freaer gave him a strange look, but turned away

without question.

Kai waited for Freaer to vanish around a corner, and then returned to Maeven's chambers and drew Elcon aside. "We should use caution with one another, even in private. One unguarded word could put Shae's safety in doubt."

Elcon lifted a brow. "What's prompted your concern?"

"I found Freaer in the outer chamber. I think he heard nothing, but we'll need to take more care."

Elcon rubbed his chin. "Let's discuss this later. This saddens me, for I've found this day a sister I cannot claim."

"Not yet, for Shae's sake."

"Do you believe the Contender remains among us still?"

"Recent events should provide your answer."

Elcon's eyes widened at Kai's words. "Do you think he's behind all the unrest? But how can he remain alive after all this time?"

"By fell arts. Meriwen of Old lengthened her own life and her son's. Even so, she couldn't cheat death forever. We can hope her son will also find a mortal end. Remember the advice given in *DawnSinger's Lament*: For when the DayStar shines while discord darkens Elderland, hearken to the signs and rest within Lof Yuel's hand."

Elcon's posture relaxed a little. "We have yet to see the DayStar."

"Not yet. But I think it can't be far off."

∂∼∽

Craelin hailed Kai, although his words were lost in

the revelry as shouts and laughter mingled with lively music. The great hall rocked with merriment. Even the fires in the yawning fireplaces danced about.

Kai returned Craelin's greeting and joined the group clad in the green and gold of the guardians. By birthright, he could seat himself upon the dais at one end of the chamber, where stone tables and carved chairs waited alongside massive sideboards. But Kai preferred to join his fellows at the strongwood tables below the dais. Through smoke-hazed air laden with the tang of resin and the fragrance of meat roasting on spits, he could see that most of the guardians had already eaten. But they would linger in one another's company.

Those seated across from Craelin—Aerlic, the archer, and Guaron, the wingabeast keeper—engaged in animated conversation, understanding one another despite the rising din. Kai spoke near Craelin's ear. "Elcon looks for us soon."

Craelin nodded while Kai signaled a serving maid laden with a steaming platter.

From the minstrel's gallery, a new tune pierced the air, its tempo increasing with each verse. Afterwards, the cheers and applause grew to such volume that the din threatened to cover any further sound the musicians might make. When it died down, they played another tune, and then another. Feet stamped and hands clapped until those with strong backs lifted a number of tables out of the way. Dancers leaped and turned in the torchlight.

Kai ate venison and, when the others tried to draw him into the dance, smiled his refusal. He could not join in frivolity while his heart beat heavy in his chest. He recognized grief at Maeven's releasing him from service but rejected the notion his sorrow had anything to do with Shae. Deep down, though, he couldn't deny the truth. No more secrets now joined him to Shae, and there no longer remained even the illusion of blood ties between them. Would she reject him for deceiving her?

❧

Misliking the cloying honeyed sweetness of the mead, Shae set the silver cup on the bedside table. She'd eaten little of the repast Chaeldra had brought. Shock at Maeven's revelations must have affected her appetite. How would the truth alter her associations with Aeleanor and the rest of those she had long called family?

She pushed away the idea that her upset came from losing Kai, but the thought returned unbidden. She blinked away a mist of tears. He had always been part of her life. She could not imagine that changing. *Kai has seemed too alone and little given to tender mercies — except, of course, when duty calls for tenderness.* Daelic's words haunted her. Had Kai given her his tenderness as mere duty? And what would happen now that his duty ended?

"Will you not take more?" Chaeldra asked. "You've eaten little."

Shae demurred, but Maeven ate a little of the thick fine bread and musty cheese, and she let Chaeldra refill her cup. After a short sleep, Maeven had declared herself ready to recover.

Eufemia, who embroidered near the fire, refused refreshment. Her needle, threaded with blue silk, flashed in and out of the crimson linen she worked. She made a pretty picture in the soft firelight, garbed in yellow, head bent, long fair hair bound in a plait that fell over one shoulder to her waist.

Chaeldra perched on a cushioned bench opposite Eufemia. How strange that Eufemia, in constant motion, possessed an air of calm, whereas Chaeldra, who held herself in utter stillness, did not. Now that Shae thought about it, Chaeldra seemed somehow different this night. Color flared in her cheeks and a bright expectancy radiated from her, making her look suspiciously like a certain chambermaid at Whellein right before she ran off with a groomsman. How *had* Chaeldra spent her afternoon? Shae decided to question her servant later in privacy.

A low moan came from the bed, and Shae turned to find Maeven with her eyes rolled up and her face ashen. Her chest rose and fell in an uneven tempo.

"What ails you?" Shae rose—or at least she tried to stand. Her legs refused to take her weight. She grasped the arms of her chair for support."Ha!" Chaeldra stood over Maeven, her delighted smile and triumphant look lending her a strange beauty. "She'll not order me around again. No one will when I'm Lof Raelein."

"What have you done?" Eufemia jumped to her feet. The embroidery that fell from her hands seemed to take a long time to slide to the floor.

Chaeldra tossed her head, and honey-colored hair spilled unchecked from her cap. "Only what needed doing."

Eufemia stood as if she braced against a wind. "You are mad!"

Chaeldra laughed. "If so, I prefer my madness to your sanity. Look at you, living your life for another with little to call your own. You disgust me!" Chaeldra's arm jerked back. As her slap reported through the room, Eufemia spun around. She caught herself on a chair and stared at Chaeldra with horror. A red stain spread over her cheek.

Struggling to her feet, Eufemia lurched toward the door.

Chaeldra followed

The two fell together, locked in a deadly embrace. Chaeldra's hands clawed Eufemia's throat but ran with blood as Eufemia's nails dug into them.

Vomit pressed at the back of Shae's throat, and her knees gave way. She slid to the floor and retched.

Eufemia bucked, casting off Chaeldra, but when she tried to rise she rolled into the flaemling cage.

It tilted and crashed, and the cage door opened. A cloud of bright birds burst forth. The linen cage cover fell over Eufemia, as if to conceal her, but Chaeldra jerked it aside and threw herself onto Eufemia. Her breaths quickened as she squeezed Eufemia's throat.

Eufemia's strangled cry cut away into silence.

Chaeldra stood, panting.

Eufemia lay motionless.

Shae closed her eyes and stilled her breathing just as Chaeldra's shadow fell across her. After what seemed an eternity, it withdrew. Even then, Shae held her breath until she could endure no more. Gasping in air, she opened her eyes a slit.

Chaeldra was nowhere in sight. Beyond the gaping outer chamber door the deep timbre of a masculine voice mingled with Chaeldra's high-pitched tones.

Shae curled around another cramp and could not repress a moan. She turned her head and retched again, and then darkness shut her in.

13

Death and Life

The door to Elcon's outer chamber creaked, and Benisch peered at Kai and Craelin through the opening with an expression of disdain. "Do you visit the Lof Frael so late with business?"

Kai hid his amusement, for Benisch often kept Elcon late with business.

"Let them in!" Elcon called from within the room, a note of relief in his voice.

Benisch yielded but muttered beneath his breath as they brushed past him.

Elcon warmed himself near the hearth. His posture and the abstracted tilt to his head stirred for Kai a vision of Timraen. What thoughts belabored the Lof Frael? Kai didn't envy Elcon his duties, having observed the lives of those who ruled Faeraven long enough to understand the twin burdens of sacrifice and privilege they bore.

Elcon speared his steward with a glance. "We can resume tomorrow, Benisch. Weightier matters than *chrins* of oil and *bursels* of barley require my attention this night."

Benisch frowned and opened his mouth as if to speak, but closed it again and executed a bow. "Until tomorrow, then, Lof Frael." The outer door shut with a firm click.

Elcon turned to Craelin. "I'm anxious to hear what you learned in your questioning of the guardians, Craelin, and I would know more of this strategy you plan."

Craelin crossed to Elcon at once. "The questioning proved fruitful. The wingabeast keeper, Guaron, noticed of late a disturbance among the creatures that might confirm the wingabeasts used in the raids came from Torindan. All the guardians, when questioned, spoke with integrity. I would swear..." Craelin's voice choked off.

Kai bolted the door before joining Elcon and Craelin at fireside. He welcomed its warmth, for drafts chilled the chamber.

Craelin recovered himself and continued. "We think it's safest to take our spies from outside the guardians—from among the trackers."

"You have chosen them?"

"We have selected two trackers—the brothers Dorann and Eathnor. They should arrive soon."

"What can you tell me about them?"

"They come from the household of Nimram in Torindan proper—an honorable family. Their father Jost leads those who track and hunt to supply Torindan's table. Dorann and Eathnor have learned well their father's skills. Erinae, their mother, often helps the *Ewaeri*, the priests and guardians of justice, to distribute alms to the poor. Jaenell, their mother's mother, used her knowledge of herbs to aid the unfortunate until her own death at a venerable age."

Elcon crossed his arms. "And do Dorann and Eathnor share a knowledge of herbs?"

Craelin's brows drew together. "I don't know, but

I cannot see how—"

"We may have need of one with such skills soon."

Tapping came at the door, and Kai admitted the trackers. Eathnor entered, with a bounce in his step bespeaking stores of exuberant energy held in check. His gaze, clear blue and piercing in a sun-browned face, went at once to Elcon. He made his bow. "Lof Frael."

Dorann followed his brother into the chamber and bowed also, but did not speak. Of the two, Eathnor had the claim to age and height. Hair streaked in hues of light brown swept his brow, cut in the short style hunters adopted to prevent any intrusion upon their vision. By contrast, Dorann's hair flamed red and freckles peppered a short nose beneath intense amber eyes. He spoke little, but seemed to miss nothing. He would, Kai had learned, allow his older brother to speak for them both.

Craelin greeted them. "Thank you for attending my wishes at such a late hour. Did my directions lead you through the keep without trouble?"

Eathnor gave him a frank look. "We found it easy."

Kai hid a smile. They were, after all, trackers.

❧⚜

"Shall we sit?" Elcon indicated the strongwood table that dominated the room and waited as Kai took his place beside Craelin. The trackers pulled out chairs on the opposite side of the table and glanced around the rich chamber with bright curiosity. Torches flamed, and a small fireplace on the rear wall corralled flames that bunched and splayed, casting dubious heat. Maps of Elderland hung on the hewn stone of the side walls, suspended by tasseled cords. Behind Elcon, a massive tapestry depicted the Battle of Pilaer.

"How much have you told them?" Elcon asked Craelin.

"They know they are to watch over the wingabeasts and report any disturbances without acting upon them."

"That's important," Elcon acknowledged. "We don't want your parents to suffer the loss of two sons."

Eathnor leaned back in his chair. "We will use caution, but our parents would accept such a loss in service to Torindan."

Elcon inclined his head. "Well spoken. Let us hope they will never need to make such a sacrifice." He swung a glance to Craelin. "How will you situate them?"

"During the day they can sleep in quarters above the gatehouse. They already dine often in the hall, so none will question their presence at meals."

"Will their absence among the huntsmen be noted?"

With a glance, Craelin deferred the question to Eathnor.

Eathnor gave a nod. "'T'will. Father has in mind to tell them we've gone into service to the hold."

"It will suffice." Elcon hesitated. "Craelin tells me your grandmother, Jaenell, possessed skill in herbal healing. Had she apprenticed either of you in this skill before she died?"

Eathnor nodded. "Dorann has the proper knack for such, but I know a little also. Enough to get by on my own, if need be."

Elcon sent Kai a sideways glance. Kai took his

meaning, for he knew Elcon looked ahead to Shae's visit to Lohen Keil, which lay within Caerric Daeft, the Cavern of Death. These two, who possessed skill to track, hunt and heal, might make the difference between success and failure for her journey.

A pounding came from Elcon's outer chamber door, a summons that demanded entry.

Craelin found his feet first. His hand grasped the hilt of his dagger.

Kai moved more swiftly. He yanked open the meeting room door and rushed into the outer chamber. Elcon's servant, Anders came through the door from Elcon's inner chamber, and Kai held up a hand to halt him. "Who knocks?" he called through the door.

"In the name of Lof Yuel, let me in at once!"

"Daelic?" Kai fumbled with the latch and threw open the door.

Daelic rushed into the room with Shae motionless in his arms.

Kai's chest constricted. He quelled the onslaught of panic only with the skill of long training, although he'd never found a task so difficult. As it was, he could not seem to move. He forced out words. "What's happened to her? Does she live?"

Daelic puffed from exertion, but managed to speak. "I think she ingested poison, but she lives."

"Attarnine." Dorann spoke with certainty.

Daelic pierced Dorann with a glance. "How do you know the name of the poison?"

"It's used to kill rodents. It has a certain odor..."

Daelic's face whitened. "I pray you are not right." He swung back to Elcon. "She needs to lie in a place of safety."

"Put her in my bed." Elcon nodded to Anders,

who followed Daelic into the inner chamber.

Dorann, his expression alive with sympathy, stared at the shut door to the inner chamber. "Use Kaba bark for attarnine poisoning."

Kai drew air into his lungs. "The Praectal will know best, but I'll mention it."

Craelin turned to the two trackers. "You may go, but say nothing of what you have seen or heard."

Dorann followed his brother from the room.

Kai secured the door behind them and leaned against its support for a span measured in heartbeats.

Daelic rejoined them. At first he didn't speak, but ran a hand through his hair with a gusty sigh. Lines of strain etched his face. "She's comfortable. Anders watches over her."

Elcon halted his pacing before the fire. "Now tell me what happened?"

"Such a scene of devastation! And to think that a mere servant—I could scarce credit what I saw."

"You speak in riddles!" Elcon snapped. "Explain yourself."

"If only I need not bring sorrowful news." Daelic took a breath before going on. "Lof Raelein Maeven has passed from this world, and with her, the servant Eufemia."

Elcon went white.

Kai's stomach churned, and he thought he might vomit.

Craelin stepped forward. "How came this to be?"

Daelic's face crumpled, and tears traced a pattern down his cheeks. "Poison. Given, no doubt, by the servant Chaeldra, whom I met as she fled the Lof Raelein's chambers. Shae emptied her stomach, and so lives. Had I not come to check the Lof Raelein when I did, Shae might have died in the same manner as Eufemia—not of poison but of strangulation."

A second wave of nausea surged over Kai. How could he have been so careless as to leave the Lof Raelein unguarded and vulnerable? And he had done so, to his shame, while discussing matters of security.

"And the servant, Chaeldra. Has none detained her?" Craelin spoke in a voice terrible for its softness.

Daelic shook his head. "I could not, with Shae living. I chose healing over vengeance. You are the first to learn what happened."

Elcon's eyes widened. "Have you any question that my mother and Eufemia lie dead?"

"None." The single word fell away to silence.

Elcon pressed his lips together and clenched his fists at his sides.

Kai hesitated. "We should tend them."

Elcon stirred. "Yes. I must have my mother and her maid tended." He turned to Daelic. "Remain with Shae until you are certain she's out of danger."

Kai remembered the young tracker's advice. "Dorann suggests the use of kaba bark to ease attarnine poisoning."

Daelic frowned, but then his face cleared. "I've heard of this home remedy. It's worth a try, for I don't know how else she'll recover."

"She must recover." Kai heard the panic edging his voice and willed himself to calm.

Elcon touched his shoulder. "Go to her. She'll want you if she wakes. I will return"—He squared his shoulders—"I'll return after I see my mother's body laid upon its bier."

"Lof Frael!" Craelin's voice halted Elcon on his way to the door. "Let me accompany you. You must not venture forth alone."

Elcon stared at Craelin. "Change has indeed come to Torindan."

❧

The stone stair climbed into darkness. Flailing at cobwebs in her hair, Shae swayed and fought to keep her balance. At the edge of hearing, someone screamed. A pair of flaemlings escaped a gilded cage to fly past her. She wept, although she didn't know why she found sorrow in their freedom. Darkness searched her soul, seeking entry.

As she climbed, a strange keening grew in pitch and volume. On a landing partway up, Eufemia, an expression of infinite sadness on her face, waited with lanthorn in hand. Shae started toward her.

"No!" Kai's cry echoed through the cavern. "Live!"

As Shae looked for him her steps slowed, and then halted. She turned from Eufemia, only to trip and fall into blackness. She fell for a long time, faster and faster, until she landed in a feather tick, and sank into its suffocating softness. She fought to free herself, to breathe, to see.

Arms caught her. She woke, clammy and shivering. Cool air bathed her lungs. A blurred face hovered above hers. "Who are you?"

"Rest, Shae."

"Kai?"

"Daelic and I will keep you in safety."

Safety. The word settled over her. As hands lowered her into a feather tick, she yielded to sleep.

She opened her eyes to daylight falling through tall arched windows in paths of light across a floor covered in lush mats. She did not know this room or how she came to wake here. This seemed her whole difficulty until memory intruded with images of Maeven, Chaeldra, and Eufemia. She closed her eyes, but could not shut out the pain of the memories. Did Maeven now lie dead? Would Eufemia never take up her embroidery again?

"She wakes."

Shae turned her head toward Elcon's voice. He sat nearby, beside Kai. Both wore expressions of weariness and concern.

Kai leaned forward. "How do you feel?"

She considered his question. "Weak and strange—and my stomach pains me." She didn't speak of the other sort of pain that throbbed within her soul. "Chaeldra—"

"Yes," Elcon said, "we know. Daelic saw her leave Mother's chambers. Craelin searches for her now. Eufemia—did not live."

An image of Chaeldra's hands on Eufemia's throat rose before Shae. "And Maeven?"

The tears sliding down Elcon's face gave answer enough. "Our mother will lie beside Timraen by morning."

Shae's own tears welled. "And so I have lost her again."

Elcon sat on the edge of the bed and took her hand. "We have lost our mother, but let us hold fast to one another." She turned into his arms and wept with him.

When Shae withdrew at last from Elcon's embrace, she noticed the glint of tears in Kai's eyes. She longed to comfort him, but held back, for she didn't know her welcome. She touched Elcon's arm. "Where does our mother lie? Let me go to her."

Kai and Elcon exchanged glances, and Elcon shook his head. "You are not well enough to walk."

"Whether or not I can walk, I must go to her." Determination gave her voice a hardened edge despite her weakness. "I have promised to sing her death song, and I shall do so."

"Well spoken," Elcon approved. "You shall sing for her tomorrow as she wished. I'll allow you to see her before then, but you must take care, my sister. You almost joined her in death." He stood and looked down at her. "Praectal Daelic watched over you most of the night. I'll have my servant wake him. He'll want to check you. Let Daelic tend you, and spend this day gathering your strength." Without waiting for her response, Elcon left the room.

Kai touched her forehead. "I am sorry for what you have endured. If I could, I would take your grief on myself instead."

His words brought a fresh onslaught of tears. "I know your heart, Kai. But we must each bear our own burdens. You have shouldered mine too long."

He sat in the place Elcon had vacated on the edge of the bed and took her hand. "Things have changed, I know, but I still love you, Shae. That remains true."

She couldn't meet his eyes. "I love you too, Kai."

He cradled her hand. "Can you remember—did Chaeldra say anything? It could be important."

Shae cast back in memory, frowning when she recalled things she would rather not remember. "Yes. She said something about becoming Lof Raelein. Kai, could the Contender be female? What do the legends tell?"

"I don't think it's likely."

Elcon spoke from the doorway. "It makes no sense! How can Chaeldra, a mere servant, make such a claim—"

Kai spread his hands. "Perhaps madness afflicts her."

Chaeldra had laughed after Eufemia accused her of succumbing to just this malady. A suspicion crept over Shae. "What if she doesn't act alone? Could someone have promised to make her Lof Raelein?" Had the Contender, whoever he might be, orchestrated Chaeldra's actions?

Kai went to the window. "That does make sense. We can hope Craelin finds her and that she'll provide answers."

A servant with faded red hair appeared in the doorway. "Lof Frael, I pray you will forgive the intrusion, but Steward Benisch waits to conclude last night's business."

"Send him away again, Anders. I can't think of such things now. Tell him I will summon him when I can. Meanwhile, I'll trust his judgment on household matters."

Daelic entered as Anders withdrew. The Praectal looked fresh, despite the fact that he had spent a foreshortened night in a strange bed. "Greetings, Shae." He laid a hand on her forehead and peered at her.

Shae murmured a reply and submitted to Daelic's examination. At length, he straightened. "You will improve little by little, with rest and a gentle diet. Already you've made gains." He glanced at Kai. "I must thank Dorann for his suggestion to use kaba bark as an anecdote. I might not have come upon a remedy otherwise."

At the sympathy in the faces around her, Shae blinked away tears. "Dorann? Who is Dorann?"

"A tracker present when I brought you to Elcon's chambers. His advice may have saved your life."

She raised her eyebrows. "Then I must thank him."

Shae looked about the lavish room and guessed that she rested in the shraen's inner chamber. It could be no other, for no other bedchamber would match this opulence. Marble gleamed at mantle and hearth, and gilt-painted carvings adorned all wooden surfaces save the strongwood floor. Tapestries wrought in jewel tones and depicting feats from history hung on the walls. The white and blue ceiling arched overhead with a carved and gilded rose of Rivenn at its center.

She returned her attention to Daelic. "You have my thanks as well."

Daelic's cheeks went pink.

Elcon joined them beside the bed and gave Shae a gentle smile. "You will meet Dorann and his brother Eathnor soon. Meanwhile, you must take Daelic's advice and rest."

But she resisted the tug of sleepiness. "What of Eufemia's wake? May I not attend it? Without her intervention, I might not now live."

Elcon glanced at Kai, who shook his head. "She lies already beneath the sod. They put her to rest early this morning. What little family she claimed dwells far to the south in Morgorad. The messenger we dispatched will not soon reach them. We could not delay."

The idea of the quiet, willowy maiden lying in a grave brought tears to choke Shae. Her mind crowded—not with scenes of death but with images of life. She saw again Eufemia's youthful grace and the beauty of Maeven's smile. Her tears spilled over, flooding her with a new resolve. She would fulfill Prophecy and defeat the Contender, or die in the attempt.

Part Two: Journey

14

Decision

Maeven of Braeth lay upon a draetenn bier in a bed of early flowers, bathed in the light of many candles. She looked as beautiful in death as she had in life. Arrayed in white-and-gold splendor, her burnished hair woven with flowers, she might have been a bride awaiting her bridegroom's kiss. Shae smiled through tears at the notion. Maeven journeyed to *Shaenn Raven*, the Land Beyond, to join Timraen, the bridegroom she'd lost in youth.

Shae stood beside Kai in the Allerstaed. In times past, she would have leaned into his support without thought. Now she held back, for much remained unspoken, and she no longer knew the timbre of their love.

She climbed the steps to stand beside her mother's bier on the dais before the altar. As she approached, a trick of light made Maeven's eyelids seem to quiver, but the pale cheek felt cold against Shae's lips. *One last kiss, Mother, to release you in forgiveness.*

Kai waited in the shadows, affording her privacy, but she knew he wouldn't leave her alone for safety's sake. Chaeldra had eluded capture and might still mean Shae harm, or others could attack.

Shae knelt and rested her forehead on the edge of the bier as the cloying scent of early flowers closed about her. Their scent would ever bring her to her dead mother's side. Sketchy prayers came to her lips and spilled over in soft murmurings. *Lof Yuel, let her pass to You with ease... Bring justice to lend peace... Thank You that I could know her love... Help me live as a true daughter...*

Standing on legs that wobbled, Shae steadied herself against the bier and gazed at her mother's face to commit it to memory. As she stumbled away with tears blinding her, Kai caught her elbow, and she let herself lean on him at last.

❧

Kai gave Shae over to Craelin and Daelic, who waited just inside the side door at the rear of the Allerstaed. The two guardians bent toward Shae as they progressed along the short, vaulted corridor that connected to the great hall.

Formality required that the Lof Raelein's body remain under guard, so Kai ignored his sudden urgent desire to follow and comfort Shae. Steeling himself for a long vigil, he returned to his post to perform this last, bittersweet service for Maeven.

Gazing at her still features, he searched for signs of the vibrant soul that had enlivened what was now a silent corpse. He couldn't find them in the face before him, sunken into lines it would not have known in life. Maeven no longer inhabited this shell.

Where did she abide now? Had she already gone

to Shaenn Raven, the land beyond the veil, or did some tenuous connection to her lifeless body remain? Perhaps her spirit kept its own vigil beside him. A tingle laddered up his spine, but he pushed the odd fancy aside. He could not let imaginings unnerve him. Wherever Maeven dwelt now, he wished her the peace life had denied her.

Images drifted to him, disjointed by the passage of time. Maeven rode, as when he'd first seen her, sidesaddle on a white charger, her long burnished hair flying about her. His young heart had roused at the sight. He smiled now, to think of the futility of his childish passion. Even if their difference in age had not separated them, Maeven's glances were only for Timraen. They made a striking couple. Timraen's large frame dwarfed Maeven, his fair hair bright against the muted copper of her tresses. They contrasted in other, less obvious ways, too. Timraen's calm nature sparked at Maeven's zest for life. In turn, his measured introspection settled her tempestuousness. Kai outgrew his childish infatuation, but never the admiration Maeven inspired.

The memory of Timraen lying wounded after taking a poisoned arrow from an unknown bow made Kai frown. Despite her grief and rage, Maeven had accepted the Sword and Scepter of Faeraven from Timraen's hand. The rousing speech she'd given at her coronation had stilled the tongues of those who objected to a Lof Raelein ruling the alliance of Faeraven alone.

Without reserve, Kai had bent both knee and heart to Maeven's service. Now she needed him no longer.

None can command the allegiance of a guardian of Rivenn. It must be surrendered of free will. But I do ask that you give yourself to Elcon's service.

Kai's mind recoiled. He had wanted to grant Maeven's request, but caution held him back, just as it had when his father asked him to serve Whellein. In truth, Kai would rather keep his freedom and search for answers in Daeven's disappearance. Unlike his father, he could not let go of the hope his brother might yet live. It rankled to embrace Daeven's death with no more proof than the board from the side of a ship and the assumptions of a grizzled sea captain. He sighed now in the knowledge that, no matter how pressing, his quest for the truth of Daeven's disappearance must wait. He knew his course now.

❧◦❧

The Allerstaed could not hold all who came to honor Maeven in death. They crowded into the nave, jammed the side corridors behind the pillars, and spilled into the rear archway. Maeven, veiled now in a pall of silk gauze, her bier engulfed in great drifts of flowers offered by many hands, waited before the altar.

Kai and Craelin, in gold and green ceremonial garb, stood at opposite ends of the bier. Elcon, near the black-robed priest on the dais behind the bier, watched a procession of Kindren file by to anoint, with flowers and tears and prayers, their beloved Lof Raelein.

Shae, seated in the *quire* with the musicians, knew that Dithmar and Weilton watched over her from nearby. But for the secrets that bound her, she could take her place on the dais beside Elcon. Freaer, who played a dirge among his fellows, glanced her way, but his gaze held no pull for her today. She felt little save the sharp pain of loss.

A priest entered from an archway behind the chancel, waited until the last of the mourners passed the bier, and then took his place before the altar. His very bearing commanded quiet. "We gather this day to honor Maeven of Braeth, Raelein of Rivenn and Lof Raelein of Faeraven. She lived well and honorably."

The priest spoke at length to describe Maeven's early life and capture by garns, her rescue by Timraen, and her rulership of Rivenn and Faeraven. Shae tried to listen but, as weariness clouded her mind, she struggled to pull her attention from the vague pathways it wandered.

The priest called for others to acknowledge Maeven, and Elcon stepped forward. "She never faltered in her duty."

Others spoke also, but Shae heard little of what they said. Elcon's words preoccupied her wholly, for they seemed the sum of Maeven's existence. Whether it had been right or wrong for her to send Shae away at birth no longer mattered. Maeven had, at great cost, done what she thought was right.

In a sudden silence, the priest signaled Shae, and she went forward to join her mother's body before the altar. But the small exertion made her head swim, and she swallowed against a dry throat as she waited for the chamber to stop tilting.

You will sing my death song. Promise me this.

She couldn't remember the words.

Why had she thought she could do this? She should have asked Maeven to release her from her promise.

But then, as her heart pounded, a soft touch soothed her mind.

She met Elcon's sea-green gaze across their

mother's bier—and understood. Here, then, was the other soul that had touched hers with peace in the night.

She drew breath and sang, trembling with the effort. The ancient song, the mael lido, said to provide a soul's safe passage to Lof Yuel, eddied through the Allerstaed. The melody climbed in pitch, and then fell to conclude on a sustained low note. Shae bowed her head.

I have longed to call you daughter.

❧

"Come in and bolt the door. We have dark matters to discuss,"

Kai obeyed Elcon's instructions and leaned against the strongwood door as he glanced about. He wasn't surprised to see most of the faces grouped around Elcon's meeting table.

"Would that we could take time to mourn my mother before addressing matters of state. We don't have that luxury. The blame for the wingabeast riders attacking Norwood and Westerland has been laid by the Elder at my door. All trade with them has ceased." Elcon sighed. "And now I hear rumors of discord within Faeraven itself."

In the silence that followed Elcon's announcement, a strain from *DawnSinger's Lament* sang in Kai's memory: *The Contender fell 'til the wane of Rivenn, for then released, he will bring division. He will gather armies and bring forth war to devour Elderland forevermore...*

"The time for heroism has come."

As Kai looked into Elcon's face and saw Timraen's son, Elcon paused to look at each of them in turn.

"I have chosen all of you to guard and guide Shae of Whellein on a journey of great urgency and peril. I count upon you to lay down your lives, if needed, in her aid. Make preparations now, but in secret. Tell no one, except to provide an excuse to cover your absence. Shae's life, and your own, depends on secrecy and stealth. You will depart in a matter of days for *Maeg Waer*, the forsaken mountain where Caerric Daeft lies."

Aerlic tilted his head. "What business can a maid have in the Cave of Death?"

Eathnor gave a low whistle. "Is there no other way?"

Dorann, if possible, became even more still.

Guaron's chair thudded as he sat forward, his hair lifting in a straw-colored halo. "No one has ever returned from Caerric Daeft!"

Besides Kai, only Craelin did not react. Kai guessed Elcon would have already told him the secret of Shae's identity. His stomach knotted at the thought. He knew he could trust Craelin with Shae's life, but a secret told can never be untold.

"I ask that you freely give your service." Elcon's voice rang out as the protests died down. "I would have you set both hand and heart to this task. It will not succeed unless you do. The very fabric of life for all Elderland rests upon this journey."

Silence followed, so thick it pressed the ears, as those about the table exchanged glances.

Elcon waited in silence.

Craelin stood. "You have my service."

Aerlic pushed back his chair and stood. "Tomorrow I pledge fealty to my new Lof Shraen. I will follow your wishes with all my heart."

"I don't know your purposes, Lof Frael." Eathnor

rose with lithe grace. "But I trust you."

Dorann stood beside his brother.

Guaron pressed a finger to the cleft in his chin, slanted a look at Elcon, and then stood. "You'll need me to tend the wingabeasts."

Kai, standing with the others, stated the truth. "I will protect Shae with my life."

ঔৎৎ৶

Whispers hissed, on the edge of hearing.

"Who's there?" Shae peered into the shadows behind her, the lamp she carried faint in the cavernous darkness. Something scuttled away just out of range, but when she turned her head, nothing showed itself. A shriek rent the air, then fell into echoes.... Her lamp flickered. Something caught in her hair but freed itself with a piercing whistle. Small creatures ran across her slippered feet.

She raised the lamp high and peered into the dimness.

Eyes gleamed back at her, accompanied by the sound of laughter.

"*Stop!*" She rushed down the stairs, but her foot found no purchase, and she lurched forward. She tried to cry out, but only croaked. Tears slid down her cheeks. Flames shot upward from a great chasm, bending toward her.

A whisper breathed through the air. *"Walk in the light, Shae. Trust..."*

She came to herself with a jerk and lay still as her heartbeats slowed. *Only a dream.* Such dreams troubled her often of late.

She'd earlier dismissed Laela, the servant Elcon

had provided her, and had fallen asleep without drawing the bed curtains or window hangings. Light now penetrated the window at the edges of its shutters and glinted in bars across the wooden floorboards.

Something in the quality of that light called her to the window. She threw open the shutters and gasped.

Low in the dawn sky over Torindan hung an orb of surpassing brightness. Shae shielded her eyes and stepped back.

This could only be Brael Shadd, the DayStar of Prophecy.

15

Coronation

"Elcon, son of Timraen, son of Shaelcon, son of Talan, son of Kunrat, son of Aelfric, son of Rivenn, receive the Circlet of Rivenn." The priest lowered the ancient circlet of bejeweled gold to Elcon's head.

Kai shifted to see better from within the ranks of the guardians of Rivenn waiting beneath the great clerestory window arches.

Elcon, arrayed in blue and gold ceremonial dress, rose from his knees and faced his people.

"A new shraen rises over Rivenn." Kai barely caught the priest's announcement in the crowd's uproar.

When the tumult ebbed, the priest laid a scabbard in Elcon's hands. "Elcon, Shraen of Rivenn, receive the Sword of Rivenn."

Elcon unsheathed the famed weapon, forged for Rivenn in the Viadrel, the Flames of Virtue at Lohen Keil. He raised the sword, and as it gleamed along its length, Kai almost fancied the blade lit with fire at Elcon's touch.

As the applause faded, Elcon kissed and sheathed the great sword.

"Elcon, Shraen of Rivenn, receive the Scepter of Faeraven." Rubies, diamonds, and emeralds glittered against the glint of gold as the staff passed into Elcon's hands. When he turned back to his people, gasps came at its beauty. Elcon raised the scepter, and its jewels winked in many colors beneath a rampant gryphon clutching a star-sapphire orb.

"Worthy Kindren, receive Shraen Elcon of Rivenn, Lof Shraen of Faeraven," the priest pronounced. Another wave of applause and cheering, more fervent than the first, broke over the crowd and deafened Kai.

The guardians, clad in surcoats of green and gold, their banners ablaze with the unfurling rose of Rivenn and the rampant gryphon of Faeraven, advanced by regiment and bent their knees in a unified pledge of fealty to Elcon.

Kai waited his turn, putting from his mind the unhappiness his choice would cause. Like Craelin and Weilton, he would face Elcon alone. When at last Elcon called his name, he walked across the shape of a gryphon laid into the floor and climbed the steps to the platform. Kai bowed before Elcon, who stood at its center on an inlaid unfurling rose.

"Do you, Kai of Whellein, give your fealty to Elcon of Rivenn, Lof Shraen of Faeraven?" The priest intoned the inquiry.

"I give it and will keep it with all my heart." Kai gave the ceremonial answer and knelt before his new Lof Shraen. He'd not anticipated the relief that now eased his burden of sorrow. He hoped his parents would come to understand the choice he'd made. The new Lof Shraen, as an untried youth, already faced opposition in certain quarters. He needed the benefit of Kai's experience. Besides, Kai couldn't bring himself to abandon Shae with the fate of Elderland resting in her hands. He would remain at Torindan in the hope of helping her.

"Rise."

Kai obeyed and squared his shoulders.

Elcon extended a sword by its hilt. "This sword can defend both flesh and spirit, and it can guide the lost to safety by its light. Shaelcon wielded Whyst in many conquests of garns, for it was forged to glow at their approach. Timraen recovered this, his father's sword, at the rout of Pilaer, but it has rested until now. Take it and carry it in my service."

Kai's throat tightened as his hand closed over cold steel. He hoisted the sword, enjoying its balanced weight, and a cheer went up. Kai faced the crowd, but his smile faltered.

He couldn't name the thing that alerted him, but something was terribly wrong.

☜☞

Shae smiled through a haze of tears. Kai had never seemed nobler than when he bent his knee to Elcon. Murmurs of approval came from the crowd around her, but also murmurings of another sort. She exchanged uneasy glances with Eathnor, who stood beside her, and Dorann, on her other side.

The presence chamber overflowed with Kindren, but as whispers hissed and faces tensed the crowd seemed on edge.

How she longed for the ceremony to end. The pageantry dazzled, but she wearied of standing, although she would not let on to Eathnor and Dorann—at least not yet. She'd only just convinced Elcon of her ability to attend his coronation. She didn't want to admit to weakness so soon.

Two carved and canopied seats reposed on the throne platform, framed by three arches in the wall behind them. Above the throne arches, scenes from the ballads Kai had taught Shae unfolded. Here dwelt Shaelcon in full battle array, as yet undefeated, Timraen brandished Sword Rivenn in the ruins of Pilaer, and Talan subdued a bucking wingabeast. Above these paintings sprawled a depiction of the Kindren entering Elderland at Gilead Riann.

Light fell in beams through tall clerestory windows above pillars that marched down the chamber on either side. Beyond them, leaves swayed in treetops, but no cooling breeze reached Shae here in the press of bodies. Her scalp prickled, sweat beaded her brow, and she sagged against Dorann.

His head turned in solicitude. "Are you well?"

She pulled away to stand alone, but clung to his arm. "It's warm in here."

Eathnor and Dorann exchanged glances and, without a word, turned toward the rear arches. She went with them without complaint, for she must lie down or fall down. Her attendance of the coronation so soon after the funeral had proven unwise after all. She should marshal her strength for the journey she would soon make now that the DayStar had appeared.

The two trackers fought through the crowd, shielding her, but a sudden murmuring halted them. Shae looked back. Freaer stood at the foot of the throne platform, commanding the eye not only for his beauty but also for the strong emotion that highlighted him. Without thought, she reached across time and space to touch his soul.

The darkness of bitterness, pride and exhileration flowed into her like rising bile. How had she missed the arrogance that defined Freaer? Her heart pounded. She had to break free from the tide of emotion or drown.

She found Kai among the other guardians and tried to catch his eye. He didn't notice but, with his body held as if coiled to spring, he seemed to need no warning.

Freaer stepped forward without a summons. "Lof Shraen Elcon!" Freaer's voice ripped through the crowd. "I have come to collect my reward!"

Elcon's eyes narrowed. "Reward?"

"Yes. Lof Raelein Maeven allowed me a reward for forgoing my right to sing her death song."

The crowd roared, and Elcon held up a hand for quiet. "I know nothing of such a promise, Freaer, but we can discuss this in private."

"I will take my reward now, as Lof Raelein Maeven wished." Freaer spoke in a casual voice that belied the excitement Shae felt drumming within him.

Three cloaked and hooded figures stepped from the front of the crowd to surround him.

"I choose Shae of Whellein as my reward."

The blood rushed in Shae's ears. Instinct warned her to flee, but her feet wouldn't budge. The crowd around her turned, and bone crunched on bone. Dorann slid to the floor. Eathnor, knife in hand, faced off against three assailants. The mob closed about her. Rough hands grabbed her, pulling in different directions. Shae moaned.

"Hold off. You'll kill her." A voice with a burr from the south of Elderland spoke above her head. Hands caught and hoisted her into restraining arms. The odors of sweat and foul breath overpowered her, but at least she could see what was happening.

Several guardians with drawn swords already moved to help Eathnor, who was holding his own. Others rushed toward her captors.

Elcon still faced Freaer. "Leave this madness! My mother would never give you authority to make such a claim, and you shall not do so by force!"

"I have a letter by her hand and stamped with her seal stating I may name my compensation."

"By forgery or trickery, I'll warrant!"

"You have no proof of that. By doubting your mother's authority, you call into question your own. Indeed, a prior claim to the thrones of Rivenn and Faeraven exists."

Freaer motioned, and those standing with him threw back their hoods. The names of three shraens from ravens to the south—Veraedel of Glindenn, Taelerat of Selfred, and Lenhardt of Morgorad—rang through the crowd.

Elcon signaled the guardians, and the scrape of swords unsheathing carried throughout the chamber.

Kai held Whyst at the ready and his shield before him as he surged to the platform and positioned himself between Elcon and Freaer.

Freaer drew no weapon, but Shae felt the raw whipcord of power that lashed Kai, making his sword arm waiver. One of the three shraens lunged toward Kai with sword drawn. Although Kai parried and shifted, he lurched back. Blood marred the beauty of his green and gold surcoat. Whyst clattered away as he fell.

"*Kai!*" Shae's cry came out a whisper.

Kai lay motionless.

The three shraens rushed from behind Freaer to cut Elcon off from the guardians' protection. Amid the cries and clangor of fighting, the crowd pressed forward.

With Sword Rivenn glinting in his hand, Elcon faced the three shraens. The priests sank to their knees behind him.

Aerlic, Guaron, and several other guardians Shae didn't know joined Eathnor to challenge those who held her. As a maelstrom raged around her, Shae's captor carried her toward the entrance but, in the crush of bodies, made little progress.

Freaer unleashed a thunderbolt of power that left her gasping. Elcon went to his knees before the invisible blow, and Freaer's rush of triumph slammed into her with savage force. She drank unwillingly of Freaer's lust for Elcon's blood and understood what she should have guessed before. A soul laden with such darkness could only belong to the son of Meriwen of Old, the Contender of Prophecy. He claimed her in order to destroy her, to bring her into his depravity, to darken her soul. She saw with a shudder what he meant her to become.

She had to free herself.

The hands on Shae lifted her across her captor's shoulder, and as her face rammed against his rough woolen jerkin, the stench of smoke and sweat assaulted her. Gripped by despair, she struggled without heart. If only she'd spoken of her misgivings about Freaer to Kai. Why had she allowed his web of fascination to bind her? The image of a bloodstained whispan tree rose before her. *She had seen but not understood its warning.*

Rousing herself, she looked inward to the place only Lof Yuel could touch. The clamor of fighting faded, and she no longer saw outwardly or felt arms binding her. White light flared to life within her and grew to a blazing fire. With the ease of thought, she sent it forth.

Freaer cried out, and his inner eye swung toward Shae. The backlash, when it came, did not touch her. Instead, her captor screamed and fell. The floor rose up to smite Shae, and she slid into enfolding darkness.

⤳⤲

Kai forced himself to lie still and listen. He'd fallen as much out of confusion as from his injury, which could not be deep. His chainmail had saved him, but his side throbbed and blood-loss leached his strength. *Why had he lowered his guard?* He remembered now…a sweetish stench of death…the image of a new tomb opening…. He almost had not defended himself. The hair on the back of his neck still lifted in warning.

An uproar told him the guardians advanced, and he opened his eyes. The three shraens approached the throne platform—and Elcon.

He settled his breathing. *He could not let this happen.* Neither could he move before time. He shifted his head by measures. Could he find Whyst? The cool luster of metal caught his attention. He marshaled his strength and rehearsed the move he would make.

A sudden bellow from Freaer chilled his blood. *Now!* He rolled, caught Whyst, and staggered to his feet. He'd planned to strike the nearest of the three shraens, but he hadn't realized the room would spin or calculated for his sword arm wavering.

Shraen Taelerat turned and smiled, almost as if they exchanged pleasantries.

The chamber righted itself, and relief shot through

Kai. He rallied his strength.

Taelerat shifted, gathering himself for a blow.

Kai feinted left. As Taelerat followed, Kai shifted right in time to nick his opponent's sword arm.

Taelerat roared and thrusted, but Kai parried and pulled back. Pain made him pant. He followed with a lunge, but his balance betrayed him.

Taelerat's expression grew smug, but Kai kept his own face blank, for he saw his opponent's next move. Taelerat did not disappoint him. With a battle cry, he jabbed toward Kai's injured side.

Kai spun to the left and, before Taelerat could recover, Whyst cut toward his side.

Taelerat's eyes widened as blood oozed from a new wound. He reeled away.

But the maneuver had cost Kai his remaining strength. He fought to pull Whyst upright with arms that shook. The great blade lowered, and Kai fell to his knees.

With a smile, Taelerat gathered himself for another attack.

Although he faced certain death, Kai didn't bow his head. The clang of steel from the throne platform told him that Elcon still fought. But how long could he hold out? Bile burned Kai's throat. If he gave up, he would fail Elcon and leave Shae when she needed him most.

He groaned, straining. Sweat poured from him. In his hands, Whyst lifted and steadied. With no strength to do more, Kai waited.

Taelerat charged with a roar, too fast for proper balance.

Kai saw his chance and took it. He parried, but Whyst left his hands, wrenching his wrists. He dropped and rolled.

Taelerat fell over Kai and landed with a grunt, a victim of his own eagerness. With enough strength, Kai could leap on his opponent and disarm him, but such an option lay beyond him now. Instead, he drew his dagger and waited.

16

Flight from Torindan

"She lives." As voices and touches recalled Shae, she fought to lift heavy eyelids, aware of two kinds of pain.

"*Kai.*" The name came on a breath.

"Open your eyes, dear one."

She managed the feat with a gasp. *"You died!"*

Kai smiled. "Ah, but I live."

She squinted to see him in faint light. "Do I dream? I saw you die!"

He put a finger to his lips. *"Keep your voice down!* I'm a little worse for wear, but still with you."

She sat up and, needing to reassure herself, reached out to cup his cheek.

He caught and kissed her hand.

Shae sobbed and leaned into his arms. Kai swayed as he took her weight but cradled her against his heart, which pulsed steadily. She gave way to tears, but then hiccupped on a laugh. "Don't scare me like that again!"

"My apologies." His voice throbbed beneath her ear.

At the memory of blood flowing from his side, she arched away to look at him. "Are you well? And Elcon?"

"You must lower your voice, Shae. Elcon fared

better than I, for he received no injury. If Taelerat hadn't thrown himself on my dagger I would not now live. Pain and blood loss weaken me, but Daelic tells me I'll recover. And you? How do you fare?" His arms tightened. "When I saw that mob take you…"

"My head hurts." She pulled away, afraid that by leaning against him she was causing him pain. She strained to see in the dimness. Guaron and Aerlic, their faces limned by the moonlight beneath clerestory windows, kept watch near the rear archway. She knew this place. "Why are we in the Allerstaed?"

"It's a precaution, after all that's happened." Kai answered her in a quiet voice. "Guardians hide outside, watching the entrances."

"Dorann… Eathnor…"

"They fought well but sustained injuries. They sleep, there." He waved toward two dark shapes lying motionless in the nave below the chancel.

"And what of—" She halted on the name.

"Freaer?" Kai read her thought. "This day saw much letting of blood, but not his. He escaped with the three shraens who accompanied him—traitors all." His voice took on a rough edge. "But at least one of them did not come away unscathed. Taelarat had to be carried."

Footsteps sounded in the corridor outside. Aerlic and Guaron flanked the entrance.

The door opened to admit Elcon, still garbed in blue and gold ceremonial clothing. Beside him, Daelic held a guttering lamp, its flame turned low.

As Elcon approached, Shae struggled to her feet, but swayed as the room tilted. Kai rose when she did and put a hand to her elbow.

Elcon took her hands in his. "Shae, I owe you my

thanks. Had you not blocked Freaer with the shil shael, I might have succumbed."

She couldn't at first find her voice. "Shil shael?"

"Forgive me, I should have realized you would not know about the soul touch—Lof Yuel's gift to those of Rivenn's blood."

"Tell me of it."

"Long ago, the first Kindren who came through Gilead Riann inhabited secret places within Maeg Waer and named the mountain's hollow core Caerric Baest, Cavern of Wonder. After garns drove out the Kindren with much bloodshed, the cave's name changed to Caerric Daeft, Cavern of Death."

Shae knew the story, having learned as much in her early days.

"When the garns invaded, they took Rivenn, Daeramor, and Glindenn captive and chained them in a dark cave. They knew of Gilead Riann and would not believe the gateway remained closed. In their lust for unearned wealth, the garns did not content themselves with wreaking destruction in Elderland—they yearned to pillage Anden Raven too. Daeramor and Glindenn died with the truth on their lips. Only Rivenn remained alive. The garns hunted his family, for they meant to torture them in front of him so he would give the location of the gate. They wouldn't believe that he couldn't, for it had vanished. That's when Lof Yuel gave Rivenn the shil shael, the soul touch that enabled him to comfort and warn his family from afar.

"The Kindren freed Rivenn and drove the garns away, but then welkes migrated from lands across the salt waters of Maer Lingenn, making Maeg Waer their roost. The Kindren no longer wished to shelter within Maeg Waer, and so they abandoned Caerric Daeft to its dead. They moved into *Weithein Faen*, the salt marshes along the coast, where they built Pilaer.

"Rivenn never lost the shil shael. It passed to his children, and then to his children's children." His voice turned bitter. "Freaer among them."

Shae caught her breath. So Elcon also saw the truth. "Yes?"

"Yes. You've heard the story of Meriwen of Old?"

"I have."

"Kunrat fathered an illegitimate son by Meriwen—Faendenn, who grew up filled with his mother's poison. When he reached adulthood, Faendenn vied with his father for the thrones of Rivenn and Faeraven. He almost won his campaign by fell arts, but Kunrat carried his misbegotten son with him when he fell into the flames of Lohen Keil, flames said to burn with virtue. But Faendenn has escaped the well to hide among us. I am certain that Freaer and Faendenn are one."

Kai stirred and the lamplight cast his face in relief. "I've come to the same conclusion. I wish we'd realized before this!"

Shae frowned. "But what of Chaeldra?"

Craelin shook his head. "I believe Freaer used her for his own ends. She has vanished, and I wonder if we will ever find her. "

She shivered at the implication. *No one will ever tell me what to do again.* Chaeldra had cried with passion as she watched Maeven die. Perhaps her prediction had come true in a way she had not intended. Shae looked at Elcon. "The shil shael...differs when Freaer uses it. He makes it into a weapon."

"Freaer has corrupted it, perhaps by dark arts he learned from his mother." The flame in Daelic's lamp flared in a draft, the sudden illumination revealing the weariness that robbed Elcon's face of its youthful vigor. But his eyes gleamed with purpose. "Daelic will tend you, Shae. You'll depart at first light; although I wish you and your protectors had more time to recover before undertaking such a difficult journey."

His words took her breath away. "By first light?"

"We can afford no delay. You must reach Lohen Keil before the DayStar completes its arc of the sky. "

"But are we well enough to travel?"

"Despite their injuries, these I have chosen are still the best to guard you. But I'm concerned about you, Shae. I want Daelic to examine you again now that you've awakened. He will do all he can to strengthen you. Dorann also has skill to tend injuries and will look after you on the journey."

She frowned. "You are right, of course. We must leave at once."

"I've come to give you my farewell...and this." Elcon drew a dagger from his sleeve, jewels glistening in its hilt. "*Leisht* belonged to our mother."

Blinking away tears, she took the weapon, and its small weight comforted her hand. Questions pressed her lips, unspoken. *Tell me of our mother. Did she hold you when you were small? Spend time with you? Talk of our father?* She sighed. Such words might find utterance some day, but not now.

"Its swirlstones light to reveal magics of all kinds. Leisht cuts enchantment."

Her fingers caressed the smooth hilt. "I'll treasure it."

"I wish I could come with you and keep you safe, but duties place me here—even more so now. We've secured Torindan, but we must watch and wait for

what comes. Guard yourself, Shae. Never forget—
Freaer desires you."

She shivered. "He lusts for your death as he does
for my life."

He kissed the palm of her hand. "Lof Yuel will not
forsake us."

❧

Kai settled onto his good side, and the rough
canvas tick rustled as the sweet scent of straw wrapped
around him. A woolen blanket staved off the cold
dampness of the stone building. Tomorrow, a simple
bedroll on the hard ground and the thick perse of his
cloak would have to do. He fought to keep his eyes
from drifting shut. He had lain down at Craelin's
insistence but would not rest fully until he knew Shae
had sustained no lasting harm.

Daelic bent over Shae, his head pale in the
lamplight.

The memory of rough hands seizing her haunted
Kai. He could not have reached her in time, and his
first duty lay with Elcon, but when he'd turned away
from her peril, a part of him had died.

Daelic stepped away from Shae, his posture
relaxed, and Kai remembered to breathe. He had not
understood his feeling for Shae before, but his
reactions now told him more than he wanted to accept.
They'd not been raised together, and knowing the
truth of her birth from the beginning, he'd never
thought of her as his sister. He'd loved her nonetheless,
without pausing to wonder at the depth of that love.
Until now.

Such foolishness. He'd lived much of his life

charged to protect Shae. Of course he would have a strong reaction to her danger. But that didn't explain the fierce joy that had gripped him at embracing her. He knew the answer to that riddle, but couldn't face it. Not now.

Daelic departed with the lamp, and Shae tiptoed toward Kai. As moonlight fell across her, she seemed more wraith than maid.

He said nothing, but closed his eyes to block the sight of her beauty and to stop the sensation, almost of pain, that grew within him.

She knelt at his side, and with gentle fingers smoothed his brow. "Rest well." Her whisper stirred the air.

Lof Yuel, help me preserve her in safety and honor.

❧

"It's time to wake!" Kai called.

Shae tried to roll over, but the hand on her shoulder prevented her. Clawing her way to consciousness, she opened an eye. When darkness met her, she moaned. It was still night! The makeshift bed of wilderein fur had kept her warm despite the damp chill, but restless dreams had impoverished her sleep. If only she could sleep a little longer...

"Shae, we have to leave!"

As memory returned, she groaned and pushed to a sitting position in a feeble shaft of moonlight. Self-conscious under Kai's scrutiny, she put her hands to her hair.

"I have your comb, but there's no time to use it now. I wish you could have a maid to tend you. It isn't proper for you to travel alone with such a rough lot."

She smiled. "I can always count on you to consider my honor. But this time propriety must bow to necessity. No maid should make this journey for the sake of my grooming. It is hard enough that I do so."

The others had already gathered their belongings and now waited for her. "You should have wakened me sooner."

"I didn't have the heart, you slept so soundly."

He helped her to her feet and led her to a small vestry behind the chancel. "You can tend yourself here in private. Elcon had traveling clothes brought for you."

She smiled when she discovered Aeleanor's cloak waiting for her in the vestry. She donned the simple tunics beside it, and then gathered the cloak to her and pressed her face into its marmolet fur lining. Who would know if she allowed herself a few weak tears?

When she rejoined the others, she found that either her eyes had grown used to the darkness or else it had lightened—perhaps both. She could see Dorann's black eye and cut lip, the way Eathnor held his arm, and the gash on Guaron's cheek. How would they fare on an arduous journey when already taxed with injuries? And yet, the tilt of Eathnor's head and Dorann's quick smile reassured her. Guaron looked a little rough but made no complaint. Craelin and Aerlic, beside him, seemed better rested than possible.

Craelin led them into the vestry, where a small door hidden in the paneling opened under his hand. Raising a lanthorn, he passed through, swallowed at once by the dark maw gaping behind it. Aerlic and Guaron followed. From the doorway, Kai turned back to Shae.

She took his hand and stepped into the bracing

chill of the secret passageway. They descended a hewn stone stair to a small landing where Craelin and Aerlic paused to light and distribute torches.

Torchlight wavered across Craelin's face. "This stair leads through the motte to the watergate where wingabeasts await us."

As they traveled down a long flight, the deep scent of water rose to Shae. Like the others, she kept silence, but the sound of their passage echoed in the enclosed space. Their feet stirred clouds of dust, and Shae smothered a sneeze. Grateful for torchlight on the uneven stair treads, she followed Kai. Aerlic, Guaron, and Craelin led the way. Eathnor and Dorann came last, so quiet she glanced back to make sure they followed. She did her best to keep up, but her strength flagged, and she had to catch up when those ahead paused to rest.

A memory, jarring in its urgency, hid just out of reach, and as the hair on the back of her neck lifted, she shifted closer to Kai. He had not spoken of it, but she knew by his strained expression he suffered.

They resumed the long descent but paused at times to keep together. Shae trudged on in mindless misery, through the dank passageway that seemed to have no end. Strange fantasies exercised her mind, based more in fear than logic. Perhaps the guards who held the wingabeasts at the watergate had met death at the hand of Freaer's forces. Attackers might even now wait for them to emerge or worse—block the way out. Perhaps the door above did not open from the inside but allowed only egress. They could find themselves entombed forever. She shivered and, with an effort, pushed such vain imaginations away.

Kai slowed to a stop in front of her. Metal

screeched in the stillness. Just ahead, an opening widened to let in the predawn light, dazzling Shae after so much darkness. The torches extinguished, one by one.

Shae stumbled behind the others into the sweet air. She blinked to clear her vision and caught her breath in wonder. On platforms above them two guardians watched over a small herd of wingabeasts.

The graceful creatures shone like pale ghosts, each saddled and laden for a journey, although not overburdened. She recognized Kai's Flecht, named for the sound an arrow makes in flight. His white coat glowed beside a Gray, just fanning and folding its wings. A pair of Silvers glistened against the deeper tones of a Blue. She made out two other dark shapes against the light stone behind them. One of them shifted, and she caught the gleam of hooves.

A quiet whistle from Guaron set wings aflutter. As one, the wingabeasts pranced to greet their keeper. Craelin beckoned. "Hurry, dawn comes too soon. We need to reach the canyons of *Doreinn Ravein* before dawn."

"Come Shae." Kai guided her up stone steps that ran from the river's edge and between the platforms to the upper gate.

Flecht nickered as they stepped onto the platform. Kai greeted his wingabeast, then turned Shae by the shoulders. "Come and meet *Ruescht*. Elcon has given her over to you. Don't let her small size dismay you. She can fly with speed, thus her name. Did you know the Elder have no word for ruescht? They use only one word, 'wind,' for all winds and must needs add other words to tell them apart."

"What do they call ruescht then?"

"Rushing wind."

She stepped toward the dainty Silver, at once enthralled. When she offered her hand, the wingabeast's moist breath warmed her palm. Delicate ears flicked forward, and liquid eyes gave Shae a look that melted her heart.

Kai helped her mount. "She will carry you well. Give her spoken commands, direct her with the reins, or do both."

Shae's mouth went dry. Although she had ridden Flecht with Kai, handling a wingabeast on her own would demand concentration.

Kai swung onto Flecht's back with a smile of encouragement. "Don't worry. She understands the command *Follow*, and she knows the other wingabeast's names."

"Follow Flecht." Shae instructed Ruescht in a steady voice, although her stomach turned over at the thought of riding a wingabeast on her own. Ruescht obeyed at once, following Flecht to the edge of the platform with a gait so smooth Shae almost believed they did not move. Kai's smile widened, and Shae relaxed her fingers on the reins.

Craelin's Silver flapped into flight. Flecht followed, wings spread and legs folded. Ruescht leaped behind Flecht. The wind of their passing tugged at Shae's plait and stole her breath but, at the heady sensation of flight, Shae's fear melted into exhileration. She might even have laughed aloud but for the severity of the occasion.

Although they flew low, she could see all the way to the Maegran Syld, the misty hills of home. The kaba forest stretched westward from there to the shores of Maer Ibris, and her heart sang as she glimpsed the ocean gleaming through reddish trees. Weild Aenar wended a tortuous route south and east to the mist-shrouded canyonlands of Doreinn Ravein. To the east, a great desert sent purple shadows across blushing sands and thick-trunked purr trees huddled around blue watering holes. But they would not venture there. The desert heated to extremes by day and vicious pyreks, birds of prey she hoped never to encounter, swooped out of the purr trees to fell prey that came to drink by night.

Though she could not see it from this distance, Graelinn Hold sat somewhere within the grassland beyond the desert. They would travel south through the canyonlands and break their journey at Graelinn Hold. By now Katera would have wed Enric of Graelinn and taken her place as his Raelein. How strange to have forgotten so important an event.

Morning dawned as they flew into its mists, and the eastern sky washed over in pale colors—lavenders and pinks and blues. Massive walls of rough stone rose above the haze to close Shae in, and she glimpsed the sky only as a gap between canyon walls. In time the veil of mist thinned to reveal the canyon's pink and blue hues and the white, green, and mauve of tiny windflowers nodding in windswept crevices.

A winged, white creature flew apace beside them. Shae swallowed a scream and laughed to find a *whirlight* accompanying her. Ruescht quivered at first, but seemed undisturbed by the presence of the ungainly bird, which croaked as it dipped and flapped. In time, the whirlight wheeled away, no doubt in search of other sport.

Shae's back ached and her legs cramped. She sighed with relief when Craelin halted on a high ledge beneath a sheltering overhang.

Ruescht landed with delicate grace behind Flecht , and Shae slid to the ground on weak legs. She sat on a sun-warmed rock, content to wait for the cramps in her legs to ease. At least the sun reached them here, and they could rest and eat a rough meal while sheltering from the worst of the wind ravaging the canyons. Kai offered her waybread and cheese, which she took with appetite. She would have relished a hot ginger drink, but found only flat water carried in elkskins and tasting of them.

Bees buzzed in a nearby patch of anemones, combining with the smell of sun-warmed soil to lull her. She sagged against the boulder at her back and let her eyes drift shut.

ᔑᦊ

Craelin nodded to Kai. "Rest while you may."

Dorann squinted a black-ringed eye at his brother, astride his ebony wingabeast, *Roaem*, named for the sound of thunder. "Take care, you."

Eathnor, his light eyes shining in a dark face, sent his brother a swift smile. "That I will." With his head tilted at a rakish angle, Eathnor seemed ready for anything.

Roaem lifted into the air beside Craelin's Silver, *Mystael*, named for the wild wind.

"How soon before they return?" Dorann asked.

Kai refrained from pointing out that they had scarce vanished from sight. "Not long, I think. They'll climb out of the canyon and find a high place so they can see the lay of the land and check our course. We must fly low through Doreinn Ravein for secrecy, but all the twists and turns and branches can prove disorienting."

"What of danger?"

Kai smiled. "They shouldn't find any. Come. You and I can offer our best service by following Craelin's instruction to rest."

Kai smiled when he found Shae sleeping upright with a crust of bread in her hand. He pried it from her fingers, then stretched out on a slab of sun-warmed rock. He didn't intend to sleep but the droning of bees lulled him.

He woke with a start. The droning had grown louder. He raised his head. Perhaps a piece of honeycomb dropped during their repast drew bees. But the ledge, half in shadow, showed itself bare of food. Even Shae's crust of bread had vanished, perhaps snatched by a greedy bird. He peered about but found no bees except those feeding in a patch of anemones.

Guaron stood in the sunlight brushing his Blue, *Raegnen*, named for the summer rain. His hands lingered over the simple task. From the look of the others, he had already provided this same service to Flecht and Ruescht. *Argalent*, Aerlic's Silver, named for the luster of his coat, and *Sharten*, Dorann's Gray, which truly did resemble a deepening shadow, waited their turn. Shae and Dorann slept in the shade cast by the outcropping of rock above the ledge.

The lengthening shadows caught Kai's attention, and he pushed to his feet. How long had he slept?

Guaron nodded at his approach, straw-colored hair lifting.

"Where's Aerlic?" Kai asked.

Guaron gestured with his curry comb toward the outcropping above them.

Kai's gaze traveled the sheer face of rock that Aerlic must have climbed to gain a vantage point. On a different day, Kai might have followed him, but not now. The thought alone made his side ache. He left Guaron to his task and returned to Shae, who stirred at his approach. He smiled. "You look better for having slept."

She sat up and returned his smile. "What did I look like before?"

"Always beautiful, but too pale."

"Have you my comb?"

He gave the mother-of-pearl implement to her and lounged against a boulder, watching as she untangled her unruly locks. "Your beauty glows from inside you, Shae. Never waste it on the undeserving."

The comb halted in its course down the pale copper river of her tresses. Her brows drew together. "I should not have let you think I considered Freaer. I don't know why I worried you in that way. I'm sorry."

"Did he...harm you?"

She stared at him, and then drew breath on a laugh. "Not in the way you mean. He took me to a strange place, Kai—an opening in the curtain wall that led to a passage with hewn stairs beyond. He called it a...a sallyport. The secret passageway from the Allerstaed is like to it, and so nudged my memory, but I didn't connect it fully until now."

Kai angled his head. "Perhaps that is how Freaer and the three shraens escaped after the coronation."

"Do you think Elcon knows of the sallyport?"

"Secret passageways riddle Torindan, created against the need for a stealthy escape, so Elcon might already know of this passage. Perhaps Craelin can tell us."

Bemused, he watched Shae's fingers weave her gleaming hair into a plait.

The rock beneath him vibrated. Understanding dawned in an instant, and a sick feeling soured his stomach. He rolled to his feet and motioned for silence. What a fool he'd been, so focused on Shae he'd failed to notice the scolding of birds or that the droning of bees had strengthened and deepened. It had become something of which no bee was capable, a repetitive thudding that filled the air and shook the ground.

Shae looked to him, her eyes wide.

Dorann woke and jumped to his feet with a look of confusion.

The wingabeasts stirred, but Guaron hissed a command that settled them.

Above the ledge, Aerlic hung from a rope like a spider, pressing himself flat against the overhanging stone, his attention riveted on something in the canyons beyond.

The din swelled and grew, unmistakable now. Kai had heard the sound of marching in his early days when the guardians had defended against garn attacks.

Shae tugged his sleeve. "What is it?"

He spoke near her ear. "An army."

Her face paled. "When will Craelin and Eathnor return?"

"Don't worry about them. Craelin is First Guardian of Rivenn. He can take care of himself. And, if I'm not mistaken, so can Eathnor."

"But what of the wingabeasts?" She stood, and the pitch of her voice rose. "Why don't they panic from so much noise?"

"They are trained to keep Guaron's commands. He won't allow them to panic."

His words at once found their test. A welke screeched from the sky.

17

Canyonlands

Kai heard Shae's indrawn breath. He clamped a hand over her mouth to cut off her scream as he pulled her against him. The wingabeasts stirred, but Guaron's swift signal brought them shuddering into stillness.

With slow movements Dorann eased his hunting knife from his boot.

The light in Shae's eyes told Kai she understood his action. He lowered his hand but kept a protective arm about her.

The welke glided overhead, its talons curled against its leathery underbelly, and Shae pressed into his side.

Kai suppressed his own urge to flee and waited as the bird of prey's ragged shadow fell on them like the curse of death. It was too late to pull his sword. If he moved, the welke's eyesight, like that of any avian raptor, would activate. If the wind shifted, the welke would catch the scent of wingabeasts. Time hung suspended, like Aerlic on his rope. How the rider could fail to spy the archer, dangling against the overhang, Kai did not know.

The leather-clad rider flicked the reins and turned the welke. With a flap of wings, the giant bird of prey descended into the next canyon and passed from view.

Kai let out his breath. The sun, hanging low in the sky, must have blinded the rider.

He caught Shae, trembling like a small bird, into his arms but shifted her away from his injured side.

The marching grew until it thrummed through the very air, then silenced.

Aerlic lowered himself to drop with scant sound onto the ledge before Kai. "Freaer leads armies carrying the banners of Glindenn, Selfred, and Morgorad."

"It's no surprise Freaer would come against Elcon," Kai said, "or that the Ravens of the three traitorous shraens would rally behind him, but they descend on Torindan with such speed it must have been planned in advance. Elcon will not expect a challenge so soon."

Aerlic dusted off his hands. "They break their march for the night in the next canyon. We should speak little and keep our voices down. There is yet danger, for they are sure to keep watch."

The glow of campfires tinged the sky to the north and west, confirming Aerlic's observations. It grew late. Already the westward sky flamed with dying fire and purple shadows lengthened across the canyon walls. The wind had changed direction and now searched the ledge with cold fingers.

"It will take several days' march for the armies to reach Torindan, which must be their destination. That they risk lighting fires shows they don't fear discovery." Aerlic stretched and flexed his fingers, which must hurt after his long vigil on the rope. Kai nodded to him. "Let Dorann tend you." An archer needed his hands.

Two shadows glided to them from across the

canyon in the twilight—Craelin and Eathnor returning.

Craelin dismounted. "I must warn Elcon of Freaer's army, which camps very near. Be careful. I wish I didn't have to leave you."

Kai clasped arms with Craelin, and then stepped back. "Your duty is clear. Elcon will need time to gather the forces of Faeraven. But take Eathnor with you. Returning to Torindan through Doreinn Ravein holds danger, and you could become lost. Dorann should remain with Shae, for he can act as both guide and healer."

Craelin turned to Eathnor, who came to stand near him. "It seems I have need of your services once more. Tell Dorann the way through the canyons, but hurry. Much depends on our speed in reaching Elcon."

❧

Shae twisted her hands together as Craelin and Eathnor, astride their wingabeasts, vanished into the mist. If only she'd summoned the courage, she might have warned Elcon through the shil shael instead. But the soul touch remained a mystery she feared to explore. What if by using it she alerted Freaer to her presence while so near him? A sinking feeling settled over her, and she fought tears. She would not cry, not now. Nor would she lean on Kai. He already carried burdens enough, for in Craelin's absence, he led them.

In the last failing light, they rolled out sleeping mats and packed for an early departure while Guaron settled the wingabeasts. When Dorann gave out rations—a crust of bread and a portion of moist white cheese—Shae took her share from his hand with a smile. He appeared tough, this flame-haired trapper, but his shoulders slumped. He must already miss his brother.

Darkness closed in around rising mists. Shae pulled the hood of Aeleanor's cloak over her head, warmed by its fur lining. Her lips curved at memories of Aeleanor of Whellein, who would ever remain a part of her. Some things went beyond blood. Her thoughts turned toward Katera who, warm and safe with her new husband at Graelinn Hold, would never find herself hiding from welke riders. How would Katera receive them if, filthy and bedraggled, they managed to reach her fireside?

They had no fuel with which to build a fire now, even if wisdom did not deny them such a comfort. Shae huddled with the others in the lea of the overhang and did her best to sleep despite the cold.

Shae trudged across a forsaken landscape by the meager light of a new moon. Water ran in rivulets down her skin and dripped from her garments. Shivers racked her body.

She was utterly alone.

Freaer drew near. She felt his presence. He searched through the night. In time he would find her.

Darkness glided toward her. A welke's screech raised her hackles. She called for Kai without hope, for he was dead.

"Shae?" Kai's hiss woke her. "Are you all right? You cried out."

It was yet night, but close to dawn, just at the time when owls cease calling but graylets have yet to coo. The wind stilled, but cold and damp crept from the ground. The breathing of the others sounded loud.

"Strange dreams haunt me, Kai. And Freaer searches for me—I know he does. It's as if he looks upon me, even now."

"The shil shael makes you vulnerable. I wish that I

could shield you."

"I must find a way to shield myself, if I can. But Kai, we should leave soon. Only danger can come from waiting. I know it."

He made a shushing sound she remembered from her early days. "Calm yourself. You're overwrought. Leaving before first light, in darkness and mist, would put us in a different kind of peril. Rest now and I'll check that all is well."

Shae opened her mouth to protest but shut it again. "I'll trust your guidance." She lay down again, certain she would never sleep.

"Wake, Shae."

She sat upright, blinking in thin light at Kai, who bent over her. She smiled at him and opened her mouth to speak.

Wings flapped.

Aerlic's warning whistle pierced the air.

Kai's head jerked up. "Welkes!"

Shae came fully awake. She struggled to her feet, and Kai caught her against him. He half-carried her toward the dark shapes of the wingabeasts.

Ragged breathing and the thud of feet overtook them. Shae's own feet left the ground as Kai hoisted her onto Ruescht's back.

Aerlic leaped onto Argalent and, in what seemed a single movement, drew his bow. An arrow thwanged upward into the mist, followed by the thump of impact.

A shriek rent the air. A welke dropped to writhe together with its rider on the ledge behind them.

A wingabeast screamed and, under Shae, a great shudder rippled through Ruescht.

"Follow Flecht!" Kai, on Flecht, leaned over to slap

Ruescht's flank.

The small wingabeast shrilled and took to the air.

The flapping of wings drew nearer. But for the mist, Shae would see the welke riders chasing them.

Ruescht twisted and dipped, making Shae's head reel, but she held on. Plunging headlong through the mist while pursued by an unseen foe, she couldn't escape a strange sense of unreality. The wild ride took on the quality of a nightmare. She longed to wake, safe in her bed at Whellein, to face no more trouble than she made for herself. She saw, then, how she must appear to Kai—heedless and willful. Had she really argued with him for warning her away from Freaer?

Fighting the uneasy sensation that she and Ruescht careened through the mist, alone and lost, she willed herself to calm. She could not see, but somehow Ruescht could. Although it made their passage more difficult, the mist saved them from the welke's sharp eyes. She felt better when stray currents tore holes in the shimmering veil to reveal Kai and Flecht just ahead and Dorann behind.

They slipped into a side canyon and spiraled downward alongside roaring waters that fell into darkness. Icy spray combined with mist to penetrate her cloak, making her shiver. She clutched the reins with hands gone numb, for she'd left her doeskin gloves behind beside her bedroll. Would she ever again find warmth, taste a hot meal, or sleep in a soft bed?

She chided herself for such unworthy thoughts. She should be grateful to escape the welkes at all. Many comfortless nights remained before them. How would she survive if she dwelt on her privations?

Ruescht followed Flecht to the canyon floor. She

landed with the others in the midst of *keirken* trees. As the flapping of welke wings grew louder, Ruescht stomped her hooves and snorted. Caught off-guard, Shae jerked the reins, and the small wingabeast reared. Shae clutched the pommel, just managing to keep her seat. As soon as her front hooves hit the ground, Ruescht bolted.

Forced to duck branches, Shae bounced sideways in the saddle. Ruescht turned onto a deer trail, and Shae tried to rein in her wingabeast. Foam flecked from Ruescht's mouth and her sides heaved. Hoofbeats told Shae that the others followed. A small creature scurried into the underbrush, and Ruescht skidded sideways. The small wingabeast broke through the trees—and reared. Obscured behind rainbow clouds of spray that stole Shae's breath, the waterfall plunged beneath them into a churning pool. Ruescht could go no farther.

The others reached them, and Guaron dismounted. He caught Ruescht's reins, although the fight had already gone out of the small wingabeast, who bowed her head as if ashamed. Shae slid from her back and stood on shaking legs.

Kai dismounted and hurried to her. "Are you unharmed?"

Wrapping her arms about herself, she gave a brief nod. She remembered their pursuers, and her eyes widened. "But the welke riders—"

"They're gone, at least for now. The waterfall's roaring must have covered the sounds we made."

Aerlic dismounted and joined them. "We have your wingabeast to thank for one thing, at least." He nodded toward a cave in the canyon wall. "We should be able to shelter there."

Aerlic went first into the cave. At his signal, Shae followed through the gaping hole that smelled of moist stone—and passed into darkness. For in that instant Freaer touched her soul. She shrank from his touch, and it slid away. Crouching in the dark cave with the others, she kept what had happened to herself. Freaer would never give up searching for her.

The flapping of welke wings echoed through the canyons all that day, so they stayed put. Nightfall made little difference to the cave's blackness. Kai gave his bedroll to Shae. He, in turn, would borrow the bedroll of whoever stood watch. She slept at once, untroubled by dreams and lulled by the waterfall's muted roar.

Shae roused to Dorann's whisper. *"Infectious… Wait it out… Poultice…"*

A tiny light highlighted Dorann's and Aerlic's faces. It also showed Kai, who tossed and turned.

Shae sat up. "What's wrong?"

Dorann shifted nearer to her. "His wound has gone septic. Fever wracks his body."

As Kai thrashed and cried out, Aerlic restrained him.

She crawled toward Kai and touched his heated forehead. Water sloshed, and Dorann placed a cloth on Kai's brow. His thrashing eased, but Shae wanted to weep, he looked so gaunt.

When Dorann wrang out another cloth, she reached for it. "Let me."

Dorann relinquished the damp cloth and brought the bowl of water closer. "That's well, then. Aerlic should return to watch, and I need to search for plantains."

"Plantains?"

"They're often found growing in moist places. I should find all I need for a poultice to draw the infection from Kai's wound."

Dorann bent, and soon another flame flared to life. Shae blinked in the light of the lanthorn he lifted. "Rouse Guaron if you can't contain Kai's thrashing, although that's not likely, he's so weak."

When Kai stirred again, she cooled his brow with a fresh cloth. Her touch soothed him, but before long he called Taelerat's name and struck out, as if fighting a foe. She restrained him until the fit passed, and then bathed his brow again.

He fell into a deep sleep, and she cradled him. When his breathing became labored, fear caught her by the throat. Kai couldn't die!

Dorann returned just as welke wings flapped overhead. The wingabeasts stirred in their corner of the cave, but Guaron hissed a command and they quieted. Shae recovered enough wit to extinguish the lanthorn. Moonlight limned Aerlic, who watched at the mouth of the cave, bow in hand. But the beating of wings faded into distance.

They ventured out at midday. Guaron led the wingabeasts to water's edge, where they drank their fill and spread their wings in the sun. Aerlic and Dorann supported Kai between them, to lay him on a flat rock beside the pool so he could stretch out. Shae sat beside him and touched his brow, now clammy. Shivers wracked him even in the warmth of the sun.

"The fever has passed," Dorann said. "Fresh air and sunlight may bring its own cure."

"It's no wonder he became ill in that damp place." Shae wished they could leave the murky cave behind. Brael Shadd glinted above the trees even now, a reminder that her time was limited.

Kai watched her with dull eyes. "Leave me and go."

She started, for he spoke as if he followed her thoughts. She shook her head. "I'll not."

"Shae, you have no choice." He sighed. "I meant only to bring you help, but I've slowed you down."

"You do help me, Kai. Now, speak no more." She did not say what filled her mind to distraction. They would leave tomorrow, whatever Kai's condition. But she couldn't imagine going on without him.

"What's this?" He caught a tear that fell to her cheek.

Birdsong trilling from a thicket of wild roses pierced her heart. She pulled away but felt his gaze follow her to the pool's edge, where she bathed her feet. She did not turn her head to meet it.

∞∞

Kai watched Shae wade into the bright waters, her hair, slipping from its plait, ablaze in the sunlight. Just now he'd seen something in her face—a recognition that frightened her. Fair enough. He shared her reticence. But he could not contain the rush of joy that lit him at the sight of her.

Right or wrong, he couldn't bring himself to let Shae go on into peril without him. At least a measure of strength returned with another night's rest and Dorann's continued efforts to cure his wound of its poisons. But Kai stayed astride Flecht more by his wingabeast's skill than his own power. Letting Aerlic take the lead, he fell back to ride beside Shae.

With dawn reddening the shoulders of the eastern

canyons, they lifted out of the narrow side canyon and followed Weild Aenor as it coursed from Maegrad Ceid toward the great southern marshes of Weithein Faen.

The mist thinned and shredded. Although the sun beat down, Kai shivered. He knew they journeyed in gentle stages for his sake. Tomorrow he would tell them not to spare him, but today he made no protest.

కారింగ్

Dorann waded into the shallows with a net. Aerlic joined him, and the two soon strode past Shae with a catch of rainbow-colored *percken*. She hummed while combing her hair in the fleeting warmth of the sun. Shielded in the canyon's lea, she could forget for a time the terrible journey before her.

She flicked a glance to Kai, who slept in the shade of nearby keirkens, his wound newly dressed with a poultice of *aergenwood*. In the meadow behind her, the wingabeasts cropped green grass.

A sun-warmed boulder countered the brisk wind that blew in from the water, and Shae settled against it with a sigh. The tang of keirken leaves, damp rock, and humus filled her senses. How small she felt as she gazed into the sky where high clouds scuttled. Her eyelids grew heavy. The rushing of the weild grew louder, and then faded….

Spiders touched her face.

Shae bolted upright and fought the arms that restrained her.

Kai laughed. "It was but the petals of early flowers. I thought only to wake you."

She pushed him away with a glare. *"Don't ever do*

that again!"

Her anger only made him laugh harder.

She turned her back to him but could not prevent the smile that tugged at her mouth. She scooped up a a handful of the petals he'd dropped and threw them into the air. Some of them landed in his hair. She laughed now, too.

Kai shook the petals from his hair, and then combed through hers. At the sensation of his fingers against her scalp, the laughter died in her throat. His expression bemused, he caressed her cheek with a feather-light touch. At the light in his eyes, her breath hitched and her pulse beat a wild rhythm.

The corners of Kai's mouth quirked upward. "May I have the pleasure of escorting so beautiful a raena to the hall?"

She smiled at his nonsense but stood with him and rested her arm in the crook of his elbow. Together they walked toward the camp. The aroma of roasting fish mingled with the sweetness of burning Draetenn wood from the cooking fire to tantalize her. As the fire crackled and smoke curled to meet the gathering mists, she ate her fill.

She curled up in her bedroll as the fire fell to embers and daylight softened into moonlight. The wind that seemed always to blow through the canyons came now as a cooling breeze, and the river sang a lullaby.

Morning arrived, too soon.

Once mounted, Shae leaned down to scratch behind Ruescht's ear. "I wish we didn't have to leave this place." She straightened and took a last look at the green grasses swaying in the morning breeze.

Kai reined in his wingabeast and tossed Shae a

smile. "Perhaps, in happier times, we can return."

Aerlic flashed his rogue's smile. "We'll have to come back so Dorann and I can fish again."

Dorann laughed. "Still hoping to catch a bigger fish than mine?"

Guaron smiled at the two, but then sobered. "I wonder how Elcon fares."

Shae frowned. Faeraven's loyal shraens might join the guardians and the town's inhabitants to defend Torindan in the present crisis, but real deliverance would come only if she succeeded in releasing the DawnKing at Gilead Riann. "We must go on." She eyed Kai. He looked stronger today, but pale.

He answered her unspoken question. "I will endure. We should reach Krei Doreinn this day and, if we hurry, the ruins of Braeth in the Smallwood of Syllid Mueric on the morrow. Don't spare me."

She stroked Ruescht's mane to hide her sudden fear. "Must we sleep at Krei Doreinn?" The ancient battleground where three canyons met carried its share of specter tales. She had also heard stories of enchantment within the Smallwood of Syllid Mueric.

Kai shrugged. "Syllid Mueric is too large to cross in a day, even on the back of wingabeasts, but we can make it with only one stop if we camp in the meadow at Krei Doreinn."

All eyes turned to him.

"We will sleep in the Place of Blood?" Dorann asked in shocked tones.

Kai shrugged. "I mislike *Paiad Burein* myself, but at least its trees offer cover."

Aerlic stilled Argalent's prancing. "Trees cannot hide us from some things,"

Kai gave a tight nod. "True enough, but do you

prefer spending two nights rather than one in Syllid Mueric?"

Shae said no more but she would rather not sleep in Paiad Burein. She preferred meeting flesh and blood adversaries over those who dwelt in shadow. But the weight of Maeven's dagger, Leisht, in its sheath beneath her sleeve comforted her as she sent Ruescht into flight behind Argalent.

At least the welke riders searched for them no more, although she thought she understood their disappearance. Why should Freaer search for her when Prophecy itself told him her destination, and he could find her anyway with the shil shael? She must learn to guard herself, even in sleep. She suspected Freaer would try to overcome Torindan first, then her. They must press on with speed, even if it meant sleeping among the restless dead.

18

Battleground

"I don't like this place."

Kai gave Aerlic no response. What could he say? He didn't like it either. Prickles of awareness ran over his skin as the ruckus of battle pressed, just at the edge of hearing. It seemed the very air could not forget what had happened here.

Flecht shifted beneath him, and Kai put a soothing hand on his wingabeast's neck as he gazed across the turbulent waters of Krei Doreinn. A tributary of Weild Rivenn fed into Weild Aenor here, the two rivers colliding in a mad frenzy amid much roaring. Whirlpools and eddies worked through the waters. Submerged stones thumped. Floating logs spun, crashed, and went under only to surface further south. Beyond Krei Doreinn, the torrent spilled out of the canyons and fanned into estuaries where it merged with the salt waters of Maer Syldra to spread into the great marshland of Weithein Faen.

In the fall, the rivers would recede, but now in the early spring they swelled to overflow their banks, running right to the edge of deep fern-encrusted canyons. No traveler could reach this place in safety by land or water when the rivers ran high. Even the air currents played tricks where the three canyons met, and it required resourcefulness to guide the wingabeasts through them.

Kai led the way into a lush grassy area starred with gentians in shades of white and blue. Overgrown keirkens blended with draetenns along the edges of the meadow. They could hide here, if need be, beneath a leafy canopy and amid tangled undergrowth rife with sweetberries and wild roses.

A sheer graystone face bruised with purple shadows reared overhead. Mute, the canyon could not testify of the blood spilled in the peaceful meadow called Paiad Burein, the Place of Blood. Here Timraen, in times past, met garns invading from Triboan, their stronghold in the south. Here Seighardt, brother of Maeven, fell and died beside his father, Raemwold of Braeth.

Kai dismounted. None of his companions followed his action. He turned away from the look of dismay on their faces. *Would they now lose heart?* Even Flecht seemed to reproach him, tossing his head and refusing to sample the long grass.

All the wingabeasts needed a quieting hand. Fluttering wings, flaring nostrils, and stomping feet expressed their feelings with eloquence.

Guaron gave them a command, and with obvious reluctance, the wingabeasts stilled.

"Surely we should take the wingabeasts' reaction as warning against this eldritch place." Aerlic's voice sounded small, as if swallowed by emptiness.

Kai had seen Aerlic face down a welke, climb an impassable cliff, and leap from a bluff into the waters of Weild Aenor. He saw no trace of that Aerlic in this fidgeting youth who cast uneasy glances about him and jumped at shadows. "Eldritch or no, we must stop here," he snapped "A trail leads from this meadow through a narrow fissure in the graystone and into a canyon. *Syllid Mueric* and the ruins of Braeth wait beyond. Even if we would continue, the light already fades. Only a fool would venture across such terrain without full light. And let's not forget the benefit of stopping here."

"It's hard to think of this stop as a benefit." Shae slid to the ground and patted Ruescht's neck. "But let us make the best of things."

Kai swept a hand to indicate the meadow's edge, where spreading keirkens brooded. "We'll camp there but make no fire. Even if welke riders no longer pursue, other threats lurk within these canyons."

Shae eyed him. "Other threats?"

"Flames from even a small campfire would light the sky, and garns hunt within these canyons. There's also the chance that some of the Feiann, the smallfolk of Syllid Mueric, might slip through Braegmet Dorien out of curiosity and find us." He did not mention that, beyond these creatures of flesh and blood, he knew not what walked Krei Doreinn by night.

Aerlic turned a white face toward him. "I have heard tales…."

"Let's not dwell on tales, but keep ourselves in vigilance."

Silence followed this pronouncement.

Guaron dismounted and, with a nod to Kai, gathered the wingabeast reins.

Aerlic followed. "I may not like where you bring me, but I will let you lead."

Kai inclined his head. "Well said. You and Guaron may keep Whyst beside you in your watches this night."

Guaron at last quieted the wingabeasts and even persuaded them to crop the green grass. He remained with them, for they lifted their heads and stirred whenever he tried to leave them.

Dorann uprooted several gentians, broke off the blue and white trumpet-shaped flowers, and presented them to Shae with a shy glance. She thanked him with a smile that wrenched Kai's heart, and he turned away. An unseen dagger cut him deeper than the wound in his flesh. If only he could steel himself against such foolishness!

Dorann cut the gentian root into tiny pieces atop a flat stone, adding the fragments to a small vial of liquid he pulled from his pack. After it steeped, he removed Kai's bandage and washed his wound, then applied the tingling mixture as a poultice beneath a fresh bandage.

Light leeched from the sky, draining color from the landscape about them. Roiling clouds moved to seal the dome of sky overhead. The wind, ever-present in the canyons, stiffened. The *wingabeasts* grew more restless with the advent of night. Guaron made an effort to settle them and laid his bedroll beneath a spreading keirken nearby.

Kai huddled with the others who shivered at the edge of Paiad Burein, jumping at small sounds as night devoured the last remnants of day.

Shae pressed into his side. *"What's that?"*

He caught her in his embrace, and she twined her arms about his neck. His senses filled with the scent and feel of holding her. But he hesitated only briefly before setting her from him. "The wind moans, Shae. It's only the wind." He hoped he spoke truth.

The hair on the back of his neck lifted, for it

seemed the wind cried and the river muttered. Indeed, the tumble and thump of stones in the riverbeds became the "river voices" of legend. And even a stouthearted warrior might imagine moans in the wind. He was near enough to Shae to feel her tremble. He knew a desire to protect her—so fierce his voice strangled when he spoke. "We're better served to try and sleep."

"We'll need a light to find our way, but a small one." Dorann rummaged in his bag. He bent and stone scraped. When he stood again, a small light wavered in a cup between his hands.

Shae made a pleased sound. "I sometimes forget you are a tracker."

Dorann laughed. "I learned this trick at my *mahm's* knee. Sometimes it comes in handy when I hunt. I should have thought to light it before, but darkness came on quick. "

Shae pulled away from Kai to look at the small light Dorann held. "How do you make it?"

"You use oil and a bit of cloth tied around a button placed in a bowl or cup."

"Your grandmother - does she live with you at Torindan?"

"Nay, *Mahm's* passed on, but not before she taught me the old ways."

"Did she teach you of herbs, then?"

"Aye."

The small light moved away toward camp and their voices faded. Kai followed their retreating figures, fighting his discomfort at sight of Dorann bending toward Shae in solicitude.

He slept badly, but lay as still as possible so as not to disturb the others. He caught the glow of Dorann's cup flame lighting the blackness and was glad he had relented enough to allow the night watch a small light. He wished, yet again, that he and Dorann could lighten the load for the other two, but they must first recover their strength. With that thought, Kai forced his mind to quiet and gave himself to sleep.

Aerlic's cry dragged him awake.

❧❦

A shriek wrenched Shae from the mists of sleep to the thud of running feet. With heart pounding, she opened her eyes to blackness.

Someone wept nearby.

The hair on Shae's arms stood on end. She struggled to rise but her bedroll tangled in her legs. Fighting free, she lurched to her feet. "Kai?"

He did not respond.

"Dorann?"

No response. Where could they be? Surely, if her companions were near, they would answer.

A blue light flared in the meadow. The dark figures gathered around it must belong to her companions.

Grass wet the bottom of her tunics as she stumbled toward them. Not certain she wished to reach the source of the weeping, she was even more loath to remain alone in the darkness.

The sobbing grew louder as she approached the light, which resolved into Whyst, its blade aflame in the hand of Aerlic, who stood with bent head.

A dry wind lifted her hair as something brushed past her. The weeping sounded close to her ear, and then ceased. She strained, but could see nothing in the darkness. Chills ran up her spine. *What had just touched her?*

She stumbled forward to reach the others, grouped around Aerlic. His head jerked up at her approach, his eyes wild until recognition dawned. *Who—or what had he thought approached?*

"Are you well?" She joined her question to those of her companions.

"I saw myself—" Aerlic heaved a breath. "I saw myself in death. A specter came to me—my own."

"How can that be?" Her light voice carried above the deeper masculine tones. "You live."

"I wish I knew." He shook his head. "Perhaps I saw only what may be rather than what will be, but the specter had my face."

"I hope you will not take harm from a deceiving spirit." Dorann's voice came out of the darkness.

"I should not have made you stop here," Kai said. "I should not have asked it."

"I'll take the watch now." Guaron pried Whyst's hilt from Aerlic's fingers. "You've done enough."

"I-I dropped the button light," Aerlic said.

"Never mind; it's here." Dorann's voice came at the edge of the circle of light.

Kai put an arm around Aerlic's shoulders. "Look, Whyst's light dims. Whatever spirit troubled the night leaves us now. Come and take your rest."

"Who can rest after such a sight? And in such a place?" Aerlic's voice sounded raw.

"At least try." Kai offered Shae his arm and led her back toward camp. "Are you well?"

She shrugged, not sure how to answer. "Something happened to me as I crossed the meadow. I heard weeping, and then felt —" A shiver crawled up her spine. "Something uncanny touched me."

He pulled her into his arms. "I should not have left you alone in camp, even for so short a time. I will not do so again."

She placed a hand on his chest. "My welfare is just one of the many burdens you carry now."

He put a hand over hers. "I don't think of you as a burden, Shae."

She stepped out of his embrace. "I'll be glad when we are quit of this place. It brings confusion to us."

"Well spoken. Tomorrow we enter *Braegmet Doreinn* — the Chasm of Confusion."

19

Ruins of Braeth

Rock walls rose about Shae, shutting her in with the musty odor of dampness. The narrowness of the twisting canyon precluded flying, and tumbled stones underfoot made riding treacherous. They might have flown above the canyons altogether but for the risk of being sighted by welke riders following Freaer's armies in the east. She led Ruescht with care through narrow places so close as to appear impassable, pausing often as Aerlic, Dorann, and Kai cleared the way of fallen rocks. When they emerged at midday, relief at passing from the canyon's bright heat into the green shadow of Syllid Mueric left her a little light-headed.

At sight of rolling hills clothed in draetenn and keirken trees and threaded by gleaming brooks, Shae halted in wonder. But as she recalled whispers she'd heard about soft places in time that swallowed wayfarers, a shiver ran up her spine. Indeed, some who had gone into Syllid Mueric never returned. Others spent but a day in the Smallwood and spoke of having passed there a lifetime.

They paused to rest in a meadow beside a rill that wended through rocks skirted with ferns. She bent and caught handfuls of cold water in her cupped hands.

When its sweet effervescence burst against her tongue, she sighed with pleasure. In truth, she longed to submerge herself in water—to bathe. What would it be like to wash away the dust and grime of travel in water such as this? She repressed a sudden longing to find out.

She shouldn't linger.

But daydreams tantalized her. She could see herself beside the sparkling rill, counting the petals of early flowers at her leisure. The urgency of their quest evaporated like summer mist.

No! She had to stop letting her mind wander.

Syllid Mueric had seemed in her imaginings a place of murk and gloom, rife with the growls and howlings of darksome creatures. But this place of burgeoning life permeated with the smell of wild mint was both wonderful and terrible in its beauty.

The ground rose at a gentle grade as birds sang from sweetberry brambles and water splashed and played. Although storm clouds threatened, the rain held. She knew a deep yearning to linger beneath the dainty *weilo* trees dripping moss into the water and to lose herself in the dappled shade that spread over green hills and valleys.

She lagged behind and, lured by the ruby glow of sweetberries, turned into a meadow at the edge of the path. Dorann, just behind her, stopped too. She slid down from Ruescht's back and crammed her mouth until her cheeks bulged and juice ran down her chin to stain her clothing.

When she thought of Dorann again, she found him sleeping in the shade of a draetenn. Nearby, Ruescht and Sharten cropped the meadow grass. Shae called to Dorann, but he didn't wake until she prodded his shoulder.

When he opened glazed eyes, a silly expression of glee covered his face. "I could idle away my days gazing upon your beauty."

Her face heated. "You speak amiss."

He stood and took her hand. "Let's stay here, Shae."

She pulled away. What was wrong with him? What had happened to them both? The pull to remain in Syllid Mueric gripped her almost beyond endurance, but caution whispered within her.

She pulled on Dorann's arm. "Come on! We need to catch up to the others."

"*Shae!*" Relief flooded her at the sound of Kai's voice. He waited with the others at the edge of the meadow.

She ran toward Ruescht, but paused when Dorann lagged. "Come *on!*"

Dorann followed with slow steps.

A chill ran over her. "Are you well?"

"Syllid Mueric holds him captive, and I see its spell on your face." Kai called. "You must resist, Shae, and let Dorann come away on his own."

"With a little help from me, of course." Aerlic leaped from Argalent and hoisted Dorann onto Sharten.

Kai waited for Aerlic to return to his wingabeast. "Let us quit this place as soon as we may."

They set off with Kai in the lead and Aerlic stationed as rear guard behind Dorann, not pausing until they reached a channel of Wield Rivenn that trended from the northeast. She found it hard to reconcile this lazy waterway fed by rivulets and cascades with the torrent she'd seen at Kei Doreinn.

She devoured what she could of the dry, cold rations enlivened by a few delicate mushrooms Dorann gathered. Afterwards, she lay on her stomach on a flat boulder and drank from a stream that cascaded over rounded stones.

The back of her neck prickled.

She sat up. Where had the others gone? A feeling of comfort edged with a curious discomfort assailed her. She didn't trust it.

Light streamed from the sky and fell across a figure outlined against the backdrop of trees—a delicate maiden garbed in glistening cloth—so beautiful she seemed to shine.

Shae had no doubt she beheld one of the Feiann. She picked her way towards the bank where the maiden waited, steadying herself when one of the rocks underfoot tipped. When she looked up, the maiden had vanished.

"Why do you and your companions wander here?" The words seemed to come from the syllid itself.

Shae's pulse pounded in her ears, but she gathered the courage to answer. "We journey to visit my sister at Graelinn Hold in the grasslands to the east, although I seem to have lost my companions. Can you not show yourself?"

"Be still!" The trees shook their leaves. *"You approach uninvited. Why should I grant your request?"*

Shae swallowed against a dry throat. "I'm sorry. I meant no harm. Stay hidden if you wish. I only thought to talk face-to-face. I am Shae of Whellein. Will you tell me your name?"

The woman emerged from the shadows to stand before Shae. *"I have more than one name, as do you, but you may call me Sharian. Come and meet my fellows, Shae of*

Whellein. Remain and dwell with us."

A wave of calm washed over Shae, but she could not allow herself to succumb. She had lost something—or someone—although she couldn't think who or what. And she had something to do—something important. She fought to remember.

Sharian's breath hissed, but a smile lit her small face. *"Why do you resist? Do not concern yourself with the others."*

Shae remembered now. Her companions—she had to find them. They needed to leave Syllid Mueric. She pulled Leisht from her sleeve, surprised to find that no light swirled about the blade. She didn't understand, for surely enchantment dwelt in this place. She raised her head to find Sharian gone. "Do you hold my companions?" Shae called after her. "I demand you release them!"

Laughter carried from the shadows. *"How little you know, Shae. Put away your dagger."*

Shae came back to herself. She still lay on the flat rock with one hand in the cascade, the other clutching Leisht.

"Are you well?" Dorann's voice drifted to her.

She sat up and blinked in the glare from the surface of the weild.

Dorann offered her his hand. Behind him, Aerlic waited for his turn to drink. On the bank where the golden maiden had stood, Kai and Guaron watched over the wingabeasts.

Shae took Dorann's hand and stood. She touched her forehead. "I'm...I'm not sure, but pray don't trouble yourself." She ignored Dorann's look of concern and hastened toward Ruescht. How could she explain what had just happened when she didn't understand herself? The sooner they left this place, the better.

The wingabeasts surged into the air and followed the weild upstream. Vista after vista enticed her eye, and the draetenns whispered her name. Streams shone with beguiling light and mists danced across green glades that called her to return. The very air sparkled.

A deep ache wrenched her soul. She had to go back!

When they landed on the banks of the river to rest and water the wingabeasts, she slipped into the forested shadows—alone. She would remain with the Feiann after all. She could not recall why it had seemed so important to leave them.

"Shae!" Kai's call broke her thoughts. She hesitated. Kai called again.

The trees before her shook as if gripped by a giant hand. She backed away and into a pair of arms. A scream ripped from her throat.

She struggled, but the arms tightened. "Shae, you're safe!"

What had she almost done? She turned into Kai's embrace and sheltered there until her trembling eased. As they lifted into the air once more, weariness from the long journey and her foreshortened night's rest caught up with her. Not wishing to fall from Ruescht's back into the waters below, she fought to remain alert.

When the ruins of Braeth stood out in the distance, she rejoiced. The day's journey would end there, although the prospect of a night at the forbidding stone monolith tempered her joy. She knew from her early studies that Timraen had burned the timber roofs to hasten the stronghold's fall to ruin, thus preventing its use by garns against the Kindren. It would not be habitable.

They reached Braeth Hold in the late afternoon. The square shell still stood, weathered but intact, defiant in the face of time. Shae could picture its heyday, with the stronghold's bulk a daunting contrast to the Smallwoods its walls kept at bay. She could almost see lights in the windows and flags fluttering atop the great towers. But the windows now gaped, sightless, and the towers thrust toward the sky, unadorned.

They landed below the silent gatehouse on a circular patch of green grass ringed by a cobblestone path. Dark walls encompassed the outer bailey, but the sun beat down here, in the open. They walked by unspoken consent across the cobblestones and into the shade of a lone strongwood.

Shae's heart thudded and she gave a small cry as a pair of large birds burst from the tree and weaved toward the hold in ungainly flight. Their feathers shone in the sun, pure and white, and their long tail feathers streamed behind them. They could only be—

"*Kaerocs.*" Aerlic lowered his bow, arrow slotted but unfired. "We had them in the woodlands of Glendenn Raven." He smiled and shook his head. "I can remember trying to catch them in my early days. They roost in tall trees."

She followed Aerlics' gaze a long way up to where gnarled branches twisted, and pendulous leaves rustled in stray breezes. The tree stood near an external ramp which ran upward to a gatehouse.

Kai gathered them with a gesture. "Aerlic and Dorann, remain with Shae. Guaron and I will search the inner ward. I doubt we'll find anything, but we don't want any surprises this night."

She shivered, for his words reminded her of the dry wind and the thing that had brushed past her at Paiad Burein. She misliked these places of ruined lives and broken dreams. Did Braeth possess its share of restless dead? "Must we sleep here?"

Kai turned back to her. "Either here or in Syllid Mueric. Braeth Hold can hide us and provide a measure of security."

She tossed her head. "You might be right about the advantages of sheltering here, but I fear these walls will prove more trap than refuge."

Kai gave her a tolerant smile. "I'll make sure it's safe before taking you inside." He turned away but glanced over his shoulder at her.

She shook her head even as a smile tugged at her lips. Retreating into the shade, she turned her back on the devastation created by hatred and let herself rest, for a time, in the strongwood's shadow.

ॐ৽ঌ

"Careful there!"

As if to illustrate Kai's warning, the trapdoor he and Guaron skirted slid from its rotting hinges and fell with a faint thunk into the dark pit below. They navigated around fragments of wood and rusted metal—all that remained of the twin portcullises which had once secured the gatehouse. A strongwood log with a pointed metal tip lay amidst the splintered wood, telling the story of what had happened here.

A short flight of graystone steps that bowed toward the middle brought them into the inner bailey, where stone paths edged a rectangular cushion of grass sunken over what Kai knew was a mass grave. These paths, built with care and trodden by many, now kept silence.

No hooves or voices rang out from the stable's stalls, which stood open to the sky. They turned away.

Even now, the smell of burning lingered in the great hall, and marks of fire blackened the high graystone walls, darkest at the tops. They stepped around piles of unburned cinders at the base of scorched remnants of fallen roof timbers that canted across the central wall and into a scene of utter devastation.

Partially burned boards would serve no more diners, for they lay akilter, having fallen from collapsed trestles. Candle branches, spoons, and knives littered the chamber where they had fallen long ago. It seemed Braeth's remoteness kept it from pilferage, or none had the heart to touch its remnants. Neither would Kai disturb them, for he could not fight the feeling that they visited a tomb.

They left the great hall as they found it and move on to the keep. The main archway opened to a square entrance chamber. Beneath their feet stretched a marble floor, scoured dull by wind and weather. The hangings at the tall, slender windows rotted to dust. Bleached benches, one of them overturned, flanked a cracked marble fireplace still bearing a raised relief of rampant gryphons. Guaron shook his head at the sight.

A sound came then—faint, like the scrabbling of bird claws.

Kai drew Whyst and signaled Guaron to follow him through the largest archway and up a short flight of marble steps.

Screeching and a flurry of batting wings greeted their entrance into the presence chamber—more kaerocs. Great nests, constructed in part from stuffing plucked from the tattered blue and gilt throne cushions which had somehow escaped the fire, sat atop the walls.

They backed out of the chamber and glanced into other rooms before taking a flight of marble stairs to what remained of the upper stories. Most of the floor timbers were gone. The two front corner towers had fared little better, although the marble steps remained intact.

With a feeling of relief, Kai stepped from the keep into the inner ward. "There's only the chapel and kitchens left to check. Are you ready to return to the wingabeasts?"

Guaron made no reply. Behind Kai, sunbeams broke through the clouds and slanted across wind-ruffled grasses above sunken graves.

Guaron was nowhere in sight.

Shae slumped against the strongwood's trunk. Better to sleep here in the open air than trapped somewhere within the inner ward. Perhaps, after exploring the ruin, Kai would agree. She lapsed into a state between waking and sleeping but could not relax into true slumber in such an uneasy place. She woke to shifting shadows and, as a movement claimed her attention, sat up. In the circular sward nearest the outer curten wall, one of the wingabeasts, Aerlic's Argalent, fanned silver wings.

How much time had passed? And how long before Kai returned?

The strongwood's leaves rushed above her. The

wind had picked up while she slept. Muted light streamed from the sky and the heat no longer held an edge. Kai should have returned by now.

Aerlic bent over his bow, oiling its string with deft fingers. He spoke in quiet tones to Dorann, who sat beside him. Shae caught the timbre, if not the words, of their conversation, and a fist of fear clenched in her stomach. "What's wrong?"

She encountered two pairs of eyes, one green and the other amber. Aerlic gave her a nod. "Kai and Guaron should have returned by now. Perhaps they have forgotten us amid the wonders within." She could see he did not believe his words either. "We've decided Dorann will search for them while I remain here with you."

She cast a glance at the hold looming above them, which, in the changing light, seemed to gather mysteries. "I'll come with you."

She waited for their protests to die before speaking. "It's no safer in the outer bailey, and Kai would not want us to separate." She did not say what they must also know. Kai would want them to continue without him. "We're better together."

Aerlic inclined his head. "Well spoken, but I'm sure Kai would not want us to take you into peril for his sake."

"With Syllid Mueric just outside the walls, peril can as easily creep upon us here, especially at night. I've heard tales."

Aerlic's expression told her he'd heard them too. He lifted his bow in a decisive movement. "We'll stay together then. May Lof Yuel protect us."

In a movement both graceful and rapid, Dorann drew a knife from his boot. As the light glinted off the blade balanced in his hand, he looked altogether dangerous.

She drew Leisht from her sleeve and gasped. The swirlstones in its hilt glowed with many colors. *"Magics."*

Dorann's amber eyes gleamed. "Don't concern yourself, gentle maid. Aerlic's a trained fighter, and I know a thing or two."

"I well believe that." She accepted the lighted lanthorn Aerlic extended to her and did not say that the best of fighters might find themselves helpless against magics.

Aerlic commanded the wingabeasts to wait, then took the lead. With reluctance, Shae turned from Ruescht, who watched her longingly, and climbed the long ramp behind Aerlic. The lanthorn swinging from her hand lent her courage. Darkness would soon fall. Dorann followed.

They entered the ruined gatehouse and emerged into the inner ward. Shae shuddered at sight of the uneven bailey sward, remembering something about hurried burials after the fall of Braeth. She followed Dorann along the path. Her every nerve tingled. Her fingers ached, and she eased her grip on Leisht. The dagger would do no good if wielded by a cramped hand. The stables were empty, so they paced toward the great hall.

Something warned her, although she couldn't say what. Perhaps she sensed it when Aerlic's posture changed to slackness, or in the fact that Dorann drew even with her and no longer acted as rear guard. Why did they drop their vigilance just as chills crept up her spine? Something was very wrong.

Aerlic bypassed the great hall and slogged toward

the keep.

The knife slipped from Dorann's hand to fall against the stone path with a ring that penetrated, but he trudged onward as if nothing had happened, his footsteps heavy.

"Wait!" Shae retrieved the weapon. "What are you doing?" She caught up with him, but he didn't acknowledge her or take his knife.

She stepped in front of him. "Are you well?"

His face blank and his eyes unfocused, he stepped around her without pause.

She gasped and turned to Aerlic, only to find the same vacant look on his face. Realization hit her like a fist in the stomach. Dorann and Aerlic had fallen victim to an enchantment.

The crimson of sunset lay across the tops of the walls and stained the silent buildings as Aerlic and Dorann walked on. Shae had never felt so alone. As her companions entered the keep, she trailed behind, but hesitated in the entrance archway.

Dusk fell with breathtaking suddenness. Standing alone at nightfall beside a mass grave of slaughtered innocents held almost as much terror as following her companions. She hurried after them with fear behind and before her.

The entrance chamber tilted, then righted. The lanthorn slipped from her grasp and crashed on the marble floor, extinguishing. Dorann's knife fell, too. She had no time to search for it. Already the others left her behind. She forced air into her lungs. She would not faint now. She had to know what had happened to Kai. *It could not be too late.* There must be a way to save them all.

"Lof Yuel, help me!"

Flashes of light swirled from the dagger in her hand to encompass her like a multi-hued shield. *Leisht cuts enchantment.* The truth made her giddy. Here lay deliverance, if she could but find its path.

Dorann and Aerlic moved as one across the dim entrance chamber and through an archway to climb a marble stair that circled upward into a corner tower.

Something calls them.

She left the broken lanthorn where it fell and followed. Light sparkled from Leisht's hilt and swirled before her. She heard the others ahead, their feet trudging onward and upward. She followed, but resisted the urge to call out to try and wake them from this nightmare. Reason would not work against magics. Perhaps if she bathed them in the light from her dagger also, it would free them.

They halted at what must be the top of the stair. She waited on the steps below. The marble stair remained largely intact, but the tower's floor timbers had burned or fallen. She looked down and wished she hadn't. The dimness did not conceal the long drop to the floor below.

A shriek rent the air. Dark creatures skittered over the tower, claws at the ready, long antennae twitching. *Waevens.*

How could this be? Such monsters lived only in stories kept for the dark of night. Those tales told of spider-like waevens weaving webs of enchantment to entrap their prey. They injected a numbing poison which stole the souls of their victims but left their bodies intact. The waevens would return at leisure to suck a victim's lifeblood.

The picture of such a fate for Kai and her other companions girded Shae. When Dorann and Aerlic stepped onto a wide stone landing leading to the battlements at the top of the tower, she followed. She was not prepared for the sight that Leisht's many-hued light revealed.

Kai stood on the landing near three waevens perched atop merlons on the battlement wall. One of the many-legged creatures dangled Guaron in the embrace of its jointed legs, purring as its fangs punctured the skin of his forearm to drink his blood. Another reached its antennae toward Kai. Why didn't he pull away?

Shae did not pause. As she stepped around Dorann and Aerlic and advanced toward the waevens, Leisht's light swirled more brightly around her. Panic babbled in her mind, but she silenced it. She must prevail.

The third waeven's foul breath rolled over her. Its atennae clutched her almost caressingly around the waist.

White-hot light flared from Leisht.

The creature's shriek filled her mind…. *No!* She gripped the dagger in both hands and waited.

The waeven emitted a low hum. She sensed it meant to strike.

Reacting without thought, she thrust her dagger into the creature's soft middle.

Its scream rent the air. The atennae gripping her slackened. She pulled Leisht free with a sob. Black liquid spurted from a gash in its chest and dripped from the blade. With no more than a faint hiss, the waeven fell from the wall to thud in the bailey below.

The remaining two waevens shrilled. They released their captives and emitted a low hum as they skittered sideways across the merlons—toward Shae.

Kai stood quiet. Guaron slid to the stone walkway, still as death.

With terrifying swiftness, both waevens lunged toward her. Before Shae could react, multi-colored light lashed at them.

They hesitated.

Shae's hands trembled and the light wavered. Her knees shook, her head reeled, and she could barely think. She steadied herself and renewed her focus on the light. She rasped in a breath and offered herself into the embrace of the nearest waeven.

As her blade struck its neck, its hum turned into a shriek. Black blood ran down her arm to stain her sleeve. The waeven fell away.

She barely had time to gather her strength before the last waeven's antennae caught her ankle.

A wave of nausea washed over her. Somehow this touch unsettled her more than the others she had endured. Sucking in her breath, she just stopped herself from swatting at the antenna. She would lose such a battle. She must defeat the whole creature.

"Shae!"

Kai's cry broke her concentration. Her gaze locked on the terrible humming monster. Its antenna jerked her off her feet, and she slid toward its cricking claws. A scream tore from her and she swung her dagger toward the fell creature's soft underbelly. The second antenna lashed around her wrist.

Leisht clattered away, its light fading.

20

Waevens

Kai watched himself, as if from a distance, go into the evil embrace of the *waeven* that held him captive. But as the waeven hissed and died, Kai's confusion loosened along with the creature's grasp of him. He no longer held Whyst. Casting back, he recalled the flash as the great sword fell from his hand. He'd turned from its light, already befuddled, and entered a darkness of the soul. He'd drifted, lost in shadows, until his captor hissed and died. Shae's scream had dispelled the last of his confusion.

Leisht glowed with fading light against the marble floor near the head of the stair. He dove for the dagger, rolled, and regained his feet.

The waeven released Shae, and she backed away. The foul creature faced Kai, humming. He could not let himself look at Shae, although concern for her tore at him. There would be time enough to make sure of her safety if he defeated—*when* he defeated—the waeven. He must not fail.

To press the advantage of surprise, he struck at once. Leisht's light flared forth and the waeven shrieked. Multi-colored light swirled backward to touch Kai. Heat reached deep within him but brought no pain, and the last lingering traces of enchantment burned away.

Guaron moaned, but Kai did not turn his head. Fully restored, he stood square against the waeven. But the creature recoiled from the light and hummed louder. Kai followed, advancing step by step.

The creature turned on him with fangs bared, despite its obvious aversion to the light. Its thrumming vibrated through the air, threatening to overwhelm Kai's senses.

Teeth gritted, he drove the dagger into the monster's black heart. Keeping hold of Leisht's hilt, he stepped away as the waeven fell. Black blood ran from the blade as the creature roiled and died. The light from Leisht faded and extinguished. Darkness pressed him.

Kai sucked air into his lungs. Shae's embrace replaced the waeven's, and he pulled her closer. Her arms clasped his neck, and for a time he knew only the sensation of holding her.

She gasped on a sob. "I thought I'd lost you—again."

"I thought the same of you." He couldn't stop touching her—her face, her hair, her arms. He wished he could see her, but they stood in darkness. "Are you unharmed?"

"I am well. The waeven had no time to...to hurt me before you saved me."

"*I* saved *you*? Had you not slain the waeven that held me I would still remain under its spell."

"We saved one another then, by Lof Yuel's grace."

"Kai? Shae?" Aerlic's voice carried to them.

"We're well." Kai put Shae from him with reluctance but didn't release her hand.

"Wait," Dorann said. Amid the sound of scuffling,

a small light flared. "I thought my cup light might come in handy."

"It's well you brought it, my friend." Aerlic's voice held the sound of a smile.

Kai sighed. "It will do, but I must find Whyst. Have you and Dorann recovered enough to carry Guaron? He's suffered harm."

Dorann held the cup light aloft. Guaron lay where he'd fallen.

Kai touched Guaron's sleeve and found sticky moisture. By the odor, it could only be blood. He felt for a pulse. "Guaron, do you live? Answer if you can."

Guaron moaned and muttered. "Who will care for the wingabeasts now?"

"You must recover." Kai's tone brooked no compromise. "The wingabeasts need their keeper."

∂∾≪

"Where are they?" Shae halted at the top of the long ramp. The outer bailey's waving grasses and cobblestone paths lay in moonlit relief below — devoid of life. Beyond the outer wall, blued light mantled the rounded shapes of Syllid Mueric's canopy. Nothing stirred. "The wingabeasts are gone!"

A hand touched her shoulder. "Steady, Shae." Kai murmured near her ear. "The wingabeasts are trained to endure. Something warned them away, perhaps the waeven's cries. They will have scattered and hidden from danger." When they reached the base of the ramp, he gave a soft whistle, but the wingabeasts did not respond.

They waited out the night beneath the spreading strongwood. Guaron, tended by Dorann and Kai, rested in fits and starts. Aerlic kept watch. Only Shae had opportunity to sleep, but found she could not. Of its own volition, her mind replayed her encounter with the waevens over and over. She tossed and turned, then dropped into light slumber, only to wake at a moan from Guaron.

Pale shadows spiraled out of the lightening sky—the wingabeasts returning. Eased by their presence, she settled to sleep at last, but at Kai's call awoke with an aching head.

She kept to herself and tried not to snap at anyone, but Kai sought her out.

"Come, Shae. Let us leave this place of death. We'll ride the wingabeasts as far as Graelinn Hold, where we can rest before going on by foot."

"We'll leave the wingabeasts at Graelinn Hold?"

Kai nodded. "It's unthinkable to take them where welkes hunt. We could only fly at night and, even if we found cover enough to hide by day and the wingabeasts didn't panic and flee, the welkes would soon scent them and find us all."

"Will they not scent us?"

"Their senses are not so tuned to us as to the wingabeasts, but no, we have no assurance they won't find us, too."

Shae said nothing. Neither welkes nor the thought of crossing the lost plain of Laesh Ebain terrified her as much as the shifting, nameless thing of her nightmares—the evil she had discovered in Freaer. In the watches of the night, it still reached for her.

She squinted into the uncertain light of a gray morn. Brael Shadd glowed above swirling mists on the horizon. The DayStar had sunk lower since she'd last marked its position. "What of Guaron? Can he travel?"

"He must. We cannot linger, especially since we'll travel by land now to avoid detection by the welkes as they fly out by day from Maeg Waer. For my part, I'm glad to leave this tomb."

Shae gazed at Braeth Hold, stark against the cheerless sky. She had thought to learn more of her ancestors here, but this ruined husk could not summon them. She turned away. Time carried on, and nothing could stay its hand.

Kai placed an arm around her shoulders, and she turned to meet his silvered gaze. Something unspoken bound her to him, but also drove her from his side. She pulled away to prepare for their journey.

They gathered astride the wingabeasts, all save Guaron, who rode before Dorann on Sharten. Guaron's Blue, Raegnen, needed no instruction, but followed close behind his stricken rider. Traveling with grim faces a half-erased track through rampant underbrush, they spoke little and rested less. Draetenns laced slender branches overhead, providing cover to all who passed into their green, scented shadow.

Once or twice, Shae caught a flash of movement out of the corner of her eye, but spied only leaves twisting in a breeze. Small *flitlings* followed as she passed, jumping from tree to tree. No other wildlife appeared but she could not escape the feeling of being watched.

She sighed in relief when, about midday, they paused to rest at the edge of a stream. She bent to sip the cool water from her cupped palm and wished for something to eat. But they'd taken their last waybread with greenings Dorann had gathered the day before.

"We dare not delay!" Kai urged them, and indeed Guaron looked more drawn than ever in the patch of sunlight where they had laid him. For his sake, they could not reach Graelinn Hold soon enough.

Once mounted again, they passed without pause a motionless stag which watched them with liquid eyes from a wildflower dell. Shae's heart ached at the creature's grace. They hurried on. Not even the prospect of fresh venison could tempt them to linger.

The soft light of late afternoon slanted across the grassland by the time they slipped from Syllid Mueric onto the plain that edged Weithein Faen's marshes to the south and stretched eastward to the first of three stone rises. Northward, beyond vast reaches of desert, the broken peak of Maeg Streihcan stood sentinel. At sight of Graelinn Hold rising from the plain in the distance, Shae could have wept.

Flecht lifted into flight. Ruescht followed. Kai chose the safest course, for here on the plain, they had nowhere to hide. Better to reach the hold in swiftness without secrecy. The warm wind blowing off the desert flowed over her, and she abandoned herself to the fleeting joy of this last flight on Ruescht.

Part Three: Gateway

21

Graelinn Hold

Although she greeted them with impeccable manners, Katera's tone held a certain distance. Shae couldn't blame her. She and Kai had, after all, missed her wedding, however important the reason. And now they stood unannounced in Graelinn Hold's circular entrance chamber in the company of a tough-looking tracker and a flame-haired archer. Guaron already rested under the care of Graelinn's praectal.

Her bright eyes and pink cheeks proclaimed that marriage suited Katera. Arrayed in linens and silks in deep colors, perfumed and manicured, she had never appeared so beautiful—a rose in full bloom. By contrast, Shae felt herself a bedraggled waif. She could guess Katera would never cross rough lands with a makeshift band of protectors, go without food, or suffer an attack by waevens.

Katera looked her over in much the same manner as Aeleanor, causing heat to creep up Shae's neck. "I hope your journey has not fatigued you unduly. I'm sorry my lord husband Enric cannot receive you. He joins forces with other loyal shraens against Freaer's siege of Torindan."

Kai tilted his head. "Tell me—how came he to learn of the siege?"

"A group of messengers escaped from Torindan ahead of the first attack. They didn't spare themselves or their wingabeasts as they relayed news of the siege to the loyal shraens of Faeraven."

"That's well then." Kai sent Shae a look, and she read his thought. Craelin and Eathnor must have warned Elcon in time.

"I confess I'm surprised—but delighted—to see you both...and to meet your companions." Katera eyed Dorann's rough garb. "You will all stay for a visit, I hope."

Kai cleared his throat. "We can stay but a few days."

Katera lifted a delicate brow but said nothing.

"I'm sorry I missed your wedding." Shae hated the halting way the words left her mouth. "I-it could not be helped."

"Mother made your excuses."

They dined well at Katera's table as minstrels entertained them, and they would sleep that night in soft beds. Katera promised to supply their needs, but when she pressed him about their journey, Kai declined to explain, saying only that they traveled "east" at Elcon's request.

Katera's eyes widened. "There's nothing out there save barren lands, ruins, and welkes."

Kai's words cut across Katera's shudder. "And yet our course runs that way. Beyond that we cannot speak."

"May Lof Yuel keep you." Katera hesitated and seemed about to question her brother more, but then turned to Shae instead. "I've always envied you the adventures you find!"

Shae stared at her, understanding for the first time how appealing her own life must appear to someone who faced the boredom of long, golden days, melting one into another. She retrieved her voice in time to speak. "We must all accept our portion in this life."

☙❧

"His soul will ever travel in and out of darkness." Praectal Caedric's words fell like a knell. "I'm sorry."

Kai gazed at Guaron's sleeping figure. The wingabeast keeper looked as pale as death. "I don't understand."

Caedric motioned for Kai to follow him into the small outer chamber that held just enough room for hearth, bench, and table. Caedric turned to Kai. "What do you know of waeven bites?"

Kai shrugged. "Nothing."

"I see." Caedric's brow creased, and he rubbed his chin.

Time stretched until Kai thought it would snap. *But I do not!* At Caedric's look of surprise, he cautioned himself at least to silence, if not to patience. "I'm sorry."

Caedric nodded. "I wish we knew more about waeven bites, but they happen so seldom. I can tell you such bites do not heal in the same manner as those of other beasts. While the physical injury repairs itself in time, a waeven bite inflicts damage to the soul—damage that never heals."

Kai stilled. "Not ever?"

Caedric shook his head. "We know of no cure.

Other victims describe sliding from our world at times into a place of terror."

"Can we do nothing for him?"

Caedric sighed and shook his head. "We can watch to make sure he does not harm himself unawares. Beyond that, quiet surroundings will bring him a measure of peace."

"He shall have them."

Kai took his leave and searched for Shae. He found her seated on a velvet-cushioned strongwood bench before a crackling fire in her outer chamber. She looked demure in a long surcoat of white wool sashed with braided cloth of scarlet and her burnished hair plaited and falling over one shoulder. Katera had provided her with elegant chambers, resplendent with gilts and velvets in rich tones and deep, plush rugs against a backdrop of gleaming kaba wood.

He clasped her hands and returned her smile, wishing it could drive from his thoughts the place of terror Guaron visited. "I hate to tell you this, but we should leave tonight."

Her smile faded, but she inclined her head. "You are right. We have need for haste. And yet, I wish we could stay longer and that we did not travel in a windstorm. Listen to its wailing!" She paused, and he listened with her to the rattle of the shutters behind the embroidered window hangings. The squall that howled outside had sprung from the east before morning and raged all day without abating.

He cocked an eyebrow. "I fear we will have difficulty submitting ourselves to the rigors of our journey after the comfort and plenty at Graelinn."

"If it were only that!" Shae wrapped her arms about herself. "I find a different sort of comfort here.

The feeling of being hunted has already left me, and I don't relish its return."

"How I wish we were quit of this business!" At Kai's raised voice, the servant Katera had provided Shae, a gray-haired matron, lifted her head to peer at him from the bench nearest the window. Kai steadied himself, and the matron returned to her embroidery.

"As do I," Shae rejoined with quiet intensity, "and yet, we must fulfill our duty." She smiled then. "I resented it—not owning a temperament or a fate like Katera's—but now I see the truth. We each answer a different calling." Her voice softened. "What of Guaron?"

"He will live, by Lof Yuel's grace." *Guaron had done enough, suffered enough, lost enough.* "He will remain here with the wingabeasts until our return." The words dropped into silence—*until our return.*

"May it be thus," Shae agreed, but she did not meet his eyes. "What troubles you?"

"How well you know me, Shae."

Her smile tugged at his heart. "You're not hard to read when you scowl like that. Tell me."

"I have just learned of waeven bites and what they bring."

"Guaron recovers, you said."

He let out his breath. "His wound will heal." He shook his head. "I blame myself! Had I not been certain safety lay within the walls of Braeth, he would not now suffer."

"You couldn't know what would happen."

"True enough, but I might have guessed that a place with such a history would draw fell creatures to itself. I should have known, too, that a night spent in Paiad Burein could only bode ill. Aerlic has not been the same since our sojourn there." He struck the palm of one hand with the fist of the other, causing Shae's servant to stir again. "I continue to make decisions that put us in peril, and now Guaron will pay for my poor judgment for the rest of his life."

"What do you mean?"

"A body can heal from a waeven's bite, but its poison continues to fester within the soul." He swallowed the lump in his throat and turned away. "Guaron dwells halfway in shadow."

Her hand on his arm recalled him. "You cannot blame yourself for what the waeven did. Reproaching yourself changes nothing and only clouds your thinking."

He pressed his lips together and slid a hand over hers. He should not add his own burdens to the ones she already carried. "You are right." He gave her the words of comfort she needed. "Will you come with me to the stables?"

She nodded. "I should say goodbye to Ruescht."

He took up a lanthorn from the mantle and lit it while Shae donned her cloak and whispered to her servant, who nodded and resumed her needlework. He stilled a twinge of conscience. Shae came alone with him without reproach only because others thought him her brother. He shouldn't do anything that might compromise her, but he couldn't deny himself the balm of her company.

Cold drafts accompanied them down darkened corridors and made the flames within the lanthorn he carried flutter and dance. Their shadows loomed tall before them, but in the next current shifted to fall behind.

Shae turned at the side door. "I wish we did not

leave the wingabeasts."

When he reached around her for the latch, the movement brought them close. "Indeed, it's a blow to lose their speed, and already Brael Shadd stands above the horizon at dawn."

The wind tore the door from his hands and a gust swept them, making the lanthorn flame sputter. He turned to shelter Shae, his own back to the brunt of the wind, and lowered his head to speak near her ear. He meant to urge her to stay close as they crossed the bailey, but she lifted her face as he lowered his, and words fled. Wonderingly, he touched her soft lips with his own. As she sighed, he groaned and slanted his lips across hers in a firmer demand. She leaned into him, and he gathered her closer to kiss her in earnest. As she yielded, the fury of the wind could not match the storm that raged between them.

The banging of the door brought Kai to his senses. Shae pulled away with a small cry. He lifted the lanthorn. Shae looked at him out of wounded eyes, the back of her hand pressed against her mouth.

He raked a hand through his hair and took a steadying breath. "I'm sorry. I didn't mean that to happen."

She nodded, and he caught the glint of tears.

"Shae, listen—"

She shook her head with violence. *"Please!* Let's not speak of this."

He went still while he fought the urge to comfort her in his arms. Instead, he inclined his head, accepting her choice. "Lean into the wind and stay close to me." He wrenched open the door and raised his voice above the storm. "Don't worry. I'll not let harm come to you."

☙❧

Shae stepped into the howling wind and averted her face to breathe. Overhead, clouds raced across the moon. Kai secured the door, and then pulled her with him across the outer bailey. As they ran, the lanthorn guttered and flamed, making shadows leap.

They fetched against the stable, and Kai flung open its door. They hurried into a chamber filled with tack and saddles, and the wind cut away. They stood apart and silent, where before they might have clung together, laughing and warming themselves. Instead, Shae huddled in her cloak and tasted the salt of foolish tears. When she lifted her head, she met Kai's darkened gaze. Despite herself, she could not look away.

Kai broke the contact and, raising the lanthorn, led her through a second door to a long corridor with stalls on either side. She wrinkled her nose at the sharp scents of hay and straw mingled with the musky smell of droppings.

Most of the wingabeasts had settled for the night. Ruescht's silver coat glinted midway down the stalls. At their approach, the little mare put her head up and whickered a greeting. Shae put a hand to the soft muzzle, and warmth blew against her palm. Tangling her fingers in Ruescht's silken mane, Shae leaned her forehead against the wingabeast's warm neck. "Goodbye, my friend."

Shae stepped back and scrubbed at the tears on her cheeks. Kai's hand touched her arm, but she could not find her way back to him—not now. Perhaps she never would. Ruescht's luminous eyes glistened and her nostrils flared. She tossed her head. It seemed almost that the little wingabeast understood her distress.

They returned to the hold in silence. At her outer chamber door, Kai pressed the lanthorn into her hands with a curt nod. "Make your preparations. We will leave after we take food together in the hall." He walked away without a backward glance

Shae hesitated at the latch, and then lifted the lanthorn and turned away from the door.

The Allerstaed waited in silence. She moved into the graystone and marble chamber, her footsteps eager. The lanthorn cast a warm glow before her. She set it down and knelt on the step below the altar, but tears, rather than prayers, found their release. She wept for the losses she'd suffered since Kai first summoned her from Whellein. She wept for Maeven and Eufemia, but also for the shift that would come to her relationship with Aeleanor and those she had called family. She wept most of all for the change between herself and Kai. But prayer at last replaced tears.

"I knew I would find you here." Katera's voice and footsteps echoed. "The others wait for you before breaking bread."

She raised her head. She'd forgotten place and time.

"Do you sleep?" Katera asked on a rising note.

Shae pushed the hair out of her eyes. For the first time, she saw through the criticism that cloaked what Katera really asked. She spoke in a rush of sympathy. "Sometimes, when I pray, I find a deep place within that only Lof Yuel can touch."

Katera sat beside her. "Can anyone find such a place? Can I?"

"I think it must be so."

"I will pray Lof Yuel will keep you safe, then."

Shae met Katera's embrace, marveling that she felt more a sister to her now than she had when she'd thought them joined by blood.

Kai, Aerlic, and Dorann looked up when she entered the great hall. A late feast, prepared to send them on their way, had already begun. Despite little appetite, Shae ate all she could, for she would need strength to endure this night's trials. After a brief greeting, Kai remained aloof. Heat rose to her face, and she looked away.

They made their goodbyes and ventured into the night. If anything, the wind blew more strongly now. She settled her elkskin satchel over her shoulders. Although it weighted her steps, it carried a share of food and water and the few personal oddments she'd allowed herself. The others bore the bulk of their supplies.

The moon, full and round and tinged with amber, rode high to light their way. Seeding grasses tossed before them like waves in the sea and then fell in their wake. The wind, when it shifted to blow with gentleness from the south, brought the clean scent of salt and the ripe odor of wet reeds from the great marsh of Weithein Fain.

They came upon remnants of the ancient road that had once connected Braeth to Pilaer. The hard-packed surface gleamed pale blue in the darkness, except where ruts cut by long-ago wagon wheels unfurled like twin ribbons. They made slow progress, for the road crumbled here and there into the marsh it skirted. Soft places made by burrowing rodents caved in beneath their feet. Undergrowth encroached and clung or stung as they passed. A rock rolled underfoot, and Shae gasped. Kai half-turned toward her. As she stumbled, she put out a hand to him but snatched it back. He hesitated, his expression unreadable in the darkness, and then turned away. He seemed as bent on ignoring her as she was on ignoring him. Where he might once have offered his hand to help her, he left her to struggle alone. Tears sprang to her eyes, and she wished she could let herself call him back.

She trudged on, caught in a dream without end. A growing ache of homesickness troubled her, although she no longer truly belonged to Whellein. She pined for the carefree innocence of her early days, a time when nothing had changed between herself and Kai. Her ankle throbbed, but she bit her lip and did not complain. An odd pain of another sort twisted inside her, for she'd wanted to take Kai's arm, to lean into his warmth and revisit their bond of shared love. She couldn't remember a time she had not borrowed his strength. It had always been so between them, but she couldn't let it be so now. She blinked away foolish tears and pulled her cloak tighter about her, stumbling on through the night.

It took her more effort to cover the same ground as the others. When she stepped into a soft place in the road and pitched to the ground, she cried out and grabbed her ankle. She'd wrenched it again. Kai called for a rest, and after that, they proceeded at a more moderate pace.

Dorann found his way to her side, his solicitude a balm. He held back the encroaching underbrush and steadied her whenever she faltered. The road stretched before them, curving only to avoid places where solid ground gave way to mud flats and salt bogs. Night birds whistled. Water lapped and mud sucked.

A pheasant erupted from a stand of marsh grass. Shae jumped, and her heart thudded. Aerlic already notched an arrow to his bow, but the bird winged across the faen to become a shadow limned by moonlight. The arrow glinted as Aerlic returned it to its quiver. Just as well. They had no means of retrieving a fallen bird from the faen nor could they abandon caution and raise the scent of blood or light a cooking fire.

Brael Shadd glowed near the westward horizon, and the thinning darkness suggested morning. Kai called a halt near a grove of stunted draetenns where the road left the grasslands to plunge into Weithein Faen.

Shae sheltered beneath the trees, too weary to follow as the others climbed a small knoll for a view of the road as it cut through the faen.

From the small distance between them she heard Dorann's whistle and Aerlic's soft cry. "May Lof Yuel protect us."

22

Road to Pilaer

Shae stopped to rub a stitch in her side. She'd run too fast to reach her companions. Without waiting to catch her breath, she turned her head to see what held the others enthralled—and gasped.

Golden morning light fell across the faen and in the near distance touched broken marble pillars flanking a wide stair. Above the stair a marble and granite fortress overlooked the rooftops of an abandoned town. With its base still in darkness, the stronghold seemed to float above the drowned lands.

Pilaer!

Her knees went weak. The ancient fortress hung suspended in the mists of time, at least in her imagination. The reality might prove as mysterious. Indeed, rumor gave it that this ruin was haunted not only by what had been but by what could never be.

The road to Pilaer narrowed and meandered across the faen. Waters lapped over it and quick mud consumed its edges. Here and there, the road sank below the surface to vanish altogether.

Shae pressed a hand to her throat. "How can anyone cross those sunken places?"

Kai spoke beside her. "We have no choice."

She hesitated. "Can't we go around the faen?"

He shook his head. "That would take far more time than we can allow."

"I'd rather you gave a different answer."

"Then you join your wish to mine. Come, Shae, and rest. We'll pass through the ruins after all welkes return eastward—before twilight, with any luck. I don't wish to visit such a place in full night."

She shivered, needing no explanation of Kai's words.

The small stand of draetenns draped curling leaves about them and bore the brunt of the ever-present wind. Shae settled herself on the hard ground and pulled her cloak close. She shifted to remove a small stone that gouged her side, but then had to settle all over again to avoid the draetenn root bumping her feet. For speed of travel they'd not burdened themselves with luxuries such as bedding. But how would she ever rest?

Kai's touch summoned her from the depths of a deep, dreamless sleep. If fearsome birds of prey had hunted overhead while she slept, she never knew. At her smile, a pained expression crossed Kai's face. She stared at him, baffled, until memory returned and her smile faltered.

The comforting words she longed to speak stuck in her throat. Her hand itched to touch him, but already he turned away. She would not call him back.

Emerging from the trees as a flock of ungainly brown waterfowl winged across gray skies glowing with subdued light, she stood transfixed. She'd never seen such birds before.

She came upon Kai beside a raft of draetenn branches lashed together, so small it could carry only two at a time. He spoke without turning his head. "We built it while you slept."

She frowned. "Will it ferry us in safety across the breaches in the road?"

He shrugged. "We'll soon answer that question."

They set out almost at once, keeping to the road as it plunged into the faen and leveled at waterline. Kai led while Dorann and Aerlic shouldered the raft behind Shae.

She took care to keep her feet out of the ruts, which in places shone with water. Dragonflies darted through the tall reeds that closed her in. She flipped back the edges of her cloak and basked in the residual heat shimmering above the road's surface.

She avoided the edges of the road where water bugs skittered in green water. Birdsong flowed all about her, the warblers hidden in reeds and grasses. The beauty of the marsh sang its own melody in her heart. She could almost forget their destination, at least until reeds gave way to burbling mud flats affording views of Pilaer.

When they reached the first of three breaches in the road, Aerlic tested the raft, paddling across the pool that had swallowed the road. Although it tilted and sank at one edge, the raft remained afloat. They drew it back by means of ropes, and Dorann went next. He hesitated, but then offered his hand to her.

Shae looked to Kai before she thought but met a shuttered expression. With effort, she returned the smile Dorann gave her and grasped his hand.

He balanced her as she stepped onto the raft. It gave beneath her, and she sank to her knees, fearful that if she stood it would tip. Aerlic pulled the rope, his muscles straining. The water slid by, murky and silent. When they reached the other side of the breach,

Dorann offered his assistance once more. She gave him her smile and felt her cheeks go warm at the light in his amber eyes. After Kai took his turn, Aerlic and Dorann hoisted the raft between them again.

Low tide exposed great boulders laid below the surface to support the roadbed. But they'd barely begun to cross the flats when the tide rushed in to cover the sucking mud. Shae eyed the rising water and did not stray from the middle of the road. A long-legged bird landed near the road's edge and waded through the water, pausing here and there to dip its beak and capture delicacies.

Storm clouds gathered, sending shadows over the faen. Wind pierced the folds of Shae's cloak. Aerlic and Kai took the lead, while Dorann hung back beside her. Did someone call her name? She looked behind her, for her skin crawled, but only windswept marsh and rippling grasslands met her eye.

They halted at the second breach while her companions settled the raft in the water.

Kai straightened. "It's shallower here. If we catch the waves right we should make it, but we'll have to go one at a time."

Dorann helped Shae sit in the center of the raft when her turn came, and then pushed off as a wave washed toward the raft. Aerlic and Kai strained together against the rope. The raft broke free of the bottom with a scrape and bucked beneath Shae. She put a hand against her mouth to keep from crying out.

The raft glided through the water toward Kai. When she landed, she steadied herself against him. "I'm glad we don't have that to do again."

"But we have one more crossing," he reminded her.

Already Dorann pulled the other rope and the raft bumped and scraped across the breach toward him. Kai relieved Aerlic at the rope, and hauled the raft toward them. Dorann jumped from it to safety.

The sun stood low in the sky, so they pressed onward in earnest. The road meandered now, curving to follow solid ground between the reeds. Shae paused only to shift the satchel on her shoulders and to take the weight off the foot she'd wrenched when she fell. Although she tried to ignore the pain that grew in her ankle, she began to limp.

Dorann matched his pace to hers but Kai and Aerlic waited at intervals. With a sense of despair, she acknowledged the truth. She could not go on much longer. And yet she must. How cruel that, by some trick of light, Pilaer seemed to recede as they advanced.

They reached the third breech just before the road lifted onto the peninsula before Pilaer Hold. A stand of reeds stood thick before them where the road should lie.

Dorann and Aerlic set the raft aside, and Aerlic lay on his stomach to search in the muck below the reeds. "I can feel the tops of boulders!"

Shae looked away while the others removed their boots and leather leggings. After a splash, Aerlic's voice came to them through the reeds. "Follow with care."

Another splash sounded.

"You'll want to kilt your skirts and take off your boots or the mud may suck them from your feet." Kai's voice startled her. She hadn't expected him to wait for her.

She hesitated. "Turn your back then."

"I have already done so."

She tucked her skirts and cloak up at her waist and removed her boots and leggings. Putting her leggings inside them, she tied her boots outside her elkskin satchel.

"I'll go first," Kai told her. "Hold to me."

A splash came, and Shae turned to follow Kai into the water. She stepped what seemed a long way down and gritted her teeth as water rose cold about her thigh. Cold mud oozed between her toes and over her foot, and she groaned. When her foot met the top of a sunken boulder, she balanced and lowered her other foot, but wobbled and flailed. With another hasty step she slid against Kai.

He reached backward to steady her with a hand at her waist. "Are you well?"

"I am."

He took another step forward.

Water swirled around her legs and weighted the bottom of her kilted skirt as she followed, but her foot slid in the slippery mud. She lurched sideways.

Kai spun around to catch her, and they swayed together. "I'll not let you fall." He spoke above the racing of her heart, which was not entirely due to physical danger.

She pulled away although she longed more than anything just then to remain in his arms.

He touched her cheek. "Stay close."

She followed his lead, step by slow step. Something glanced against her leg and creased the water as it darted away, but she swallowed her scream. She feared a living creature in the water far less than what might await them within the ruins. By the time they found the place where the road lifted from the faen, her muscles ached and cold numbed her feet.

She rinsed the slime from her legs in the shallows along the shore, wrung out her skirt, and put her leggings and boots back on. After wrapping herself in her cloak, she joined the others on the bank with slow steps, all at once in no hurry to approach Pilaer, which watched them and kept its silence. Before they came upon it, they would need to pass the ruined town itself.

She lay beside Kai, and the rich smell of mud rose about her. Birdsong trilled from a stand of marsh grass, riding above the faint lap of water against shore. Her heart ached at its piercing beauty. If only they could remain in such peace!

She ran her tongue over her salt-crusted lips and closed eyes that stung. As clouds chased the declining sun, the play of light and shadow moved over her lids, and an image of Elcon formed. How did he fare? Had the loyal shraens reached him in time, or had Torindan fallen? A place of prayer beckoned from within—an Allerstaed not contained in a building—and she pushed past exhaustion to reach it. Her surroundings fell away and she saw in her mind's eye a white light flaring forth to find Elcon.

She did not mean to use the shil shael. She did not even know at first that she did, for it came with the ease of breath. It brought her to Elcon, surrounded by blue light. A sharp pang slashed through her with fever heat. A floodgate of emotions broke open— despair, sorrow, fear—emotions that belonged not to her but to Elcon. She could almost see him pacing. Thoughts touched by his soul drifted into her mind. Torindan lay under siege with no hint of rescue by Faeraven's loyal shraens. And he'd heard nothing yet of *her*. She curled her fingernails into her palm in quick sympathy, seized by a longing to comfort him. He paused and looked toward her across time and space. Somehow she'd touched him.

A flash of red flashed across her mind. A whiplash of power engulfed Elcon, dimming his light.

Shae tried to hold on, but the connection to Elcon faded.

The assault turned against her now, stinging her mind with raw pain. Strength drained from her like blood from a wound. She clutched her head and moaned. Did Kai speak her name? She opened her eyes to darkness. Her mouth went dry. Had the evil touch blinded her? Panic screamed in her mind.

Lof Yuel!

The inner place where the white light flamed pulled her to its heart, and she recognized the Allerstaed within. There she hid.

The evil grasp slid away.

Kai's face swam into view. "What happened? Are you well?"

"Well enough, except that Freaer found me."

He moaned and gathered her into his arms.

She wanted to protest, to pull away and keep him at a safe distance. Instead, she closed her eyes and let herself pretend nothing hurtful had happened between them. She kept silent about what she had learned from Elcon. No good would come of burdening the others with misery.

When she stood her knees wobbled, but the curtain of night waited to drop. They must not linger.

Dorann hoisted his backpack but paused before settling it on his back. "Are you ill?"

She gave him a gentle smile. "Not in a way you can cure."

His forehead creased. "You speak of magics."

Her smile faltered. "I've felt its breath. Still, I speak more of mysteries than magics."

Kai's arm encircled her, and Shae leaned against him. They set their feet again upon the road that ran straight to Pilaer Hold, but made halting progress until she regained enough strength to walk alone.

They continued their journey, but she slowed them, weakened by the encounter. The sun stood low on the western horizon as they passed empty dwellings that watched them out of blank windows. She kept her eyes forward, just stopping herself from searching those windows for movement. Anything that stirred here did not warrant discovery.

Something dark rushed at her from the side.

She jerked and turned her head. *Nothing.* Her heart beat like a wild thing. Swallowing, she fought to still her shaking.

"Magics." Dorann muttered.

A pall hung over this place, as if the mists shrouded a corpse, not a town. Sorrow lay so heavy over all that it would not have surprised her if the walls ran with tears and the stones themselves wept.

Whispers of despair invaded her mind. *We will never reach Maeg Waer. The bones of all who have tried and failed litter Laesh Ebain.*

Shae shook off the thoughts, but they returned and multiplied. *You deceive yourself. It is all for naught. Elcon will go mad under Freaer's assault. Torindan cannot stand. Elderland will fall.*

Hopelessness looked back at her from the faces of the others. She roused herself to encourage them. "We will succeed." They did not respond, and she couldn't blame them. Her words did not even bolster her own spirits.

As they approached the shell of Pilaer Hold, shivers walked up her spine, for the setting sun stained the walls and pillars blood red. Ramps and steps led to the gatehouse, where splintered strongwood doors hung agape in mute testimony to the violence that had once visited here. What sort of lives had her ancestors lived in this place before the devastation that ended many of them? Pilaer's remoteness had not saved it from ruin. In the end, unity, rather than isolation, had saved the Kindren.

❧

Kai looked away from the ruined hold towering overhead.

A rushing shadow vanished as it reached him.

He pulled Whyst from its sheath. The blade shone with blue light. Balancing the great sword in his hand, he turned to face another shadow. He needed no confirmation of what he already sensed. Wraiths hung heavy in this place of defeat.

An image of Guaron, lying pale and still as death, rose in his mind's eye. *You lost Guaron. You will lose the others.*

A hand touched his arm and he turned to meet Shae's gaze. An image of her in a bride's veil, her eyes closed in death, rose between them. He swallowed against tears. *You'll never wed. She will die. You will die.*

He reeled backwards but turned to confront the next shadow. Another loomed on its heels, only to disappear when it reached him. Strange. That one reminded him—it had looked like Eberhardt. He stabbed at another shadow. Whyst seemed only to slice air, but a faint hiss told him he'd hit his mark.

More shadows ran at him.

"I'll send you to your rest!" His shout dropped into dead air. It seemed the more wraiths he dispatched, the more came. They ringed him in, now running at him, now dancing out of reach. A terrible howl filled his ears and made him quake. He flailed, no longer able to move or see beyond the shadows.

Aerlic and Dorann shouted from somewhere near.

Shae's voice cut to him with quiet intensity. *"Stop fighting!* You're only making matters worse."

Kai glimpsed Shae. She stood with Leisht in hand, bathed in its light. He recognized the truth of her words, but he didn't know how to disengage. If he stopped fighting, the shadows would overrun him. He fended off yet another attack and fell back with a cry. The wraith had worn the face of his missing brother Daeven. *What madness ruled this place?*

"Kai, Dorann—Shae's right." Aerlic's voice lifted above the howling. "The wraiths gain strength when we fight them and fade when we stop."

Another shadow scuttled toward Kai, and he saw his own face as a boy. With tears running down his face, he swung Whyst. The shadow hissed and vanished, but two sprang forth to take its place. He understood then. The more he fought, the quicker they multiplied. They could not hurt his body—only his mind. They were shadows of nothing—wraiths of his regrets.

He held Whyst before him and, even as shadows rushed him, forced his mind to quiet. They fell upon him, shrieking. Panic screamed in his mind. *You'll suffocate!* He tightened his jaw and held his ground. If this didn't end soon, he would lose his sanity.

Their shrieks faded, and the wraiths fell away to

fizzle and vanish.

He lowered his sword arm, which trembled so badly he almost dropped Whyst. "They seem to have fled."

Dorann passed the back of his hand across his sweat-glazed brow. "Well then."

Aerlic blew out a shaky breath. "I guess that's that."

Kai restrained the urge to follow every flicker of shadow and instead turned to Shae. "Why didn't the wraiths approach you?"

"They did, but they couldn't hold me. Leisht must have cut their enchantment."

Kai gave a weak smile. "I'm thankful. Let's forsake this eldritch place before more trouble finds us. I know of a tracker's shelter that once stood a little distance away on the mainland. If it still stands, we can avail ourselves of its protection."

Pilaer and its ruined town shrank behind them as light leached from the sky. At the narrow neck of the peninsula, they crossed through the shattered remnants of a gatehouse. An ancient path led from there into the Darkwood of *Syllid Braechnen.* They entered the syllid as full dark fell. Kai kept Shae close to him, for he did not relish the fall of night in such a place. Nightbirds called from the thick brush and gnarlwoods bent twisted branches low to grasp at them as they passed.

Kai caught himself looking backward more than once. He couldn't shake the feeling that something stalked them through the night.

23

In The Darkwood

Hissing whispers woke Shae. She propped on one elbow and looked for Kai in the silvered moonlight but found only an impression in the sweetgrass where he'd lain. She sat up. Where were the others? She pushed to her feet and circled the clearing with dagger drawn, peering into the shadows. The swirlstones in Leisht's handle flared with light.

Laughter slashed through the air.

"Who's there?"

More laughter.

Shae steadied herself. Did the Feiann also dwell in Syllid Braechnen? Anger lent her strength. *"Answer me! Show yourself."*

Silence.

She calmed herself enough to speak with civility. "We are no threat to you. We only want rest and safe passage."

More silence.

Her patience snapped. "What have you done with my companions?"

The whispering returned and rose to fever pitch, but then faded into the babble of the brook that cut across the clearing.

Shae opened her eyes.

A full moon rode like a ship in the sky, shedding light like sea foam. Trees, combed by the wind, tossed at the edge of the meadow. Partway into the darkness of the syllid the collapsing tracker shelter hunched.

Only a dream—it had been but a dream.

She turned her head, and her heart thudded in her ears.

Her companions really were gone.

Freaer emerged from the shadows. Even in the dark of night she read triumph in the tilt of his head. He stood over her. *"You are mine, Shae! I bought you with Maeven's death song."*

Terror clutched her mind and weighted her legs. She opened her mouth to deny his words, but no sound came.

Freaer held out a hand. "Come." His voice echoed through the *syllid.*

She jerked her eyes open. Freaer was gone. The moon, which no longer rode high, dimmed in the gathering light of morning. She cast about in confusion. What had happened? Had Freaer found her with the shil shael? Or had she suffered one nightmare after another—a dream within a dream?

Sounds carried to her—rustlings and a sudden thump. She turned her head, and her gaze clashed with Kai's. He crouched, ready to spring. *Something was wrong.*

A scuffling sounded. Metal rang on metal. A fearsome cry rent the air.

Kai rolled and sprang to his feet, Whyst at the ready. But he had no time to take up his shield. The sounds of battle escalated.

She pushed to her knees.

Hairy, thick-necked giants had invaded the

clearing. *Garns!*

Shae fumbled to snatch Leisht from its sheath. She lurched to her feet. Kai called a warning, and she put out her dagger in an instinctive gesture.

It caught the wall of stinking, hairy flesh that slammed her backwards and against the hard ground. The garn grunted as it bled and died, pinning her to the ground beneath it.

She could barely move. Her lungs burned, and a creeping blackness edged her vision. In a surge of desperation she twisted and bucked until the dead garn shifted.

She gasped in air but when the garn's stench filled her nostrils she fought the urge to retch.

Redoubling her efforts to free herself had bought her exhaustion rather than freedom. She lay helpless beneath the fallen garn, able only to watch the battle unfold.

Kai fought with zeal. Whyst sang as it sliced the air. He took up his shield and raised it to deflect a strike from the garn's huge sword. She would not have thought the light shield could withstand such an onslaught, but it remained unmarked. Forced into a defensive posture, Kai fended blow after blow. But blood stained his tunic. His wound must have reopened. As Kai's vigor flagged, the garn concentrated its attack on his injured side.

Dorann fared better. She caught glimpses of him just beyond Kai. Small of stature and light on his feet, he seemed almost to dance in battle. As their prey darted about, the two garns who chased him bellowed, but their frenzied blows came to naught.

She could not see Aerlic.

Kai cried out. His shield spun away. He stood,

exposed and panting. A spreading stain soaked his side. He gathered himself.

The garn waited, sword ready.

No! Her cry came out a whisper. She had already watched Kai die once, or at least thought she had, at Elcon's Coronation. She could not do it again. She called to Dorann. *"Help him!"*

Tears slid down her cheeks, for he did not hear her soft cry. Besides, Dorann had his own battle to fight. With renewed strength, she shoved against the dead garn.

Aerlic stepped from the edge of the clearing with bow drawn.

Thwank! His arrow thumped into the side of the garn attacking Kai.

With a grunt, the garn turned to face a new threat.

In that instant, the dead garn slid sideways and Shae pulled her legs free.

Her ears rang but cleared as she gulped in air. She lifted to shaky knees and jerked her dagger out of the garn's body. It dripped blood. Her stomach heaved. Cold tremors ran over her. Panting, she crouched and waited for the sickness to pass.

She peered around the dead garn's body. By some miracle Kai still stood. But he swayed on his feet.

She spotted Aerlic, fallen at the edge of the clearing, his body as broken as his bow.

Tears wet her cheeks. She tried to move, gritting her teeth as blood tingled back into her legs. They would not yet serve her. She suppressed a moan at the delay, but its necessity won her time to think. She could not hope to overpower the garn, but she could provide a distraction.

As the tingling eased, she crawled away from the

dead garn and toward Kai's fallen shield, which gleamed just out of reach. The carved and twined wingabeasts adorning it, symbol of the guardians of Rivenn, remained unmarred, a testimony to its strength. She held back a sob, for she had never felt more exposed, but the garn's attention remained fixed on Kai. Her fingers touched the edge of the shield. An instant more and she would bear it.

Her fingers curved around the boss ring. She hoisted the shield, almost falling backwards, for it was lighter than it seemed. Recovering her balance, she staggered to her feet.

A battle cry raised her hackles, and she turned her head. Dorann made a running lunge and planted his sword in the neck of one of the garns he faced.

The garn's dying roar filled the clearing.

As blood spurted, Shae winced and averted her eyes. She swallowed against the acid stinging her throat and willed herself not to give way to queasiness.

Raising her dagger with a fierce cry, she charged Kai's garn.

❧❦

At sight of a screaming, dagger-brandishing Shae, fear jolted through Kai's veins.

The garn swung toward Shae, exposing its wound, blood oozing around the arrow Aerlic had placed.

Kai saw his chance. Gripping Whyst with both hands, he drove his blade deep into the garn's side. Kai staggered backwards as the garn toppled. Kai's legs buckled, and he went to his knees. Blackness edged his vision.

Shae screamed.

The garn, still living, clawed her leg. The vile creature now dragged her toward its fangs.

Kai fought to his feet, but blackness pressed him on all sides, and he had to pause.

Dorann sidestepped a blow from the remaining garn he fought. Before it could recover Dorann spun and, with a powerful thrust, embedded his sword in its side. The garn went to its knees and Dorann moved in for the kill.

When the garn lay dead, Dorann started toward Shae. Kai breathed a prayer. *"Lof Yuel, save her!"* Dorann would never reach her in time.

Shae's shrieks raised the hair on his arms. He watched, helpless, as the garn pulled her closer to its fangs. Blood ran across its hairy hand from scratch marks she made. A cold sweat broke over Kai as blood ran down her leg. He staggered toward Shae, feeling somehow weightless.

The garn moaned and its fingers relaxed in death.

Kai remembered to breathe.

Dorann reached Shae and pried her leg from the garn's death grip.

Kai sank to his knees before her.

She lifted herself to kneel with him, and he saw that she wept. *"You live!"*

"*I* live?" He pulled her into his arms. "I thought I'd lost you when that garn crushed you beneath it, and then again when you charged our friend here like Lof Yuel's revenge, and once more when he tried to take you with him in death." He drew away to scold her. "You must stop putting yourself at risk."

A strong-minded look came over her face, but, as darkness took him, he didn't hear her answer.

❧❧

"We're at risk here, but we should remain another day to recover." Dorann straightened from crouching over Kai. He touched her with a glance. "And to bury Aerlic."

Shae leaned against a Draetenn trunk. Her bandaged leg stretched before her. "And if we stay, won't other garns find us?"

"I doubt they will if we're careful. As a precaution I've hidden the corpses."

The memory of Dorann dragging the dead garns into the syllid made her shudder. "Time grows short." But her protest sounded weak.

"Travel will overtax Kai," Dorann reminded her. "And you can little tolerate it yourself. Besides, I don't like the thought of leaving Aerlic to the wolves and garns."

She shuddered again. "I can't abide the thought!"

"We will give him a proper burial—somehow." As it met hers, his amber gaze softened. "I've tended Kai. Watch over him while I gather a few herbs. Call if you need help."

She took his meaning. Leisht weighted her hand as she peered into the green shadows. Apart from the nodding of a gnarlwood bow when a flitling flew from it, nothing moved. She glanced at Kai's white face and bending over him, touched his clammy brow. *"Live!"*

At her whisper, his eyes opened and his silvered gaze sought hers. She couldn't deny the curious pull that bound her to him. *How came this?* She forced her thoughts to calm. Right now she needed her wits about her. There would be time enough for such trouble should they return from Lohen Keil.

Dorann returned with his hands full of greens. He dipped his head to Kai. "I'm glad to see you awake. I'll make a draught to soothe your ills, but I think we should move into the draetenns upstream for the night. Already *pyreks* circle."

The thought of the small, fierce carrion fowl roused Shae. The glint of wings overhead confirmed Dorann's words. She shivered, for night's chill already drew near.

Dorann supported Kai's weight as they transferred upstream to a place where the banks of the brook broadened in a wide arc. Although the blue sky faded to shades of gray, soft light filtered through the draetenns and gleamed from the brook's surface.

Shae sat on a boulder while Dorann settled Kai on a fallen log. Dorann rummaged through his pack, and then tossed her a round of waybread. She caught the bread but, as pain shot through her, winced. She ate the meager fare, although she had no appetite, and then took the steaming cup Dorann offered her. It tasted of sweet herbs. The medicinal infusion unfurled tendrils of warmth inside her, and she pushed her hair back to cool her forehead.

Kai, propped against a fallen log, looked up from his food and met her glance. He offered an encouraging smile, despite the sadness on his face, and bent again to eat. She swallowed against the lump that rose to her throat, grateful Kai would recover.

A sudden thought struck her. "Aerlic saw himself in death."

"He did." Kai leaned back against the log. "At *Paiad Burein.'*

"Did he see his future?" Shae set aside her empty cup. "Or did something in that place mark him for death?"

Dorann shook his head. "I don't understand such dark matters."

Night crept upon them in stages, so gradual as to catch them off guard. Dorann stood. "Sleep and I'll stand watch."

Kai growled low in his throat. "I am much improved."

"You must rest!" Dorann flushed. "At least tonight." He said in a gentler tone.

Shae hid a smile. How odd to hear Dorann order Kai about. While Kai embraced leadership, Dorann kept to himself.

"All right." Kai relented. "I'll surrender to your care."

Shae lay down with a yawn. Sleep caught her up at once.

She woke to birdsong and morning light. Kai sat on the log, looking much improved. Dorann knelt below him and dug in his pack.

Shae sat up and worked a kink from her neck. Her leg pained her, despite Dorann's poultice.

Dorann glanced her way. "How do you fare?"

"Much improved." She kept her aching muscles to herself.

Kai cocked a brow at her. "As am I."

She gave him a doubtful look.

"That's well, then." Dorann, speaking around a bit of waybread, sat beside Kai. "We need to leave this place soon."

Shae studied Kai's pale face. "Can you travel?"

His eyes gleamed. "I can and will. We've dwelt too long here."

Shae stretched, and then wished she hadn't. Every

part of her hurt. "What lies before us?"

"A climb." Kai smiled. "But in forest shade and by daylight."

Dorann frowned at Kai. "We'll go slowly this day, I think. But first, we have a matter to attend."

❧

Light and shadow sifted across Aerlic's cairn—a wall of rocks piled across the opening in the side of a hollow draetenn. Aerlic rested within. As she waited between Kai and Dorann, the stone Shae had taken from the banks of the brook chilled her hands.

Dorann laid his stone on top of the others there. "I did not know you well until the last, Aerlic, but I'll not forget you."

A small breeze lifted the leaves overhead. The voice of the brook surged and ebbed.

Kai stepped forward, shoulders squared. "I'll return for you if I can." His voice caught, and he paused. "I'll return you to your home in Glendenn raven."

Shae placed her rock among the others. "I'll not let you die for nothing." As she stepped back, Kai placed his hand on her shoulder, and she let herself lean into his strength. They stood for a time, brief of necessity, and then turned away from the makeshift tomb.

Emerging from the stand of draetenns, they kept to the path as it entered deep shade beneath towering gnarlwoods. Here and there, sunlight broke through weaving branches, fracturing into shafts.

Shae trudged behind Dorann and beside Kai up long hillsides where grassy meadows yielded to tumbled rocks. When downed trees blocked the way, they clambered over or found a detour. Kai couldn't endure such rigors long, and Shae's leg pained her more than she admitted. They halted early to shelter beneath a rock overhang, which was just as well, for rain came before night fell.

Dampness seeping from the edge of her cloak woke Shae before dawn. Chilled, she lay awake until dawn. When they set off again pain shot up her injured leg, but she clenched her teeth and gave no protest. Rain drove into her eyes and soaked her garments, but she pressed on, regardless.

Now that the ground angled at a steeper grade, she stopped to catch her breath more often. The path narrowed, and Kai motioned her forward to walk between Dorann and him. At times they stopped to hack away the undergrowth so they could pass. Time spun out. Shadows lengthened.

"Here!"

At Dorann's call, Shae halted but didn't look up until Kai took her hand. He gave her a bracing smile and led her into the dim shelter of a hollow gnarlwood. She sank onto the bed of dry hummus at its center, thankful for the warmth it gave.

Dorann turned in a slow circle. "I don't see any openings but the one we came in by. That will make the night watch easier."

"I'm stronger now," Kai told Dorann. "I can stand part of the watch."

Dorann gave him a doubtful glance. "You'll only exhaust yourself. I'll do it."

"I insist." The edge to Kai's voice reminded Shae of the tone he'd taken after rescuing her from a precarious perch in one of Whellein Hold's gnarlwoods back in her early days.

Dorann, who didn't have the benefit of her experience of Kai, snorted. "Stop trying to be a hero."

"Come now. It's obvious you're the one trying to be a hero. Don't think I haven't noticed why."

Alarm shot through Shae. "Kai—"

He looked down at her, pain in his eyes.

Dorann's jaw tightened. "Stand the watch then."

As the two turned their backs on one another, Shae blew out her breath. The long trek took its toll on them all. Sleep caught her unawares.

She woke to murmurs and pulled her cloak more snugly about her, ready to drift back to sleep.

Kai's voice roused her, and she picked out his words. "Our supplies are low. Besides the fact that we could carry only so much on foot, we've suffered delays and had less time to hunt and gather than we hoped. At this rate, by the time we enter Laesh Ebain, our stores will run out."

"We'll have to tighten our belts." Dorann answered.

"We may be able to reach our destination, but we won't have supplies for the return journey."

"I'll hunt and gather."

"Let's hope the Lost Plains offer something worth the effort."

Their murmuring stopped, and Shae lost her hold on wakefulness. Morning came too soon, and she woke with a groan. As she combed and replaited her hair, Kai watched with grave interest. What had he meant about Dorann wanting to prove himself a hero? Did it have anything to do with the look of admiration she sometimes surprised on his face? She hoped for all their sakes that it did not.

The trail narrowed further that day, steepening as

it wended through tall gnarlwoods and lush
undergrowth. But, when they neared the second bench,
the ground leveled and the forest thinned. Late in the
day they followed a stream through a high meadow
where the sun's warmth soothed Shae. Gazing with
longing at the waving meadow grass and cooling
waters of a small stream, she opened her mouth to
suggest they stop. Before she could speak a welke's
screech rent the air.

She searched the sky. All at once, the sweetgrass
meadow seemed too exposed.

Kai's long eyes gleamed. Although he didn't
speak, she read his message clearly. Dorann gave a
tight nod. As one, they sought cover in the serviceberry
thicket beside them.

No sooner had they hidden than a great shadow
swept across the meadow. Shae pressed the back of her
hand against her mouth. Did the creature not hear her
ragged breathing? The bushes were sparse and Kai had
to crouch so they covered his head. If the welke flew
over the serviceberry thicket, surely it would find
them.

24

The Lost Plains

"Don't move." Kai's whisper stirred the air near Shae's ear.

She pressed against him, glad for the reminder that welkes needed movement to see. A shadow rippled across the ground. Feathers rustled overhead. She held her breath. Time stretched to snapping point. And still the welke did not return.

"*Safe!*" Dorann exhaled on a breath.

Shae loosed her death grip on Kai's forearm, but he made a sound in his throat and pulled her into his arms. She leaned her head on his chest until the long shivers that racked her subsided.

His voice thrummed beneath her ear. "We must take special care from here on out. We draw near the welke's roosting places."

They started off again. Another time, and she might have taken more thought for the rugged beauty of her surroundings. The deep, dank forests and forsaken landscapes they traveled became to her now only torments to endure. From the viewpoint of Torindan's ramparts, these rises had seemed moderate. Of course, at the outset of their venture, everything had seemed much easier than it had proven.

The climb, which had started, if not jauntily, at

least with energy, wore her down. Shae could not prevent herself from slowing. She grabbed at the plentiful *ederbaer*—tiny berries that grew in abundance on bushes along the wayside. The moist fruit eased her dry mouth, its tartness tingling against her tongue. Her leg throbbed, but still she said nothing. She huddled within herself, disregarding suffering, cold, and discomfort. Nothing mattered but reaching Caerric Daeft.

How did Elcon fare? She had not tried the shil shael again, for it called for a stamina she did not now possess. Its use must drain Freaer's reserves as well. How had he kept up such a constant barrage against Elcon? But then, Freaer's ability did not match her own. Something eldritch overlaid his "touch"—a dry breath of magic. Of course, the son of Meriwen of Old would learn fell arts at his mother's knee. She had by these arts ensnared shraens and extended her own life—and her sons'—far beyond their mortal limits. What other privileges might such powers bring?

Shae would never win against Freaer on that level. The thought, somehow, made her glad. She pushed forward with renewed energy but soon gritted her teeth to keep from crying out. Each step jarred her leg.

Kai must have guessed her discomfort, for he pressed a walking staff into her hand and paused often.

Dark clouds gathered overhead and hurled icy water upon them. They slogged on, although the trail slicked into mud at once. Rain drove into Shae's eyes and her feet stuck in the mud. Even when she slid and fell onto her injured leg, she did not call a halt.

Too much depended on reaching the second bench. They'd glimpsed its naked stone surface gleaming in the distance throughout the day. By the time they drew near, the rain had ceased and the sun touched the horizon. Shae reached the bench and the brink of exhaustion together. Kai turned a pale face toward her, and even Dorann's step lacked vigor.

She sighed and leaned against the natural wall of dark stone that leveled just above her head. From this viewpoint above the stunted draetenns that persisted almost to this altitude, she thought she saw the cliffs surrounding Torindan. In the space between, the canyons of Doreinn Ravein twisted in shades of mauve and pink and gray, the tossing green and gold canopy of Syllid Braechnen stretched to Pilaer, and the ruins of Braeth hunched over mysteries. She sighed. They had already journeyed far and paid dearly to reach this lonely place.

"Come, Shae." With a hand on her shoulder, Kai urged her to enter a cleft in the wall of stone. When she hesitated, he caught her eye. "It's safer inside."

She passed through the cleft into a small cave.

Dorann waited within. A tiny flame glowed in the cup he held high as he peered into the cave's recesses. In such a dark space, even a small light illuminated well. Kai settled beside her.

Dorann completed his inspection of the cave and turned to Shae. "I'll tend your injuries while we wait."

She stretched out in the cool darkness, biting her lip against the pain as she moved her leg. She endured in silence as, with deft skill, Dorann applied a fresh poultice and new bandages.

Shae leaned her head against the smooth rock wall behind her, glad for the chance to ease her feet. The new poultice took the edge off the pain.

When he finished bandaging Kai's side, Dorann

extinguished his light. With only a few rays of fading light penetrating from the cleft, the darkness in the cave overwhelmed Shae until her eyes adjusted.

A great flapping and whirring of wings punctuated by screeches and ululating cries broke forth outside. The welkes returned to their roosts on Maeg Waer.

Shae shuddered, for the cries chilled her blood despite the relative safety within the womb of rock. Kai's hand slid over hers with quick warmth, and she leaned on his shoulder in gratitude. As he cradled her, time slipped away…

Kai's soft call roused her, and she opened her eyes with reluctance. Daylight had fled, but moonlight outlined the cleft at the mouth of the cave. A shadow shifted back and forth across it.

"Dorann guards the entrance." Kai's voice spoke near her ear, and she realized she still sheltered in his arms. "The moon stands at its apex. We should see well enough to climb the step, and we'll have time to hide again before dawn."

Shae followed him from the cave and blinked in the moon's bright light. Clouds brushed with iridescence drifted across its face and unfurled to send quixotic patterns across the lands below. The clouds filtered moonbeams that fell in paths across the stone bench. All lay in stillness save the wind, which sighed in intermittent gusts that set the draetenns below hissing.

Kai scaled the wall with grace despite his injury, but Shae hesitated. "My leg."

Dorann held out his hand to Shae. "Don't fear." He caught her around the waist and lifted her. Kai leaned down to grasp her arms and pulled her to the top of the bench.

Although Kai steadied her, she slipped when he released her. As she fell to her knees, she cried out as her leg jarred and cold, slick stone slammed against her hands.

Kai helped her to her feet as a gust whistled from the east, threatening to topple her again. Turning, he sheltered her from the brunt of the wind.

Shae pressed a hand to her stomach as she looked out across Laesh Ebain, dismayed to find the Lost Plains so barren. Even the softness of moonlight could not disguise an utter wasteland. She'd heard Laesh Ebain described thus, but mere words could not have prepared her for the reality. Without the relief of trees and studded only by the few scraggly bushes that dared brave the poor soil, the ebain offered little sustenance. Great cracks marred the ground, which would make their journey a nightmare.

To the north the broken peak of Maeg Streihcan looked utterly forlorn, but the misty hills of Maegran Syld comforted her with thoughts of home. The rocky coastline of Maer Syldra bordered Laesh Ebain to the south, wild and impassable. The ebain ended at the bench of rock beneath them and, hazed by distance, fetched against the feet of Maeg Waer to the east. That monolith cocked its dark head against a moon-washed sky. Wind searched the folds of her clothing as she stumbled and slid across the terrain between Kai and Dorann. Her ragged breathing in the face of the relentless wind mingled with the squelch of mud to disturb an otherwise profound silence. A finger of wind snatched the edge of her cloak. Shae clutched it about her with hands that stung, shivering as water penetrated her clothing and into her skin. Her feet gave little sensation anymore. Her boots, caked in mud, would probably never come clean again...if she survived this journey.

She could not remember ever suffering in this way. She walked with jerky movements, as if her body no longer belonged to her. Her mind drew apart. Did she sleepwalk?

She stepped in a rut and came down hard on her injured leg. Pain tore through her, and she gritted her teeth with hot tears stinging her eyes. A gust wrenched the hood from her head, and wet hair slapped her eyes. She clawed at it as she swayed before the buffeting wind.

Kai caught up with her and put an arm around her. When he urged her forward, Shae took a step and gasped. Kai lowered his head to catch the words she spoke with reluctance. "My foot....I must rest."

He called to Dorann, who waited ahead. "Find somewhere to shelter."

Kai bore the brunt of the wind for her.

She leaned into his arms.

Dorann led them into one of the cracks in the ground — a chasm that with any luck would hide them through the day. Her leg throbbed and she doubted she would sleep, but when Shae opened her eyes again morning gleamed on the horizon.

She woke to temperatures that drew clouds of steam from her wet clothing. The heat carried an edge, but at least her skin warmed, and she would not have to chafe in wet clothing all day. Kai leaned against the earthen wall and returned her gaze in silence. Dorann, propped beside him, still slept.

"*Water.*" She cast about, searching.

Kai motioned her to silence. "Keep your voice

down. Welkes have excellent hearing." He reached across Dorann and retrieved one of the elkskins. "Drink with care. Too much and you'll become ill."

With difficulty, Shae restrained herself from gulping the water. She handed the skin to Kai, who drank in turn. The chasm that sheltered them terrified her less by day than it had in the dead of night. The earthern walls lifted moist and dark about them, although the sun beat down through the crack overhead. A natural streambed of smooth white pebbles lay beneath them, wet now only at its middle.

A screech rent the air to echo across the ebain, making Shae shudder.

Dorann woke with a cry. Kai motioned him to caution and drew Whyst. Dorann's eyes cleared. He pulled his hunting knife from his boot and went into a crouch. Shae grasped Leisht's hilt and watched with the others the jagged crack of blue sky overhead. A tense silence stretched, but Dorann's cry must have gone unheard. Perhaps the welke's own screech had covered it.

As the day wore on, they grew familiar with the welkes' cries and even learned to gauge their distance. They could distinguish the various *carruches* and clicks and whistles the creatures made while flying back and forth to Maeg Waer. Shae couldn't become accustomed to the heart-wrenching cries, however. Whenever they pulsed through the air she cringed.

Their forced inactivity became as much a foe as any welke. As dark shadows passed overhead, Shae ignored the urge to stretch her leg to relieve its cramping and held still until, with muscles screaming, she could stand it no more. She shifted her position with care, fearful any noise she made would draw nearby welkes.

They had no choice but to wait in this wretched crack in the ground, although it heated to unbearable levels. Shae put her head on Kai's shoulder and sheltered beneath the cloak he raised to shade them both. Even so, her scalp prickled with heat and moisture ran down her neck. Her tongue clung to the roof of her mouth, and when she licked her lips, she found them cracked.

She ate the last of the waybread, which Dorann offered her, and drank a little water. Afterwards, she propped against the earthen wall and closed her eyes in prayer. Perhaps they would get further in their travels tonight since the sun must have baked the ebain dry throughout the day.

Shadows lengthened and the temperature cooled, but when night at last fell, so did renewed rain. Disheartened, they clambered from the chasm, now a streambed, to stagger across the darkened landscape. Progress came more slowly this night, for roiling clouds obscured the moonlight. Despite this, they came within another night's march of the foothills of Maeg Waer.

Toward dawn, they settled in a chasm that offered a small, overhanging shelter made by the washed-out roots of stunted ederbaer bushes, which leaned, still living, into the chasm. Shae crouched with the others, thankful to find eroded rock underfoot rather than mud. She washed off her boots in the stream that coursed down the center of the chasm and into a deep pool that swelled over a rim. From there, the water snaked away as a new stream. At least they would have water to drink in the day's heat.

The chasm was wider and shallower than the one

they'd hidden in the day before, but it would serve. The screen of ederbaer leaves would provide some shade by day, but didn't protect well from the rain. Huddled between Kai and Dorann, Shae watched droplets plunk from her hood to the ground in a steady rhythm. She pulled her cloak about her, but the steady drizzle invaded anyway. Made of wool, her garments kept her passably warm even when wet but chafed her skin. She could not sleep in such misery, not until the rain lifted with the sun and her garments dried.

She woke in sweltering heat to find the others waiting with drawn weapons. She pushed to her knees, peering with them at the strip of sky through the ederbaer branches. Kai motioned for quiet. The screen of ederbaer bushes lent a sense of security, but did little to separate them from the creatures which could so easily swoop upon them. Shrieks rent the air. So near….

A black shape blotted out the sky, but the raptor didn't pause in its flight. Shae fought to still her body's trembling. If this ordeal of cold and heat and nerves did not end soon, she might go mad.

A guttural croaking warned her. The ederbaer branch just above her dipped low. Showers of dirt cascaded over Shae. A leathery underbelly showed through the leaves.

She held her breath. She didn't dare move. A welke perched in the bush and plucked the shiny berries.

How had they not considered that the ederbaer bush might draw hungry welkes? Shae watched in a strange sort of fascination as the the dark creature tipped its head back to swallow the berries one by one. She had never seen a welke up close before—or smelled one's stench either.

The raptor *carruched* and preened, then bent to take another crimson morsel into its sharp beak. Its coat gleamed sleek and dark as ebony. Wicked talons grasped the ederbaer branch. Those claws could shred a person in an instant.

Panic suffocated Shae, and her chest rose as she sucked in a breath. She pressed a hand to her mouth to keep from crying out.

The welke's head swiveled, and its black gaze locked on her. Its beak opened and a shriek vibrated the air.

The sound went on and on in Shae's mind. She tried to move, but her shaking limbs would not obey. She opened her mouth in a soundless scream.

The welke flapped its wings and lifted into the air, poised to drop.

ॐॐ

Kai thrust his blade upward through the bush just as the creature left it. Whyst snagged in the ederbaer branches and would not pull free.

The welke hovered overhead, then dropped into the chasm beside the bush and pecked sideways through the tangled roots.

Kai pushed Shae toward the earthen wall, but she stumbled and fell. And then a blood-curdling cry from the welke claimed his whole attention.

"We will die if it breaks through!" Dorann, sword in one hand and hunting knife in the other, crouched beside him.

Kai fought to free Whyst, but the welke pecked at him through the bush. Dorann thrust his knife upward.

A horrendous screech tore from the welke, and it lifted a bloodied talon. Far from giving up, however, the fiendish creature renewed its attack.

Kai's hands and forearms ran with blood, but he set his teeth and heaved. Whyst gave way all at once, and he fell backward. He rolled and regained his feet, but halted. Chills crawled over him.

Whyst wavered in Shae's hands as she stepped from behind the *ederbaer* roots. With a bloodcurdling battle cry similar to the one she'd unleashed on the garn, she charged the welke.

The giant raptor swung to intercept Shae, and Kai's mouth went dry. Horror kept him frozen in place.

Dorann sprang from cover and arced his sword toward the welke's exposed side. His sword thrust fell short, but he'd diverted attention from Shae. The raptor gave a series of high-pitched clicks and made a small retreat. Head tilted, it watched both Dorann and Shae out of round, black eyes.

Kai managed to get his legs to move. Coming up behind Shae, he placed his hand beside hers on Whyst's hilt and spoke near her ear. *"Let go!"*

She obeyed, and he shoved her behind him, haste making him less than gentle. He parried a black beak. "Shae, *get back!*"

Dorann rushed in, and the welke turned on him.

Kai lunged toward its undefended side, but the bird lifted into the air to hover above him with talons spread. He raised Whyst and braced for its attack.

Answering cries rang across the ebain.

❧

Trembling, Shae willed her knees to hold her

upright. What insane impulse had caused her to charge the welke? She released Whyst to Kai, but when he pushed her behind him, lost her footing. A cold shock of water closed over her. She came up in the stream, gasping and shaking water from her face, to the shriek of approaching welkes. She caught her breath on a sob. They could not overcome so many. Death would find them here, after all. Letting the water bear her where it would, she wept for herself and for Kai and Dorann. She wept, also, for Elderland—for the devastation that would follow unfulfilled Prophecy.

The current picked up speed, hurrying downstream toward the deep pool and the cataracts beyond. She hadn't sought escape, but the chance of it came nonetheless. A flicker of hope revived, although turning her back on her companions tore the heart from her. But she had to go on.

The stream deepened. She gulped as much air as she could and dove underwater. If she escaped notice, she could hide there until after the abominable creatures—until they left again. She slammed into hidden rocks as she slid through the murky water. A boot came off and her skirts hampered her, but she surfaced, gasping in air. The current sucked her back under only to spew her out further downstream. Its roaring drowned out the screeches of the *welkes*—and any other sounds. Shae plunged into the pool with such force she sank deep and fought to surface. She looked around her, shuddering in anticipation, but nothing pursued. Shae plunged back to the depths and pulled with strong strokes for the shadowed green recesses farthest from the feeding stream. She discovered her mistake too late, for the turbulence held her under until her lungs burned and darkness threatened to overtake her. Just when she thought she must drown, the current bobbed her to the surface. As she pulled air into her burning lungs, she drifted toward a stone lip.

She plunged, screaming, through the falling water into another pool.

Light drew her upward, and with bursting lungs she kicked for the surface. She emerged to the deafening roar of a cataract. The sun lay low in an empty sky, tinting the pool she approached with reds and mauves. Staying away from the edge this time, she dove deep and came up behind the water falling from the pool above.

She pulled herself from the water onto the shelf of rock at the edge of the pool. The wind misted her with spray and, although she wound her arms about herself, she could not stop shivering.

She crawled into a cleft behind the waterfall. She could hide from the welkes here but not from her thoughts. Images of Kai and Dorann intruded. Had they perished? Putting a hand to her mouth to quiet her sobs, she curled into a ball and fell into a half-sleep troubled by dreams of Freaer. She felt his "touch" at the edge of awareness, just out of reach. Instinctively, she shielded herself. And then blessed oblivion came.

She opened her eyes. Silver water, ruffled by the night wind, cascaded before her. She gazed at the waterfall in bewilderment but as memory returned closed her eyes. Emotion rose to choke her, but she clamped down on it. For all of their sakes, she had to survive. Wriggling out of the cleft, she halted when her tunics caught. A rip answered her tug. She crawled forward and pulled to her knees. With cupped hands, she reached into the waterfall. Icy water eased her dry throat. Her stomach growled in protest. With no food to give it, she drank again.

She staggered to her feet. One bootless foot peeped from beneath the ripped tunics lying sodden and heavy against her legs. Shivers racked her, and her teeth chattered. She wound her arms about herself and fought the strange numbness that dulled her senses. She had to think.

Her cloak remained behind in the chasm. Survival demanded she retrieve it. Besides, she wouldn't get far in Caerric Daeft without a lanthorn. Bile rose to the back of her throat. How could she look upon the remains of the welke's *feast*? And yet she must return or perish from the cold.

She had sensed she would finish her journey alone but had not understood what that would cost. If she had known, she would have left Graelinn Hold alone and in secret to spare Kai and Dorann. She pushed the thought away, for it brought a hitch of pain. She would not be able to go on if she dwelt on her sorrows. She must not delay, or her courage might fail.

Brael Shadd glowed steady upon the horizon.

She raised her fist at the star. "*Lof Yuel!* Do you mock me?"

Even as she spoke, rage drained from her. She hung her head. "You ask more than I can give."

Peace. The word whispered across the ebain — or did it speak only in memory? She lifted her head.

A wayfarer of Elder blood had comforted her in the Allerstaed. *You are not alone.*

Clinging to handholds, she tackled the bluff. Pain slashed her leg and her fingernails tore, but she reached the lip of rock at the top of the waterfall. She paused to gasp in air and looked out over the ebain, where spirals of mist eddied above the chasms like specters shifting in the moonlight.

She hadn't realized how far the water had taken her. The stream shone with liquid fire as it tumbled over gleaming rocks, but its banks lay in darkness. Shae made her way with difficulty across the rough terrain, despite the light of the moon. Her hips soon ached from her uneven gait, and she eased off her existing boot to relieve them. She had no real hope of finding the other, but she couldn't quite bring herself to discard the one she held. She made faster progress with both boots off, although sharp stones sometimes gouged her bare feet.

The chasm near the leaning ederbaer bushes lay quiet, limned in moonlight, but a foul odor drifted to her. Shae's feet made little sound on the naked rock. She shrank at the sight of dark bits and pieces scattered about an inky pool which as she drew closer, proved to be blood. The shredded remains of a welke ringed it about. Her gorge rose at the sight and stench, and she pressed a hand to her mouth. Its fellows had obviously set upon the welke that had attacked them, perhaps drawn by its bleeding.

She turned away from what was left of the welke and steeled herself to search the chasm. Their belongings lay scattered about, but there was no sign of Kai or Dorann. Gathering her cloak from beneath the bush where they had sheltered, she pulled its folds close about her.

What had happened? Had the birds carried her companions off? It seemed the only explanation, but she took foolish hope from Whyst's absence. If Kai were dead, surely his sword would lie somewhere at hand.

She found the lanthorn, but the oil that fueled it puddled around an unstoppered flask. The lanthorn itself held only a small portion of oil, but it would have to suffice. As she searched for flint, she caught sight of something that glinted. Her fingers closed upon the locket she'd given Kai in her early days—a silverstone on a silver chain that gleamed as she raised it to catch the moonlight.

Smiling even as grief smote her, she touched the locket to her lips. Tears choked at the back of her throat. She could not let sobs overtake her. Not here. Not now. She clasped the chain at the back of her neck, and the locket swung into place against her chest. Its small weight gave her a measure of comfort. Something of Kai would go with her.

A single tear coursed down her cheek, and brushing it away she turned eastward. She'd cross this night to the crags and boulders at the feet of Maeg Waer, and then enter Caerric Daeft.

Alone.

25

Cavern of Death

The suck and lap of water roused Kai. Rolling onto his back with a slosh, he opened his eyes to darkness. He sat upright, every muscle protesting, and his head hit something solid. As he put up a hand, his fingers grated against cold rock close above him. He pushed into a low crouch, all he could manage in this tight space, and wet sand scraped his palms.

Memory came then. Screeches and dark wings. Rent flesh. Spattered blood. Just keeping his grip on Whyst as he jumped into the stream after Dorann. The shrieking of the welkes as they devoured their wounded member.

Swept down a series of cataracts, he'd found a handhold at waterline while Dorann slid over the next waterfall. With welkes screeching overhead, he'd heaved himself into a small hole in the rock face.

The thought of Shae alone in the night, possibly injured, spurred him now. He crawled toward the blue light at the mouth of the small hole and emerged behind a sparkling ribbon of water falling into a pool of black silk.

He slipped into the pool and, staying away from the main current, struck for the bank. Bumping to the edge, he pulled himself out. Water sheeted from him as he stood upon bare rock. He shook, shedding droplets like a dog.

The cold cut like a knife. He needed his cloak, and if Shae or Dorann lived, perhaps he would find them in the chasm where it lay.

Before he turned aside, Kai peered from the edge into the dark pool below. *"Shae! Dorann!"*

A night bird exploded from its perch in some rocky crevice below and became a white blur winging across the ebain. Its plaintive whistle carried on the wind. No other reply answered him. He hadn't really expected one.

Kai's boots squelched as he walked, but he ignored their discomfort—even welcomed the distraction—for he would not soon erase the image of Shae standing bold and alone against the welke, Whyst raised high. Nor could he forget Dorann's panicked expression as the current carried him away.

Something caught his eye, a hard-edged object along the shore. Plucking Shae's sodden boot from the stream, he tasted the salt of tears. He gathered himself to trudge onward, but other images weighted his steps. Maeven lying still in death…Shae flinging early petals over his head…Aeleanor huddled in her daughter's cloak…Daeven tilting his hat as he rode away, never to return.

He reached the chasm and found his cloak near his pack. He settled its warmth over his shoulders. Dorann's cloak remained but Shae's had vanished. Hope stirred. Had she survived? The contents of their packs littered the area—strewn, no doubt, by welkes in search of food. Kai gathered his belongings. Spilled oil pooled on the ground, but he found no lamp. His heart turned over as hope, and then certainty, seized him.

Shae lived.

～∽

Shae put her lone boot back on. Better to limp than to have two slashed and numbed feet. She tore strips from her tunic and bound her bootless foot with them. Even so, cold soon penetrated the cloth. As the night progressed, her clothing had dried but she still shivered in her cloak. At times the world receded, and she fancied herself a ghost floating across the ebain. Other times, she dragged, all too aware of each painful step.

Light blushed across the eastern sky as Shae fetched against one of the great boulders in the foothills beneath Maeg Waer. She spread herself flat against the rock and eyed the mountain towering overhead. If she didn't find and enter Caerric Daeft, the welkes would find her when they left their roosts. But she held back for want of courage. How could she face the Cavern of Death alone? *Lof Yuel, help me.*

A cool touch brushed her mind across time and space. She smiled through her tears. *Elcon lived.* He would need the DawnKing's help to free Elderland.

She stood and faced the mountain.

A faint path led to a cleft marking the entrance to Caerric Daeft. At the mouth of the cave, she turned for a last look across Laesh Ebain. Even the gentle morning light could not ease the bleak landscape. Brael Shadd glinted in the distance, not troubling to rise above the horizon. A shaft of light followed her inside the cave, but there deserted her. She paused, shivering in the sudden cold, and ignited the lanthorn as she had seen it done by Dorann and Aerlic. Her fingers fumbled over the unaccustomed task. It took longer than it ought, but she at last held the lighted lamp aloft. She peered about to gain her bearings, and a frisson of fear traveled her spine. This cave resembled the one she'd visited in her dreams.

She set her fears aside and moved into the cave, but halted in wonder. A large chamber, finer than any built by Kindren hands, unfolded before her. The near walls glittered with a thousand tiny lights of gold, white, and pink. The lights seemed so luminous. Would they continue to glow if her lanthorn went out? Stalagtites hung from the ceiling like icicles, while stalagmites of the same smooth material thrust upwards from the cave floor.

This majestic cave would make a fitting tomb. She shivered when she remembered it had become just that for many of the early Kindren. What would it be like to encounter a garn in these passages?

She pushed the question away, for it would only defeat her, and followed an arched passage farther into the cave, moving as one in a dream. Each turn uncovered fresh marvels— luminescent draperies of rock, walls as smooth and white as milk, and a crystal bridge that spanned an abyss. Chamber opened onto chamber, passage gave way to passage. Almost, she forgot time and place in awe. The drip of water echoed throughout, and here and there she skirted pools that shone like glass and fell away to depths unknown. She passed great pillars of stone that rose into darkness and holes that dropped to nowhere.

Just when she lost all sense of direction, Shae didn't know, but she had no idea which way to turn to find the ancient stone stairway that climbed to Lohen Keil. She pressed on, trying not to panic, but the cave seemed to breathe, as if it lived—or as if something that lived followed her here.

She halted. The chamber before her seemed familiar. Did she travel in circles? She turned back and slammed into something warm and alive. A hand covered her mouth and stifled her scream.

The lanthorn swung in her hand, arcing light across the near walls and creating grotesque shadows before it sputtered and extinguished. A blue light remained. Although she didn't know its source.

"It's me, Shae!" A familiar voice spoke near her ear, and the arms released her.

She stepped back.

Kai's form stood before her. Whyst glowed with blue light in his hand. "Keep your voice low," he told her. "We don't know what darksome creatures dwell here."

She looked askance at the apparition before her. *Had she at last gone mad?*

He caught her shoulders and gave her a gentle shake. "What's happened to you, Shae? Do you fear me?" He touched the silverstone on its chain about her neck. "You wear my pendant."

She caught her breath. No apparition would recognize a pendant. "I thought you died!"

"You thought *I* died? *What about you?* You vanished, swept away in the stream." He paused, his hands flexing on her shoulders. "When I couldn't find you, I was certain you'd drowned."

"And I thought the welkes killed you and Dorann."

A pained look crossed his face. "They might have, but they went after the welke we bloodied first. Not a pretty sight. Dorann and I just had time to escape. We followed you into the stream. We weren't far behind, but you disappeared."

"*Oh Kai!* I crawled behind a waterfall and didn't see or hear anything. I thought—I thought…"

He tilted her face upward. "You thought me dead and mourned, did you? So much so that tears fill your eyes even now."

"Kai—"

His kiss, featherlight, stopped her words. "I love you, Shae."

She jerked away. "Can't you see that it's easier for you, Kai? You've known all along what I've only just discovered—that we bear no blood in common."

"I wish I'd never deceived you." His gaze pierced her. "And what of you, Shae—do you lock away secrets of your own?"

"I can't deny…" But her voice caught as a tide of sorrow flooded her.

He waited in silence.

She stepped back and willed herself to speak. "I do love you, but it's hopeless."

"Don't say that!" He pulled her into his arms and pressed her lips with his.

She returned his kiss, tasting the salt of her own tears. And then, lost in a labyrinth of emotion, she forgot tears. A sweet yearning seized her, and she wound her arms around his neck.

He responded with quick passion, and she followed him into realms of desire. In the flame that consumed them, every argument she'd raised to separate them blazed and died. Had she really thought to deny the love that drove them together?

He pulled away, his breath ragged, and gave a shaky laugh. "Such words belong in a garden, not in this forsaken place. I promise to speak them again when we are quit of here."

Bereft with his warmth gone, she wrapped her arms around herself. "At least we've spoken them now." A sudden thought struck her. "You've not mentioned Dorann, and to my shame I forgot to ask about him. How came you here alone?"

"The current carried Dorann farther down the cataracts. I'm not sure he lives. I called to him, but he didn't answer, and his cloak lay undisturbed in the chasm. Time presses or I could have searched for him. I thought you dead, especially when I found your boot. But when I returned for my cloak and saw yours gone, I chose duty and followed you first. We can search for Dorann upon our return."

"Let us hope for his safety. I hope he turns back. I only wish you hadn't come after me."

Kai's hands closed over hers in a warm embrace. "I could never leave you." He took the lanthorn she still held.

"It's empty."

He examined it and set it aside. "Never mind, Whyst guides the lost. It has already led me to you. We can trust its light." As he turned, the light from Whyst flared to show them a narrow side passage. "This must be the way."

They entered the narrow way that broadened into a small chamber where the walls glistened with moisture. A burbling rill cut a channel through the smooth floor. Another, invisible current flowed here. From somewhere hidden, fresh air entered the cave.

Kai stopped her beside the rill. "Wait! You limp, and I have your other boot. Here, sit down and hold Whyst."

Shae found a ledge to perch upon and angled the blade to cast light over Kai. He stripped off his pack and crouched at her feet. With gentle fingers, he unbound the strips of cloth from her foot. "Your foot's so cold. Here, let me warm it."

He rubbed her foot between his hands, and she cried out as sensation returned. Pulling her boot from his pack, he eased it over her foot, and steadied her when she stood. She could walk much better now, although she still limped.

Kai shouldered his pack and they followed the rill across the narrow chamber. It led through a small opening glowing with natural light. Kai straddled the rill and ducked to go through the opening, then turned back to offer Shae his hand.

A thin edge of rock crumbled into the rill beneath her. Kai caught her in time to keep her from going into the water, but the splash of stone echoed through the Caerric in endless cadence.

She blinked in sudden light, which spilled through a natural "window" — a hole in the rock wall. Her vision adjusted, and she stood on tiptoe to look out at Laesh Ebain, stretching away, windswept and desolate.

Turning from the hole in the wall, she fought to keep her eyes open. Her head swam, for she'd gone too long without sleep. Her foot stung as it warmed, but at least the pain from her injured leg had lessened. Still, each step came at a cost.

An opening at the back of the small chamber gave unto hewn steps. She followed Kai up the stairway, but missed her footing and slipped. As she slid, the hard stone of the stair treads smote her over and over. She lay still.

Kai reached her and helped her sit up. Scratches

welted her arms, and her cheek throbbed as if bruised. He pulled her into his arms. "We should rest before we climb. A little time remains before the dawn."

Shae recognized the truth. She had reached the end of her strength. This small chamber offered something of security, and its fresh air and light comforted her.

Kai found a dark corner and propped himself against the smooth cave wall, and Shae settled herself in the warmth of his arms. It occurred to her, before she fell headlong into sleep, that she had always sought Kai's arms. Nothing and yet everything had changed between them.

A breeze lifted the hair from Shae's brow. She stirred. Arms came around her. She fought until Kai's voice cut through her confusion.

"Wake, Shae! We've lingered overlong."

She struggled, lost in the fog of sleep.

Rage coupled with lust pounded her as Freaer's "touch" smote her mind. He would crush her soul. She tried to cry out but no sound came. She could not find the place where she ended and he began. Curling into a ball, she retreated inward.

The stranglehold loosened its tentacles and slid away. Almost, she would call it back, for her soul shredded. The sensation faded, and she breathed in the dusky scent of water on stone.

"Shae! Are you well?" Kai lifted her into his arms.

"Freaer's touch strengthens." She struggled to her feet to peer through the hole in the wall and take in the fresh draughts of air that bathed her face. Outside, storm clouds filled the sky, boiling purple. Lightning jagged and thunder boomed. A shimmer of rain obscured the ebain, slicking the clay soil.

Kai came up behind her, and she turned. "He draws near."

"Shae, you are safe."

She shook her head. "He won't spare himself to stop me. I know it. We must hurry."

Kai lifted Whyst. The spirit sword cast its light over the ancient stair. A rock wall rose on one side, and the other fell away to dark places unknown. Shae fretted at Kai's slow pace but he acted in wisdom. They would gain nothing if they tired themselves early in this long climb.

She watched her footing and, when they slowed for safety's sake, curbed her impatience. It would be all too easy to stumble over broken fragments of stone or trip on fissures.

Freaer's soul collided with hers again. Caught by surprise, she forgot to shield herself. This time the sight left her eyes, and she put out a hand in darkness. Her mind whimpered. She barely felt arms come around her. "Shae, *fight!*"

Kai's call sliced through her paralysis. With an effort, she curled into the Allerstaed within. Freaer's grasp of her slipped away. She was safe. He might rage without, but Freaer could not reach her here.

A sweet vapor drifted across her mind, pushing away Freaer's "touch." Lof Yuel!

Kai's face swam into view. She put a hand to his cheek. "Thank you."

He gave a shaky laugh and pressed a kiss into her palm. "I thought I'd lost you."

"It grows more difficult each time Freaer attacks. He's very near."

They climbed now with less caution and more speed. Water dripped all around them, and slid in channels down the walls. Small cave creatures splashed into pools at their approach, and the black waters rippled with silver. The ceiling soared out of sight far above, and a flurry of wings told Shae that creatures roosted there. As they climbed fresh currents blew over her. They passed more breaches in the side of the mountain. She breathed fresh air in these places but did not pause to look out. Would they come across openings where welkes roosted? She pushed away the thought. They faced enough perils without her imagining more.

She puffed as she climbed. As each flight of stairs broadened into a landing, always they found another that curved upwards. Her limp deepened as they climbed, and her legs trembled. The cave swung around her, and she put a hand to the wall until it righted itself.

Kai cried out and lurched backward. Stones clattered down the stairs. He dove toward the edge, fighting to hold his sword. She caught him, and they swayed together as Whyst spun into the black void.

26

Well of Light

Kai dragged Shae back from the edge, and they fetched against the cave wall. Darkness, more profound than any she had ever known, pressed against her eyes. She hid her face in Kai's cloak. Terror babbled in her mind like a lost soul. How could they go on without light? But how could they go back?

Kai moaned. "I lost my footing and dropped Whyst. There's no time to search, even if we could do so in safety."

"At least *you* did not fall. We will find a way to go on."

"*But how?* We can't see. Groping upward in darkness requires a slow pace, and the night wears on toward morning. We would risk falling to certain death for a bare chance of reaching Lohen Keil in time."

"What choice do we have? We can't stand here forever. A bare chance is still a chance." Silence followed her outburst, punctuated by the faint rustle of wings.

He drew a ragged breath. "You're right. We have to try."

Look to the light…

The whisper came with such clarity Shae thought

Kai might have heard it too. Memory stirred. *"Wait. I think...I know something."*

Retreating inward to the place only Lof Yuel could touch, she saw in her mind's eye the light that had flared within her at Elcon's Coronation. With the ease of thought, the white flame blossomed before her. "I can see."

Kai's hands tightened on her arms. *"How?"*

How indeed? "Lof Yuel's 'touch' lights the way." She edged past him and skirted past the broken step. "Take my hand."

Her fingers curled around his. She tugged his hand and started upward, but Kai stepped short of the riser and staggered toward the edge with arms flailing.

"Careful, Kai!" She caught him by the waist and helped him balance. "You almost followed Whyst."

She tried again to guide him, but he stumbled and fell to hands and knees as rocks scattered away from the edge.

She helped him rise. "I'll walk beside you this time."

"There's not room or time enough for that, Shae. It pains me to say it, but you must go on alone."

"No." She touched the rough perse of his cloak as she looked up into his face, soft in the glow of Lof Yuel's light. "I can't leave you in the dark."

His hand enclosed hers in warmth. "Shae, I'm loathe to let you go on alone, but we have no choice. You must reach Lohen Keil by daybreak and release the DawnKing...if it may yet be done."

She bit her lip, recognizing the truth of his words. "I love you, Kai."

He cupped her face and kissed her in a sweet but far too brief goodbye. She clung to him. "I love you more than I can say, Shae. As long as my heart beats, I'll find a way to follow you. May Lof Yuel keep you safe and lend you speed." He caught her hand, pressed his lips into its palm, and stepped out of the circle of light that shone before her.

Closing her hand over the tingle that remained, she tasted the salt of tears. How she longed to linger, to comfort them both, but time stood against her.

She left Kai behind with hesitant steps that steadied as she climbed, the white light ever before her.

The thought of Kai, sightless and abandoned, halted her at the next landing. She hesitated, and then turned back in sudden decision.

The white light extinguished. Utter darkness closed over her.

She flung out a hand and steadied herself against the damp stone of the cave's wall. How could she go on without a light? Perhaps if she called to Kai, he would hear and feel his way to her, and they could find their way together. Even as the thought came, she knew they'd never make it before dawn broke, before Freaer found her in person.

Look to the light...

She turned her thoughts inward and found the white flame still burning. It flared before her once more, and she could have wept.

Shae did not allow her thoughts to stray again, but kept them on the climb before her. She longed to wake, for it seemed she'd stepped into one of the nightmares that haunted her at Torindan.

Laughter floated at the edge of hearing. Faint at first, it grew until it filled the Caerric. Eyes watched her out of the shadows crowding at the edge of light. Unseen "things" brushed past her, whispering.

Winged rodents screeched and tangled in her hair. Screaming, she batted them away but teetered on the edge of falling.

The light dimmed and flickered.

Sudden terror made her pant, and she only just stopped herself from bolting. She jumped at every sound.

Footsteps padded behind her.

She turned. *"Kai?"*

Silence answered her as darkness fell.

She found the inner flame and let it fill her mind until it bloomed before her, brighter this time. She wouldn't look back again, no matter what. Taking step after step, she climbed until her chest ached with each ragged breath, but she dared not stop.

The footsteps behind her faded from hearing.

Freaer's "touch" crawled over her and passed on, but returned, searching. She gritted her teeth and shielded herself as she looked to the light, and it slid away.

Weariness made her careless. She stepped too close to the edge, and it crumbled beneath her feet. Pitching forward, she landed hard on her knees as stones crashed far below. Pain jarred through her and, as darkness descended, despair came with it.

She curled her hands into fists. *Lof Yuel! I never asked for any of this. Do you want to make me suffer? Is that it? Well, I've carried the burden you gave me this far. But I can't go on! You ask too much.*

Her own words returned to her. *In my life until now I felt a great burden press upon me. You have named it for me. I give you my promise.*

Spoken as a true Daughter of Rivenn. Her mother's answer whispered through her mind.

She'd forgotten her pledge to her mother. Would she ignore her vow at Aerlic's cairn? And what of Eufemia's death and Guaron's madness? Did they deserve their sufferings? Shae lifted her head as Lof Yuel's light flared to life once more.

She had to try.

She slogged onward and upward, her chest burning with each ragged breath she drew. When she reached a wide landing where light shifted and eddied, she stopped with a sense of shock. She'd reached the top of the ancient stair. Through a breach in the mountain's side, she could see out and a long way down across the barren landscape, now tinged with the pink of morning.

The light outlined a natural stone bridge arching across the rotting heart of the mountain. The circular chasm it spanned fell a long way to an ember glowing below—Lohen Keil, the Well of Light. The tapestries all showed the natural bridge leaping to an opening in the cave wall—Gilead Riann, the Gate of Life. But this bridge ended against a rough wall of stone. Had she come too late?

Trembling, she stepped onto the bridge and looked the long way down into Lohen Keil. Her knees went weak. Here Kunatel had fought and vanquished Faendenn. The Contendor had remained trapped within Lohen Keil until the integrity of the House of Rivenn faltered and the Viadrel, the Flames of Virtue, could no longer hold him at bay.

The ember in the chasm below leaped with fire, which stretched and grew until it ringed her about. Warmth traveled through her feet and into her injured leg. When the Viadrel receded, she pulled off a boot. The redness and swelling had vanished, and her cuts were gone.

Something blocked the light.

"Shae!"

Freaer occupied the landing she'd vacated. The shadow of the welke he rode loomed across the cave wall behind him. The dark creature fluttered its wings and bobbed its head as it waited in the breach. It perched at the edge as if ready to take flight and seemed loathe to enter the cave.

Her gaze shifted to Freaer. He wore rumpled clothing, his hair tangled about his neck, and smudges stood out beneath his eyes. His jaw tensed as if he struggled in the grip of strong emotion. His mind crawled outside hers, trying to find a way in, searching...seeking...

"Stay back!" She drew her dagger. Its swirlstones flared with multi-hued light. Light from the *Keil* flared, as if in sympathy and danced around her.

"Wait, Shae." As Freaer held her gaze, memories of his kisses flooded her mind. Light gathered around him and grew until he shone with such beauty she ached.

He held out a hand to her, and longing flowed into her. He wanted her. He would enshrine her. Just a few steps and she could enter his embrace. His smile beguiled her, but even as she started toward him, something jarred in her mind.

"I've come to save you, Shae."

෧෧෧

In the absence of sight, Kai's other senses intensified. The acrid stench of damp rock tinged with rodent leavings permeated the air. Water burbled, splashed, and dripped throughout the Caerric. A draft touched his face. His dagger weighted his hand with smooth coolness. At least he still possessed a weapon.

Balancing against the damp, rough surface of the rock wall, he explored with his foot to find the next tread. He had to try following Shae. He took the next step, and the next. A rhythm developed that leant him speed. A landing opened before him. After a search, he found the lowest tread of the next flight.

Laughter gurgled around him. Something pummeled into him from the side and sent him reeling. Hard stone slammed into him and his dagger clattered away. Jerking to his knees, he patted the stone of the landing but his dagger eluded him. Screeching, winged rodents descended upon him, and he guarded his face with an uplifted arm. When he flailed at them, the creatures fell away.

He patted the stone of the landing, renewing his search for his dagger, and winced as his hand found its cutting edge. He tasted blood while his uninjured hand searched inside his pack and closed on a roll of bandages.

He bound his hand as best he could and stood, his pulse throbbing in his ears. Did he hallucinate? Or did Whyst float toward him from below? Gripping his dagger, he watched and waited. Fell creatures shoved him and laughed as he thrust his blade into thin air.

The laughter quieted. Whyst neared, wielded by a shadow.

He strained to see. A familiar face, blue in Whyst's light, floated above the sword. "Dorann? Do you live?"

"Wait there. I'll come to you." Dorann answered. "I found Whyst below. It nearly fell on me, in fact. I'm amazed it's still whole. I gave up my cup light and let it lead me instead. I'm thankful to find you." He stopped abreast of Kai and lifted Whyst aloft. "Kai? *Where's Shae?*"

"She's gone on alone." The words tasted bitter in his mouth. He'd kept watch over Shae's safety all her life, and now, when she'd needed him most, he'd failed her.

Whyst wavered in Dorann's hand, and blue light slanted over Kai. *"Why?"*

"She could see by a light from Lof Yuel, while I could not. Rather than make her lead me, I released her to go on alone."

"You released her!" Anger twisted Dorann's face. "What kind of guardian are you? Could you not have remained with her *somehow?* I should run you through with your own sword!"

With his dagger before him, Kai backed. "Stop this foolishness."

"Aye, I will, but for Shae, not you. We have to find her! Mark me, if a hair of her head is harmed, you'll answer to me."

The truth came home to Kai. "You love her."

Dorann's hiss confirmed the truth. "'Tis not important that I do. I know she's above my reach. But I would have her safe."

"Then we have the same mind on the matter." Kai eased Whyst from Dorann's hand. "Let's waste no more time on words."

∾❦

"You belong to me." Freaer smiled and extended a hand.

Even as Shae swayed toward him, something held

308

her back.

Don't listen to him! Elcon's voice warned from within.

She hesitated. How had she come to be in this place? She couldn't seem to remember...As Freaer's beauty filled her senses and his "touch" overlaid Elcon's, she gave up wondering. Freaer waited, just out of reach, his hand extended to capture hers.

She took another step toward him.

This is wrong! Elcon's voice spoke more sharply.

She put her hands to her head in confusion. She could barely think. *Lof Yuel!*

A soothing breeze blew across her mind, driving all else before it. She pulled her gaze from Freaer and started.

At the place where the bridge had met only a stone wall an open gateway shimmered in veiled light. Behind the veil waited an Elder youth in a humble tunic and worn cloak. Although dressed in common garb, he held himself with regal grace. Ragged black hair fell over a well-shaped brow. Round, dark eyes gleamed as he smiled and lifted a hand toward her. "Come."

"*You.*" Shae had seen him once before, when he came to her in Torindan's Allerstaed. But she held back. "Who are you?"

The youth smiled. "Why do you ask what you already know?"

She considered. She had never imagined the DawnKing as an Elder. How could one of such tender age save Elderland? And yet, she could not deny the joy that sprang within her at sight of him.

Now he no longer held her mind enthralled, Freaer's beauty seemed less true. With his mask of comeliness slipping, she caught glimpses of a harsh soul. He scowled. "Shae, don't do this! Can't you see he means to imprison you in Gilead Riann?"

She hesitated, but answered back. "I'll not listen, Freaer."

"You don't know what's on the other side!"

Fear touched her, but she shook her head, "Lies. You father lies."

"You will never see Elcon or Kai again."

Her resolve weakened. As the first light of dawn penetrated the breach, tendrils of sorrow twined through her mind to crowd out all else. *Kai.*

"Don't let him sway you, Shae!" Kai's voice came as if conjured by her thought.

He stood with Dorann on the landing below the last flight of stairs, Whyst gleaming in his hand. "Ask yourself why he won't walk onto the bridge with you."

Shae understood then. Freaer could not withstand the Viadrel. He could only reach her mind. *If she let him.*

"You don't know what it's like to be trapped." Freaer no longer looked beautiful at all. Odd, but in the shifting light his face appeared fissured as with age.

"You would know. You were imprisoned in Lohen Keil until the House of Rivenn waned."

He smiled. "Poor, besotted Iewald was fool enough to betray the Kindren, weaken the House of Rivenn, and thus win my freedom."

"What do you mean? How could Iewald's betrayal weaken the House of Rivenn?"

Freaer gave an ugly laugh. "I'm not the only illegitimate son of Rivenn."

Shae gasped. "You mean—"

"Raelein Gladreinn grew impatient while waiting

to bear Kunrat's first child and so gave her maid, Illandel, to do it for her. But when she became pregnant by Talan, Gladreinn sent Illandel away to bear Iewald in quiet. Of course, the damage was already done. Mother exploited a weakness in the House of Rivenn to free me."

Shae backed away from Freaer. "You are evil."

"You wound me." He smirked. "I would have destroyed you long before this, but I find you...entertaining. It's a pity, but I can see now it would never work." He pointed to Shae. *"Attack!"*

The welke let out a screech and jumped onto the stair in front of Kai and Dorann, batting its wings to balance.

Kai confronted the hissing creature, but the welke sidestepped and launched into flight over Lohen Keil. Gliding toward Shae, it extended deadly talons.

"Shae, *go!*" But Kai's shout could not unlock her legs. She stood, rooted in terror, and gave a soundless scream.

The flames of the Viadrel licked upward from the Keil and surrounded the welke. With a shriek, the creature fell, encompassed by fire.

Freaer retreated toward the breach.

A keening wail rose from the Keil and echoed through the Caerric.

She put her hands over her ears. "When will it stop? I can't bear it!"

"You hear the need of Elderland, the sound of its heartbreak," the Elder youth said. "This cry calls me forth."

All at once, Shae understood. This Elder youth *could* save Elderland. She knew, perhaps had known all along, the song she must sing. No other would do.

.She'd last sung the Mael Lido for her mother. Tears ran down her face as she sang the death song for her own safe passage.

Her gaze locked with Kai's across Lohen Keil. He inclined his head, and she took the last few steps that would carry her beyond the shimmering veil.

27

DawnSinger's Song

Shae sang from behind a caul of light, so beautiful and noble that Kai ached with love for her. The Mael Lido echoed and eddied throughout Caerric Daeft, arresting the ear.

The song ended and silence fell. Shae bowed her head and wept.

Did she weep for herself, for him, or for Elderland? Perhaps for all. His heart pounded. He longed to snatch her from Gilead Riann, to keep her safe at his side, but he could not, would not.

The caul glimmered and spun with light. Shae raised her head and smiled at him just as the wall of rock firmed into place once more. Kai blinked. She was gone.

The Elder youth now stood on the bridge. He had passed into Elderland through Gilead Riann as Shae left it.

Kai balled his hands into fists. "Where is she?"

"She waits now in a gap between worlds, where she will findpeace and rest. She has fulfilled Prophecy and brought me into Elderland in her place."

"*You* are the DawnKing?"

Something in the youth's bearing answered Kai's question. "I am Emmerich, sent by Lof Yuel to bring peace to Elderland."

Kai leaped the last steps to the landing and bowed. From the corner of his eye he saw Dorann hesitate, then do the same. A thought intruded. "Freaer escaped."

"His time has not yet come." Emmerich said.

"Will Shae return?" Kai's words wrenched from him.

"She laid down her life by choice, not knowing what would befall her." Emmerich gave a faint smile. "And yet, in losing her life, she will find it. You shall see Shae again, Kai, although you will travel many roads before that day."

❧❦

In the Darkwood

Ruescht's neck warmed Kai's hand. The little Silver put back her ears and nickered, but did not lower her head to graze with the other wingabeasts on the banks of the brook. Kai patted her and turned with Dorann toward the stand of draetenns. A breeze kicked up and curling leaves danced overhead. Emmerich followed, lending his strength to Guaron. Kai waited for them, his heart lifting, as it always did when he thought of Guaron's recovery.

Upon their return to Graelinn Hold, they had found Guaron restored enough to join them in a feast, although he was still weak. He bit with appetite into a joint of roast crobok and washed it down with ginger beer. "The song healed me," he said. "A beautiful morning song carried on the wind and drove all poison from me."

A wandering minstrel brought news of other healings from the sweet song that echoed throughout Elderland early one morning. Enric returned from battle, for those loyal to Elcon had beaten back Freaer's forces.

An insect whirred past Kai's cheek. Trumpet flowers nodded their dainty heads on the banks of the brook. The wingabeasts lowered their heads to crop the green grass. An image of Shae placing a stone on Aerlic's cairn brought back to Kai of the promise she had made. *"I'll not let you die for nothing!"* She had kept her word. He had come to keep his own. He would bear Aerlic's body to its rest among his fathers in Glindenn Raven.

"Aerlic was faithful." Guaron spoke in a hushed voice behind him.

Kai couldn't speak around the lump in his throat. Tears blinded him, and he almost ran into Dorann, who stopped without warning before him. "What ails—" Following Dorann's gaze, he broke off.

A hollow tree yawned before them, open and empty. Rocks that had once made up a cairn lay strewn about.

Dorann's eyes flashed amber fire. "Something—or someone—has desecrated Aerlic's grave. He's not here."

Kai stared at the hollow tree and the piles of rocks. Who—or what—would do such a thing?

"Garns?" Dorann echoed Kai's own suspicion.

"Perhaps not." Emmerich said.

Dorann looked in the direction of Emmerich's voice, and his face reflected shock.

Kai turned from the tree and went still.

Beyond the draetenns in the place where the brook

widened, stood Aerlic with Emmerich beside him. His wound had vanished but his clothing still showed stains of blood, and a slash rent the side of his surcoat.

Emmerich extended a hand to Aerlic.

Aerlic stared at Emmerich, his eyes very blue against a dirty face. What he saw must have put him at ease, for he smiled and grasped the proffered hand.

Kai mustered his voice. "How fare you?"

Aerlic smiled. "I'm better now that I've freed myself from that tree. Tell me, how came I to wake there? I recall strange dreams, and then someone singing. I must have slept a long time, for I own to hunger. Have you any food?"

"We have food aplenty, Aerlic, and pleased we are to share it with you." Kai smiled through a haze of tears. "Come then."

Glossary

Aeleanor (A-LEE-a-nor)—Queen of Whellein

Aelfred (ALE-fred)—King of Merboth

Aelgarod (ALE-gah-rod)—Healer of Whellein Hold

Aergenwoad (AYR-gen-wode)—Healing herb

Allerstaed (ALL-er-stayd)—Place of Prayer

Alliance of Faeraven (FAYR-ay-ven)—High kingdom made up of low kingdoms united under one banner

Anden Raven (AN-den RAY-ven)—Other land from which the Kindren originally entered Elderland

Anders (AN-ders)—Elcon's manservant

Anemone (Ah-ne-moh-nee)—Low-growing flower with daisy-like petals

Argalent (AR-ja-lent)—Aerlic's silver wingabeast; Kindren for "luster"

Attarnine (ATT-er-nine)—Rodent poison

Benisch (BEN-ish)—Steward of Rivenn

Braegmet Doreinn (BRAYG-met DOR-ee-in)—Chasm of Confusion

Brael Shadd (BRAYL-shad)—DayStar of Prophecy

Brambleberry —Edible berries that grow in a thorny thicket

Brynn (BRIN)—Hedwynn's red-haired sister

Bursel (BUR-sel)—Dry measurement

Caedric (KAY-drik)—Healer within Graelinn Hold

Caerric Baest (KAYR-ric BAYST)—Cavern of Wonder

Caerric Daeft (KAYR-ric DAYFT)—Cavern of Death

Chaeldra (CHALE-dra)—Shae's maid at Torindan

Chrin (KRIN)—Liquid measurement

Circlet of Elder—Crown designating rulership of Rivenn

Coast of Bones— Elderland's northwestern coastline

Contender—Ancient enemy determined to destroy the Kindren and all Elderland

Craelin (CRAY-lin)—First Guardian of Rivenn

Crobok (CROW- bahk)—Small blue bird

Daelic (DAY-lic)—Healer within Torindan Hold

Daevin (DAY-vin)—Prince of Whellein, brother of Kai

Darksea—Coastal Elder kingdom

DawnSinger's Lament— Ancient prophetic song

Dithmar (DITH-mar)—A guardian of Rivenn

Dorann (DOR-ran)—Tracker for Torindan

Doreinn Ravein (DOR-ree-in RAH-veen)—Canyonlands southeast of Torindan

Draetenn (DRAY-ten)—Tree with spreading branches and fragrant bark

Eathnor (EETH-nor)—Tracker for Torindan

Ebain (ee-BAIN)—Plain

Eberhardt (EB-er-hart)—Whellein's king

Ederbaer (ED-er-bayr)—Red berry bushes that grow at the edges of meadows and in barren places

Elcon (EL-kon)—High prince of Faeraven; son of Timraen and Maeven

Elder (ELL-der)—Race of humans with darker hair and more rounded eyes; original inhabitants of Elderland

Eldritch (ELL-drich)—Eerie and malevolently strange

Emmerich (EM-mer-ik)—Elder youth

Enric (EN-rik)—Graelinn's king and Katera's husband

Erdrich Ceid (ER-drik SEE-id)—Mythical Ice Witch

Erinae (EAR-rin-ay)—Mother of Dorann and Eathnor

Eufemia (YOU-fee-me-uh)—Maeven's serving maid

Euryan (YOU-ry-an)—King of Westerland; an Elder kingdom

Ewaeri (ee-WAHR-ee)—Priests who distribute alms

Feiann (FY-an)—Elusive small folk

Flaemling (FLAYM-ling)—Tiny bird often kept as a pet

Flecht (FLECSHT)—Kai's white wingabeast; Kindren word for "arrow"

Flitling (FLIT-ling)—Tiny bird

Frael (FRAYL)—Prince

Freaer (FREE-ear)—First Musician of Torindan

Garn (GAHRN)—Goblin-like giants

Gentian (GEN-ti-an)—Trumpet-shaped flower

Gilead Riann (GILL-ee-ad REE-an)—Gate of Life

Gladreinn (GLAD-re-in)—Bride of Rivenn; one of the first Kindren to enter Elderland at the Gate of Life

Gnarlwood—Giant tree with high branches

Graylet (GRAY-let)—Medium-sized bird of prey with speckled gray feathers

Guardians of Rivenn—Highly-trained knights

Guaron (GWAR-ron)—A guardian of Rivenn and keeper of the wingabeasts

Heddwyn (HEAD-win)—Mistress of White Feather Inn

House of Rivenn—Ruling family of Rivenn; also rule the alliance of Faeraven

Iewald (I-a-wald)—Talan's trusted friend; First Guardian of Pilaer

Iewald's Betrayal—Ancient historical song

Illandel (ILL-an-del)—Glaedreinn's maid

Ilse (ILSS)—Queen of Merboth, sister of Shae and Kai

Ivan (I-van)—Captain of the Sea Wanderer

Jaenell (JAY-nel)—Grandmother of Dorann and Eathnor

Kaba—Giant tree that has reddish bark with healing and preservative properties

Kaeroc (KAY-rok)—Large white bird with long tail feathers that roosts in tall trees and inhabits ruins

Kai (KI)—Guardian of Rivenn and Maeven's personal guard

Katera (Kuh-TEAR-ah)—Shae's twin sister

Keep—Innermost and strongest building or tower within a castle

Keirken (KEER-ken)—Deciduous tree with twisting trunks and spreading branches

Kindren (KIN-dren)—Race of humans with fair hair and slightly elongated eyes who came through the Gate of Life into Elderland from Anden Raven

Krei Doreinn (KRY DOR-ree-in)—Three canyons; a place where two rivers and three canyons meet

Kunrat (KOON-rat)—Descendent of Rivenn

Laesh Ebain (LAYSH e-BAYN)—Lost plains

Lanthorn (LAN-thorn)—Lantern paned with thin horn instead of glass

Last Battle of Pilaer—Battle that marked the fall of Pilaer to garn invasion

Leisht (LEESHT)—Dagger that breaks enchantments

Lenhardt (LEN-hart)—Morgorad's king

Lof Frael (LOFF FRAYL)—High prince

Lof Raelein (LOFF RAY-leen)—High queen

Lof Raena (LOFF RAY-nah)—High princess

Lof Shraen (LOFF SHRAYN—High king

Lof Yuel (LOFF YOU-el)—High One; God

Lohen Keil (LOH-hen KEEL)—Well of Light

Lute (LOOT)—Guitar-like instrument with ten strings

Lyse (LYSS)—Shae's maid at Whellein Hold

Maeg Streihcan (MAYG STRY-kan)—Broken Mountain; a lone peak rising at the eastern edge of the Plains of Rivenn

Maeg Waer (MAYG WAYR)—Forsaken Mountain; where the Cavern of Death is located

Maegrad Ceid (MAY-grad SEE-id)—Crystal Mountains; Kindren name for the Elder's Ice Mountains

Maegrad Paesad (MAY-grad PAY-sad)—Impenetrable Mountains, located in the north of Whellein

Maegran Syld (MAY-gran SILD)—Forested Hills, Kindren name for the Elder's Hills of Mist

Mael Lido (MAYL LEE-do)—Death song

Maer Ibris (MAYR EE-bris)—Western sea

Maer Lingenn (MAYR LING-gen)—Eastern sea

Maer Syldra (MAYR SIL-dra)—Southern sea

Maer Taerat (MAYR TAY-rat)—Northern sea

Maeric (MAY-rik)—Chief Cook at Whellein Hold

Maeven (MAY-vin)—High queen of Faeraven; queen of Rivenn, Elcon's mother

Meriwen (MAIR-ee-win)—Temptress who changed the Kindren's history, mother of the Contender

Muer Maeread (MYOUR MAY-ree-ad)—Coast of Bones; the northwestern shore of Elderland

Mystael (MISS-tayl)—Craelin's silver wingabeast; Kindren for "wild wind"

Norwood (NOHR-wood)—Northerly Elder kingdom

Paiad Burein (PAY-ad BYOUR-ee-in)—Field of blood; a historic battleground

Pawel (PAH-wel)—Son of Daeramor; a kingdom east of Whellein

Percken (PERK-en)—Rainbow-colored river fish

Pilaer Hold (Pil-AYR)—Ancient stronghold of the Kindren; now a ruin

Plains of Rivenn—Grassland in Rivenn

Plaintain (Plane-tane)—Broad-leaved herb growing in moist places used for drawing poison from wounds

Praectal (PRAYK-tawl)—Healer

Purr (PUHR)—Trees with thick trunks that grow in the desert oases

Pyrek (PY-rek)—Small, vicious bird of prey

Quinn (QUIN)—Master of White Feather Inn

Raegnen (RAYG-nen)—Guaron's blue wingabeast; Kindren word for "summer rain"

Raelein (RAY-leen)—Queen

Raemwold (RAYM-wold)—King of Braeth and Maeven's father

Raena (RAY-nah)—Princess

Raven (RAY-ven)—Kingdom

Reyanna (RAY-yan-na)—Queen of Braeth and Maeven's mother

Rivenn (RIV-en)—A kingdom

River voices—Imagined voices caused by the turning of stones in riverbeds

Roaem (ROW-em)—Eathnor's black wingabeast; Kindren for the sound thunder makes

Ruescht (ROOSCHT)—Shae's silver wingabeast; Kindren word for "rushing wind"

Sceptor of Faeraven—Symbolic staff of rulership over the alliance of Faeraven

Seighardt (SIG-hart)—Prince of Braeth and Maeven's brother

Serviceberry—Small tree or large bush with broad leaves and purple berries

Shae (SHAY)—Princess of Whellein

Shaelcon (SHALE-con)—Father of Timraen

Shaenalyn (SHAY-nah-lin)—Shae's full name

Shaenn Raven (SHAYN RAY-ven)—Afterworld

Sharten (SHAR-ten)—Dorann's gray wingabeast; Kindren for "deepening shadow"

Shil shael (SHIL SHAYL)—Hereditary soul touch

Shraen (SHRAYN)—King

Shraen Brael (SHRAYN BRAY-el)—King of the Dawn; DawnKing

Strongwood—Hardwood tree

Sweetberry—Edible berry which grows on brambles

Sword of Rivenn—Sword forged in the flames of virtue for Rivenn and handed down to his descendents

Syllid (SIL-lid)—Wood or forest in Kindren

Syllid Braechnen (SIL-lid BRAYK-nen)—A murky forest

Syllid Mueric (SIL-lid MYOUR-ik)—A beautiful and terrible forest

Taelerat (TAY-le-rat)—Shraen of Selfred

Tahera (Tah-HEAR-uh)—Aeleanor's maid

Talan (TAH-lin)—Early high king of Faeraven who captured and tamed the first wingabeast

Timpani (Tim-PAN-ee)—Kettledrum

Timraen (TIM-rain)—High king of Faeraven; king of Rivenn; Maeven's husband

Triboan (TRI-bone)—Southern land occupied by garns

Turret (TUR-et)—Small projecting tower

Unibeast (UN-i-beest)—Unicorn

Varaedel (Ve-RAY-del)—Glindenn's Shraen

Viadrel (VY-ah-drel)—Flames of Virtue

Waeven (WAY-ven)—Spider-like animal

Walls of Death—Enclosed passageway that could be shut off to capture attackers

Ward—Environ within a castle; also known as a bailey

Watergate—Gate leading to and from a body of water

Weild (WEELD)—River

Weild Aenar (WEELD AY-e-nar)—Wild River

Weild Rivenn (WEELD RIV-en)—Rivenn's River

Weild Whistan (WEELD WHIS-stan)—White River; Kindren name for the Elder's White Feather River

Weilo (WY-lo)—Tree with weeping branches and long leaves that grows beside a river or in damp places

Weilton (WEEL-ton)—A guardian of Rivenn

Weithein Faen (WY-then FANE)—An estuary

Welke (WELL-key)—Giant creature of prey that is a cross between a dinosaur and a bird

Westerland—Western Elder kingdom

Whirlight (WHIR-lite)—Large; ungainly white bird

Whispan (WHIS-span)—Small tree with lacy white foliage

Whyst (WHIST)—A spirit sword, defends both flesh and spirit

Wingabeast (WING-ah-beest)—Winged horses

Wingen (WING-en)—Small, colorful bird

Wreckers—Elder who lure ships to their doom

Yellowroot—Edible tuber

Acknowledgments

A work of fiction doesn't spring into being fully-formed and well-dressed. Ultimately, many hands groom, tailor and finish a novel. Attempting to identify them all is a difficult task, so I hope anyone I've unintentionally omitted will forgive me. The following people lent their touch in shaping *DawnSinger*:

Nicola Martinez, Editor-In-Chief of Pelican Book Group, for believing in Tales of Faeraven and for creating the beautiful cover of this book.

Lisa McCaskill, my editor at Harbourlight Books, for her kind guidance, and for polishing my novel to a fine sheen.

Suzanne Hartmann, for understanding and respecting my vision for *DawnSinger*, and for helping me grow as an author.

Barbara Scott, my wonderful agent at Wordserve Literary, for lending me her expertise and believing in me.

Eric Wilson, for having the humility to encourage and endorse a new author, and for giving me his most valuable commodity: his time and attention.

Jill Williamson, **Linda Windsor**, and **Lisa Grace** for endorsing DawnSinger and providing valuable insights.

Michael Duncan, Melissa Norris, K.M. Weiland, Kerry Neitz, Anne Greene, Sharon Lavy, Pride Mutoli, Linda Yezak and **members of my NCWA critique groups** for contributions made during *DawnSinger's* inception.

Kathy Carlton Willis, my publicist, for giving me a foot up in the marketing world.

Pelican Books Marketing Staff for their support

and guidance.

I also appreciate the **test readers** who gave me feedback on how to market my novel.

Last but not least, I extend a special thank you to my husband, **John Voigt**, and my children, **Jessica**, **Zammy**, and **Jeremy** for supporting me in innumerable ways during the writing of *DawnSinger*.

Thank you for purchasing this Harbourlight title. For other inspirational stories, please visit our on-line bookstore at www.harbourlightbooks.com.

For questions or more information, contact us at titleadmin@harbourlightbooks.com.

Harbourlight Books
The Beacon in Christian Fiction™
www.HarbourlightBooks.com

May God's glory shine through
this inspirational work of fiction.

AMDG

CPSIA information can be obtained at www.ICGtesting.com
Printed in the USA
LVOW06s0021130913

352261LV00008B/254/P